"Is it my turn now?" he asked, as she reached his side. She smiled and he was dazzled by the pure joy on her face.

"Let's just dance and dance all night!" she exclaimed.

"You're enjoying yourself then," he commented, as she wound her arm through his and dragged him onto the floor.

Unconsciously, she reached up and touched the diamond around her throat. "Yes."

He took her in his arms and the warmth of having her so close hit him like a wave. He pulled her more firmly against him and they swayed to the romantic music. "You see, if I have you close like this and I never let you go, no one can steal the diamond," he whispered into her dark hair.

She pulled back a bit with a wicked grin and replied, "But we want the Ghost to *try*."

"Veronica, as you know too well, when the Ghost tries, he usually succeeds."

"Not tonight," she said with a determined look in her eyes before snuggling into his shoulder again, her perfume encircling them like a magic spell blocking out the rest of the world. He closed his eyes and surrendered to the bewitchment.

Romance Writers of America's "Heart of the West Writers Contest" Finalist.

**Praise for Lydia Storm
writing as Nicole Coady...**

Moonlight on Diamonds

by

Lydia Storm

Moonlight on Diamonds

Contact Information: info@thewildrosepress.com

Cover Art by *Daniel DeFabio*

The Wild Rose Press
PO Box 708
Adams Basin, NY 14410-0706
Visit us at www.thewildrosepress.com

Publishing History
First Crimson Rose Edition, 2009
Print ISBN: 1-60154-496-0

Published in the United States of America

Dedication

For Tom

It was the suspended hour, the hour when the sky has lost its sun but not yet found its stars. Everything in nature is clothed in a blue light.

- Jacques Guerlain

The detective by tradition and definition is the seeker after truth.

- Raymond Chandler

Prologue

Amritsar, India—1661

The temple was dark but for the flicker of tiny
candles burning at the feet of the golden goddess.
The thief stepped forward, crushing the crimson rose
petals that perfumed the pathway to her altar. In
the dim light, Jean-Baptiste Tavernier could see the
shimmer of the legendary diamond which had called
to him all the way in his native France.

Rumors of the jewel's magical powers swirled
around it until it had taken on the aura of a fairytale
talisman in his imagination and the lust to possess
the gem had become an obsession. Tavernier had
used bribes, trickery, and sometimes brute force to
uncover the location of the stone—a diamond so
precious only the highest caste of Brahmans had
knowledge of its resting place. The humble,
whitewashed building he at last discovered at the
base of the Himalayan Mountains was the perfect
home for one of the great treasures of India. Few
would have thought to search for it there. Few would
have endured the trials he had to reach it.

His yellowed flesh hung from his bones, the
result of the malaria he had contracted at a lodging
house on the shore of the Ganges River. The once
snowy linen of his shirt was torn and stained, his
strong hands were cracked from sunburn, his nails
ragged and dirty, and his fair hair hung in a filthy
plait down his back. All this was forgotten now as he
gazed spellbound with greed at the massive violet-

blue diamond sparkling like a crown in the forehead of the golden idol.

Confident in the knowledge that the priests who guarded the temple's treasure had fallen under his sword in the dark jungle outside, Tavernier took a bold step forward and stood before the altar. He would take what he had come for.

The thief reached through the veil of incense, and with his blood-stained dagger pried the shimmering diamond from the third eye of the goddess. He held the jewel in his hands, felt the weight and viewed the clarity of it up close. This was a stone fit for a king. Joy washed through him. He would sell the diamond to Louis XIV and at last take his place at court. His future was now secure.

As he stepped outside the temple, Tavernier unclenched his fist. Moonbeams struck the diamond, bringing it to life like a flickering silver flame. It seemed to burn with supernatural brilliance in the hot midnight jungle, a blue star that had fallen to earth from the heavens to illuminate even the darkest shadows of the human soul.

The cries of feral dogs howling somewhere in the blackness of the strange trees just beyond the temple rose up around him. The hair on the back of his neck prickled as he saw a pack of emaciated hounds moving ghost-like in the gloomy depths of the tangled undergrowth. Their demented yellow eyes watched him from the shadows, their fangs bared, their paws nervously clawing at the earth.

He blinked and they disappeared from view, but he brought his tattered handkerchief to his nose as the stench of rotting meat rose up like steam from the jungle floor. He could hear the twigs snapping as the pack limped through the trees. He could feel them creeping closer with every breath he took.

The Frenchman crossed himself and gaped in superstitious horror at the blue fire in his hand. Had the Indian Brahmans truly bewitched the gem with their curses and devilish spells?

Barely holding back his panic, Tavernier fought the desire to fling the jewel away as if it were a venomous serpent. Summoning all his will instead, he shoved the diamond into his satchel and leapt onto his mare, sending them both crashing through the overgrown thicket. The branches clawed at his face as his horse thundered through the jungle, but he didn't care. With his heart pounding and malarial sweat pouring down his face, he rode from the heathen temple with all the fury of a man pursued by the hounds of hell.

One year later, the diamond rested among the other sparkling baubles in King Louis' jewel box. Tavernier's fortune was made, but in his fever dreams the spectral pack hunted him down as he lay paralyzed on silken sheets, the luxury of Versailles' mirrored walls and crystal chandeliers reflecting his mute terror into infinity. The strange, sickly dogs were always just a heartbeat behind him in the suffocating jungle. He felt their ripping claws at his coattails and the acid fire of their breath down his back, branding him forever with the mark of the Thief.

Chapter One

New York City, 2003

The dusty Greenwich Village church basement was strung with Christmas lights in an attempt to improve the vibe of the Wednesday night meeting of Alcoholics Anonymous. It was already March, but that didn't deter the ex-speed-freak girl with the pixie blond hair from carefully draping lights across the exposed wood beams. Perched on a metal folding chair, she wound the cord around the pre-war metal lamps which lit up the crowd like a cast of characters from an old black-and-white noir.

John Monroe sat slurping his coffee as the bossy, transvestite meeting secretary attempted to get a pair of giggling teenagers sitting in the corner of the room to shut up. He urged the newcomers in a raspy voice to pay attention to a bald, nervous wreck of a man as he read the Twelve Steps. The poor guy was sweating through it and tripped awkwardly over his words as he recited the core philosophy of the AA program.

"Step One, we, we admit we are pow-powerless over alc-alcohol..."

John smiled encouragingly, trying psychically to cheer the poor guy on, feeling his pain every time Baldy misread a word or had to go back and start a sentence over. At last, the ordeal was finished and everyone in the room gave Baldy a round of applause, the clapping dying out almost before it had begun.

Now came the moment John was dreading—birthday cake time.

It was a tradition in Alcoholics Anonymous to give birthday cakes on the anniversary dates of each member's sobriety. The idea was to celebrate another year of living clean and sober and allow the newcomers in the program to see that it was possible to go for many years without taking a drink. John usually had no problem with this scenario. He could sing an off-key version of "Happy Birthday" with the rest of them, but this evening John was not feeling quite as positive about the birthday experience. Tonight, the whole thing gave him a sick feeling in the pit of his stomach.

The secretary cleared his throat, his Adam's apple contrasting with the matching baby-pink faux-Chanel jacket, lipstick, and mules he sported. "Thank you for reading the steps, Herman. Now, I believe we have one birthday to celebrate tonight." He stared straight at John and smiled. "John is celebrating one year of continuous sobriety and Simon will be giving him his cake."

This was it!

John stood up as the room burst into a wild rendition of "Happy Birthday" complete with bad harmonies and biker-guy hoots and hollers. Simon, John's seventy-eight-year-old AA sponsor, came to the front of the room bearing a cupcake with a single candle shoved in its center. As the song came to its crashing end, John closed his eyes and tried to make a wish. His mind went blank. The applause had died down by now and everyone was staring at him expectantly.

"Make a wish, man!" called out a fifteen-year-old punk-rock kid named Rudy, whom John had taken under his wing over the last few months.

Okay, what do I really need? John was starting to sweat like Baldy. *MONEY.*

He closed his eyes, squished up his face, and wished for money as he blew out the candle. Everyone cheered and Simon gave him a big hug. Even the secretary hugged him. He still wasn't totally comfortable with all the indiscriminate embracing that went on in AA, but if the program kept him sober, he was willing to put up with it.

John approached the podium and looked out over the crowd. Simon stood proudly smiling up at him from the front row. There must have been at least two hundred people there and they were all looking at him.

"Okay," he said aloud into the microphone and took a deep breath. "Well, I want to thank my sponsor, Simon, for giving me my cake and, um, I want to thank all of you for being here and supporting me...and..."

Out of the blue, he felt his eyes well up and his face flush. He swallowed hard and tried to get a hold of himself, but as he spoke his voice squeaked with suppressed emotion and a tear trickled down his cheek. "This is for my dad who never got the chance to get sober." He held up the little cupcake. "He died from alcoholism when I was still a kid and..." He wiped his nose with his shirtsleeve and tried to keep it together. "I just...I'm very grateful. Thanks."

John quickly stepped offstage amidst a round of supportive applause.

Simon clapped him on the back. "I'm proud of you, kid."

"Thanks," mumbled John, as he sank back into a chair next to his sponsor and gratefully became one of the anonymous masses. From all around him in the dark, people whispered their congratulations and patted his shoulder.

Rudy reached across three people and shook John's hand. "Congratulations, man, you hooked it up! One year sober!"

****

A light rain sprinkled onto Sixth Avenue as John turned the corner and began to navigate his way through the street vendors selling fake Gucci sunglasses and fluorescent plastic necklaces. He passed NYU students chatting on their cell phones, homeboys hanging out on the corner with their boomboxes, and Wall Street types flooding out of the subway station bound for cozy West Village brownstones. The streetlamps reflected off the wet pavement and the sky was a moody gray as evening fell over Manhattan.

Some instinct made John look up as he passed the crowded newsstand with its glossy fashion magazines and trashy porno rags, which were placed front and center for any five-year-old to see. It wasn't the pair of fake double D hooters that caught his eye but the headline of the *New York Post* which stopped him in his tracks:

GHOST STRIKES AGAIN!
INTERNATIONAL JEWEL THIEF STEALS PUCK DIAMOND AT ACADEMY AWARDS!

John felt his heart skip a beat. "Oh shit."

****

Marguerite Gateaux had a perfect view of the Eiffel Tower from the windows of her seventh arrondissement apartment as it shimmered with lights before vanishing into midnight darkness for the rest of the evening. Now only the warm glow of myrrh-scented candles illuminated the tanned skin and strong limbs of her lover, René. She caressed his dark head absently as she might that of her little King Charles spaniel, Voltaire, and relaxed in the semidarkness. Sighing contentedly, she stretched a pair of long dancer's legs on the divan where she and René had just made love. Thoughtfully, she pulled a tangle of dark red hair back revealing a wide sensual face that was not quite beautiful, but arresting in the raw sensuality of her knowing smile and laughing feline-green eyes. The radio, which had been throbbing with the slow erotic strain of French trip hop, switched over to a news program, almost destroying the romantic atmosphere of her tastefully appointed apartment.

Marguerite sipped from a half-empty glass of Chateau Petrus as René yawned and moved his head higher up from her bare belly to nuzzle against her breast and lay there like a sleepy child. The newscaster droned on until he came to a bit of information that made Marguerite perk up.

"The famous Puck Diamond, belonging to movie star Katherine Park, was stolen in a dramatic scene at this year's Academy Awards Ceremony in Hollywood, California. While there are no leads yet, Los Angeles police suspect the infamous 'Ghost' who once plagued many of Europe's great cities with a rash of thefts throughout the late 1980s and 90s."

Mon Dieu, the Ghost?

She quickly clicked the stereo remote and the soothing strains of baroque chamber music floated through the apartment.

So they thought the Ghost was on the loose, eh? That was certainly fascinating news, even if it was impossible. The Ghost couldn't have struck last night; Marguerite knew why, though apparently the American police hadn't figured it out. She looked down at René to see if he'd picked up the story, but he seemed so entranced with the soft curve of her breast that he hadn't heard a word.

Marguerite smiled. While she had not yet become *a woman of a certain age*, she had lived enough to know that she adored younger men. Younger men didn't try to run the show, and if there was one thing Marguerite knew how to do, it was put on a show. As the star of the Ballet de l'Aire, the French acrobatic group that had taken the world by storm, she knew how to create quite a spectacle. She'd also managed to make a splash in her other profession—cat burglar.

It was in Marguerite's nature to exceed expectations, and she loved rehearsing for each new act, pushing herself to greater and greater feats of courage and agility. She could master a triple back-flip on the trapeze or fly unnoticed past the police helicopter's searchlight with a bundle of sizzling white-hot stones clutched in her hands and the wind whipping through her flaming hair. She loved the costumes too, brightly colored, eye-catching ones for the big top and a Parisian femme's favorite of basic black for those late night prowls and yowls.

Her upcoming performance at the Diamond Ball, which was to be held in Washington DC's Smithsonian Museum, would be the triumph of both her careers. Of course, she hadn't counted on having to deal with the Ghost publicity and all the extra security that came along with it, but she'd manage to accomplish her mission to steal the museum's most valuable treasure just the same.

Marguerite almost purred in satisfaction as she pictured the Hope Diamond wrapped around Voltaire's collar as she paraded her pet through the Luxembourg Gardens on his daily walk. No one would ever guess they were watching the most famous gem in history prancing by on four little legs. How she would laugh!

She'd have to plan very carefully, she mused as she let her fingers play through Rene's short but surprisingly soft hair, especially if people believed the Ghost had risen from the dead. At least she wouldn't have to worry about Dornal Zagen, the ruthless Austrian jewel thief whom she had clashed with on more than one high-pitched rooftop. She still recalled with a shudder the look in his frosty gray eyes as he'd placed the revolver against her temple in the moonlit dressing room of the Comtesse De Vigne and slipped the majestic diamond-and-sapphire necklace from Marguerite's black-gloved hand. She was well aware only his fear of the commotion a gunshot would raise in the well-staffed chateau had kept him from pulling the trigger before he slipped through the air-conditioning vent and she sprang empty-handed out of the third-story window. It had been bad luck running into him like that. Thank God the Americans had had the good sense to lock up the cold-blooded bastard. Hopefully he'd stay behind bars, and out of her luxurious hair, for the next thirty years.

Of course, there would still be the authorities to contend with. She had always gotten along so well with the Paris police. She had found that the majority of them, and even a few venerable judges, were happy to share her spoils, or her bed, in exchange for turning a blind eye to her late night escapades.

The Hope Diamond would be another matter entirely. The gem was a United States national treasure so she'd just have to make sure she covered her tracks well and didn't get caught.

Marguerite closed her eyes in pleasure as René slipped his sensitive fingers between her thighs and began to gently stroke, sending waves of warm tingles up through her belly. She could feel him hardening against her, a signal he was ready for another round. He pulled back a strand of her blazing hair to kiss her neck. She felt his hot breath as he whispered in her ear, "*Attaches-moi.*"

She loved it when he talked dirty. René knew how to spark the flames which always burned brightly in her, but before Marguerite succumbed completely to her lover's touch, she couldn't help smiling like the cat that ate the canary. As much as the young Frenchman made her breath catch and the blood surge through her, the biggest thrill of all was her secret: after almost fifteen years of Ghostly activity, all the world longed to know the phantom jewel thief's true identity, but no one did. Only Marguerite was privy to that exclusive information.

****

The lights went out, leaving only the ominous green glow of the security lamps to illuminate the hall outside Dornal Zagen's prison cell. He had been marked present during the evening's eight p.m. roll call. Now he was expected to settle in and go to sleep like the rest of the inmates at Ossining Penitentiary.

But tonight Dornal had other plans.

The thin-faced prison guard with the pock-marked complexion and slicked-back hair had remembered to leave his cell conveniently unlocked. He'd met Dornal's stone-gray eyes for a moment, just to make sure they both knew what was going on. Then he'd walked away, leaving the notorious Austrian jewel thief's metal door slightly ajar. Dornal wondered how much his mysterious employer had bribed the guard to assist in his escape, but he had no time for speculations as the alarm system would only be down for five minutes. He'd have to hurry.

At 6'4", with a shock of white-blond hair and Nordic pale skin, he should not have blended so well into the dark shadows of the prison corridor, but with an almost robotic ability to contain his own energy and move efficiently in situations such as this, he was able to pass by the rows of occupied cells in the blink of an eye—a phantom passing unnoticed in the night.

As he reached the medical wing, perhaps the most feared area of the prison, he paused outside the door, his blood running cool through his veins. He paused just long enough to listen and make sure no one stirred inside.

All quiet.

Noiselessly, he pushed open the door and dropped to the ground, slinking toward the front desk where a nurse sat reading tabloids and smoking menthols. She wasn't supposed to be there. He'd been told they shut down the admissions room of the medical wing at night. With the alarm only turned off for a few more minutes, he had no time to dwell on her unwelcome presence.

The Austrian's nose dusted the puke-colored floor as he inched slowly past her. He didn't have time for this. He could feel the seconds ticking away as he moved one muscle at a time, silently making his way across the floor like some cold-blooded reptile stalking its prey.

At last he reached the hallway, which led into private rooms where inmates lay hopeless in their beds praying for death's release. Dornal slipped by, unmoved at the plight of his fellow prisoners. Who were they but a bunch of futureless, low-level drug pushers and street trash? The world would be better off without them.

He passed the operating room with its Plexiglass windows, which allowed spectators to watch from the hallway. The cold glint of steel caught his eye. His brain calculated like a computer how much time had passed, how much time he had left, and how long it would take to make a momentary detour.

In a flash, he was inside the operating room. His eyes swept the pedestal next to the sink where some careless or distracted nurse had left a scalpel out to dry instead of locking it securely away in the cabinet across the room with the rest of the instruments. His hand closed around the knife with its razor-thin blade and then he was back in the hall moving fast toward the fire exit.

One of the patients in a room to his right let out

a loud curse and began screaming gut-wrenching gibberish at the top of his lungs. The insane shrieking would have chilled the blood of any normal human, but all Dornal felt was annoyance. He couldn't help but wonder, as he retreated back into the operating room, why this idiot wasn't kept sedated.

He held his breath as his fellow inmate screamed pitifully into the lonely night. Surely the nurse would come through with a needle full of whatever dope they were using to shut their patients up. The seconds ticked by and no one appeared.

Dornal had no choice but to head back into the hall and make a break for the fire exit. He fingered the steel blade in his hand. If he met the nurse along the way, she wouldn't hold him up for more than a few seconds.

But evidently the nurse wasn't coming and he reached the fire exit without any more trouble. The door was supposed to be unlocked. At least it would be as long as the operating system that controlled the alarm was still down, but Dornal trusted nothing and no one. He cautiously put his hand on the knob and twisted until he felt the click. It was unlocked. The last thing he heard before the heavy door shut behind him was the whimpering sound of the patient in the room down the hall. Then he was in the stairwell flying down the steps on silent feet. When he reached the bottom, the door to freedom awaited, beckoning him. His heart was hammering now, even as his brain remained calm and cool. He'd learned over the years that he could not always control the instincts of his body, but he could always keep his mind clear.

How much time had passed? Was the alarm system still off? On or off, this was the closest he'd been to freedom in a long time and he would make his move. Forcefully, he pushed the door open.

Sirens screamed out from every direction and the giant spotlight atop the watchtower at the perimeter of the jail swung around, combing the building with a bright-white beam. The yelping of dogs let loose from the security stations raised the hair on the back of his neck. If there was one thing he didn't like it was animals, especially ones trained to go for the jugular.

He looked down and saw the storm drain his employer had promised would be there. It had better be unscrewed, because he'd never have time to unfasten the dozen or so bolts that held the cover down onto the cement. Holding the scalpel between his teeth, he grabbed the edges of the cover and pulled.

The spotlight was just bearing down on him and he could sense the bloodhounds picking up his scent as they turned in their tracks on the open field and charged in his direction. The heavy iron cover rolled away and he shimmied down into the tunnel, replacing the cover behind him only moments before the choppers roared overhead with their thermal detectors and probing spotlights.

Inside the storm drain it was pitch black and he had to crawl on his hands and knees in the enclosed space. The air was stagnant with mold and rotting debris. He could hear the unnerving scratch of little rodent feet ahead of him, but none of that mattered. What did matter was that he wouldn't make very good time this way. Unfortunately, he didn't have many options.

The prison security would have him in a moment if they had seen him go down the storm pipe. But he didn't think they had and if that was the case, he still had a chance...

****

John made a beeline for the newsstand and picked up the *New York Post,* ignoring the rain that

14

was creeping down the collar of his vintage suit and the jostle of pedestrians brushing past him.

The show before the show at this year's Academy Awards Ceremony proved to be more exciting than the awards themselves. The Puck Diamond, known for its whopping 33.19 carats and flawless beauty, was stolen from its famous owner, Katherine Park, just before the ceremony began. Because the ring appeared to vanish into thin air, there is speculation that this could be the work of the Ghost.

The Ghost first began spooking authorities over fifteen years ago when a piece known as the Winged Isis disappeared from the neck of Rachida Al-Mansure, the wife of Moroccan pasha Zaffar Al-Mansure. The crime took place aboard the pasha's yacht anchored off the coast of Alexandria during a glamorous New Year's Eve bash. Since that time, the Ghost has repeatedly staged thefts around the New Year's holiday or other high-profile events.

Many believed the international jewel thief had at last returned to the proverbial grave when cat burglar Dornal Zagen was put behind bars three years ago. Since Zagen's arrest, no new Ghost stories have unfolded, but with the theft of Miss Park's famous gem, authorities say they are not ruling out the possibility that the phantom thief is back in business.

Hollywood loves a good Ghost story, but some here in Tinseltown worry that this latest exploit could be just a trailer for coming attractions. With more than ten million dollars worth of gems stolen in 1998 (the thief's busiest year), everyone from starlets to studio heads have been reminded to lock up their loot. Perhaps the most serious threat to the glitterati will be in the nation's capital at the Diamond Ball scheduled for next Saturday. The charity event, sponsored by First Lady Lillian Spencer, is being held to raise money for a new library in Anacostia, a

DC neighborhood infamous for its urban blight. The Smithsonian will permit many of its greatest treasures to be modeled during the ball in a jewelry fashion show.

John folded the paper under his arm and handed the grumpy Italian newsstand attendant seventy-five cents. The old vendor sat morosely, blowing his nose with a handkerchief and staring out at the gloomy weather. "Rain again," he muttered, as if the world could bring nothing good to any of them.

John barely nodded in reply. He was too lost in thought for doom-and-gloom chitchat.

He reread the article on the subway ride to the Upper West Side, but as he was leaving the Eighty-Sixth Street station, he tossed the paper in the trash. The Ghost was no longer any of his business.

****

Veronica sat curled up in a worn velvet chair by the fireplace of the Upper East Side brownstone she shared with her father, celebrated archeologist, Buzzy Rossmore. She had been living with the old man since her divorce three years earlier. At first, the family home had been a refuge from prying eyes and wagging tongues, but after a while she had grown so comfortable, it seemed there was really no reason to leave.

Perhaps other twenty-something girls in Manhattan would have found living with a crusty academic a cramp to their flirtini-filled life-styles, but Veronica was more interested in Socrates than sexual exploits and happier to take long, solitary gallops through Central Park on her pure-blooded Arabian, Ramses, than intoxicated rides on some stockbroker after an intolerable Gen-Art function.

Perhaps she craved the security of the house itself, which had been her grandmother's. There was something wonderfully permanent and reassuring about the weathered brick exterior and the creaking wood floorboards after growing up in every far-flung place the globe could offer. Veronica had inhabited everything from pitched tents in the Egyptian desert to gilded Moroccan palaces filled with servants to strictly-run European boarding schools. She had lived in thirteen countries in twenty years. Now, with her mother gone and the horrifyingly public collapse of her marriage, she had only her father and this well-worn, but quietly beautiful, house to cling to. She felt at last as if she had a place to settle in for a while.

Veronica had been assisting her father in one way or another since she was the little girl who had stood awestruck by his side, gaping up in the shimmering heat at the strange paintings covering the walls of a pharaoh's forbidden tomb or gently wiping dust with a fine brush to reveal the statue of a forgotten Indian goddess in the jungles outside of Calcutta.

Now that the daring exploits of his youth were behind him, her father had at last settled into a tenured position at Columbia University as the head of the archeology department. He made no secret of the fact that without Veronica's sharp mind and organizational skills many of his ground-breaking bestsellers or the highly regarded academic papers he published would never have made it to print.

It was for an article scheduled to be published in *The American Journal of Archeology* that Veronica now studied a series of photographs taken in a recently discovered tomb at Abaydos in the lower Nile Delta. A curtain of sable-soft hair fell across the rows of hieroglyphics and her eyes started to burn as she deciphered the final lines of Egyptian symbols. A tight knot gripped her neck from leaning over her work so intently all evening.

Pushing aside the papers, she stretched,

enjoying the feel of thick silk pajamas gliding across her skin. Pulling off her cat's-eye glasses, she ran perfectly manicured fingers through her long, dark hair, pulling it away from a face so flawless she had been dubbed the "Dream Deb" of 1995. Not that she cared what the society drones thought of her, but it was what they had said just the same.

She closed her eyes and allowed the fire to warm her feet for a moment, luxuriating in the feel of the heat stealing up her toes to her bare ankles.

The chimes of the doorbell floated up from the ground floor below.

She glanced at the scarred antique clock which ticked discreetly on the mantle. It was after nine o'clock, too late for one of Buzzy's many friends or colleagues to be calling, and she was not expecting company.

Veronica rose and made her way through the dark house down two flights of stairs to the elegant, if slightly disheveled, entry hall, ignoring the chill of the marble floor against her bare feet. She was just about to open the front door to investigate when the lights flicked on in the hall. Buzzy Rossmore, wrapped in a frayed, old Japanese yukata, his usual bedtime attire, made his way down the stairs, his bushy white brows and wiry hair standing on end.

"Who's come a-calling?" croaked the old man good-naturedly.

With the lights on, Veronica noticed the envelope lying just inside the doorway where someone had slipped it through the brass mail slot. She leaned down and picked up the letter, turning it over for clues to its origin. "I don't know."

The envelope bore her name across the front in anonymous typewritten letters.

"Maybe it's a note from an admirer," chuckled the old man.

Veronica frowned and carefully tore open the

letter. Her face remained as smooth as glass as she read the note, but trying to hide her anxiety, she quickly jammed the letter back into the envelope.

"So? What does it say?"

Veronica smiled. "It's nothing." As her fingers folded and unfolded the envelope, she prayed he would let it go.

"Indulge an old man," said Buzzy, gently slipping the paper from her hand.

Annoyed, Veronica crossed her arms across her breasts, as her father read her mail. "You're by far the nosiest person I've ever met."

"Made a career of it," mumbled the archeologist as he pulled the letter out of the envelope and read.

Veronica studied her father as his face darkened and his usually good-natured expression vanished.

He looked up. "Perhaps now you'll stop being so headstrong and listen to me!" Buzzy angrily slapped the note down on the hall table. "Is this what it takes?"

Veronica's chin rose a notch and a combative fire kindled in her eyes, but she said nothing.

Shaking his head, Buzzy turned away and started back up the stairway. "I've had enough, Veronica. This Goddamn Diamond Ball! I'm going to take care of this whether you like it or not!" He turned back momentarily to glare at her. "You're still my daughter!"

Veronica bit her lower lip to keep back a sharp response as she watched her father lumber up the stairs. There was no point in arguing with him when he was in a state.

Whether in anger, or simply by reflex, Buzzy snapped off the light as he reached the landing, leaving her bathed in the moonlight spilling through the hall windows. She could hear him grumbling to himself as he disappeared into the darkened second floor.

Veronica exhaled a long breath and picked up the note again. Narrowing her eyes in the dim light, she slowly went over the short, typewritten sentences. There was nothing to be found on either the letter or the envelope to reveal the identity of the author.

Glancing up from the page, she caught sight of herself in the hall mirror. The shimmer of moonlight on diamonds played at her throat and peeped out like stars from behind the dark hair that didn't quite cover her earlobes. "Ice Princess" had been one of Derrick Chapin's favorite snide little pet names for her—derogatory and complimentary at the same time, as he had so often been during their brief marriage. She searched her own dark, India-ink eyes looking for something beyond the flawless image.

When will this finally be over? She looked at her reflection, but the cool moonlit beauty who stared back seemed to possess more secrets than answers.

Chapter Two

John stopped off at Zabar's, the famed gourmet delicatessen, on the way to his mother's house. He picked up bagels and lox, matzo ball soup, and crunchy kosher pickles—all the Jewish food his Catholic-Croatian mother was crazy about. He ordered himself a turkey and provolone sub from the deli counter and headed to the register. A pretty cashier with big brown eyes and long wavy hair rang him up.

"That'll be $22.45," she informed him cheerfully.

John scanned his wallet. It was filled with maxed-out credit cards and no cash. "Try this," he said hopefully, handing the cashier a credit card. He held his breath as she swiped it through the machine.

This is no way to live.

The register beeped and, to his relief, spit out a sales receipt for the groceries.

The cashier smiled and handed him the bag of gourmet goodies. As he met her eyes, she blushed and coyly cast down her heavily mascaraed lashes.

John smiled back. It was amazing how women could respond so positively to a smile or a polite, "How are you?" Back in his drinking days, John had come to the conclusion that women were difficult. Of course, this thought usually came while he was puking his guts out in front of a date on the pavement outside his favorite dive bar or wavering on his feet while making improper suggestions in some poor girl's ear with alcohol-drenched breath.

But, lo and behold, with the onset of his sobriety, suddenly female admiration glowed warmly toward him from all corners. Too bad Simon had strongly suggested he not get seriously involved with anyone just yet. Following Simon's suggestions had been tough but so far he was right on the money. John picked up the bag of groceries and waved goodbye to the cashier.

He sauntered down West Broadway to Eighty-Second Street, enjoying the spray of spring rain on his face. The streets were lined with dark brownstones and art deco apartment buildings with their uniformed doormen hanging out in front smoking cigarettes and waiting for their shifts to end. John nodded cordially to them as he made his way to number 224. There was no fancy-pants doorman here. Just a dusty lobby with a row of metal mailboxes and a chandelier with a few cracked crystals and one missing light bulb.

As he waited for the elevator, he couldn't help but notice himself in the smoky, mirrored wall across the hallway. At thirty-three, he didn't look half bad in the snappy vintage suit he had donned for the big AA birthday bash. His short, dark hair was neatly cut and his dimples flashed as he smiled at his one-year-sober self. The green eyes he had inherited from his Irish father sparkled with a bit of the devil in them, but overall he decided he looked like a fine, upstanding man.

A loud ding announced that the elevator had finally lumbered its way down to the lobby and John pushed open the heavy steel door. He punched the button for the fifth floor and a small wave of apprehension started at the pit of his stomach. Had he remembered everything at the store?

The elevator came to an abrupt stop, which almost sent his groceries flying. He stepped out into the familiar old hallway. When he was a kid, he used to play hockey on the shiny linoleum floors before his mother returned from work. He found himself wishing he could just stop with those memories instead of continuing in time and remembering how much she had suffered watching him destroy himself with alcohol.

"You can never pay your mother back for all the years of boozing and acting like an asshole," Simon counseled him, "but what you *can* do is be the best son possible here in the present."

John had taken this advice to heart, and slowly his mother's suspicions had been replaced by confused smiles when he showed up with potted plants for her, scrubbed her kitchen floor, and took her out for Chinese food or the symphony. Still, old habits die hard, and he knew she had her eye on him, waiting for him to screw up.

He pushed open the door and the smell of lavender talcum powder and potpourri air freshener greeted him. "Mom?"

Rose's head popped out from the den. Her hair was perfectly coifed in a silver bouffant and she had her reading glasses on. Her face spread into an annoyed smile.

"Johnnie, you didn't tell me you were coming tonight." Her Yugoslavian accent was still strong after thirty years of living in the US. "I got nothing to make you for dinner." But she gave him a kiss as he entered the den.

"I brought *you* food, Mom."

"Oh, what you got?" She peered into the bag and began pulling out items. "You got those cookies?" she asked hopefully.

"No, I forgot to get them."

The one thing he didn't get.

"Oh well, that's okay." She shuffled into the kitchen with John in tow.

"What are you going to eat?" she asked, opening

cabinets that were stocked to bursting with enough food to last through any terrorist attack they could cook up. She looked at her stash and shook her head as if the cans and boxes of food had in some way disappointed her.

"Don't worry, I have a turkey sandwich." John gently closed the cupboard doors only to have her reopen them.

"That's it?" she asked astonished. "You don't want no soup? I got extra coleslaw I made for lunch yesterday in the fridge."

"No, I'm okay. Seriously."

Rose raised her eyebrows and shook her head.

"I'm going to run now, Mom."

"But you just got here."

"I know, but I have a lot of stuff I need to take care of."

"What stuff?" she demanded. "You don't got no job."

"Well, I think maybe I need to deal with that."

"You going back to the FBI?" she asked.

"I don't know," he was suddenly getting defensive. "I don't know what I'm going to do, but I need to do something."

"Yeah," she said shaking her head. "You got to do something. Why don't you become a teacher? That's a good job."

"I'll think about it," he promised, nodding his head politely.

"Yeah," she persisted, "you could get good benefits."

"That's right, I'll think about it." He started to inch his way out of the kitchen.

"So, you gonna go now?"

"Yes, I'm going to get a good night's sleep."

She couldn't argue with that. "Well...that's good," she sighed.

He kissed her cheek, but she grabbed his arm

and said, "Oh, wait a minute. I have something to give you."

While she shuffled into her bedroom, John ripped the deli paper off his sandwich and started eating. He was halfway through the sub when Rose reappeared with a little black box in her hand and an impish grin lighting up her face.

"What's that?"

She came to John's side so they could both look from the same angle. Rose lifted the lid to reveal a Silver Star that had belonged to John's father. During WWII, Bill Monroe had sprinted through a hailstorm of German bullets to rescue a wounded soldier in his regiment. John had never heard his father talk about the incident but his Aunt Maureen loved to brag about it at Thanksgiving dinners after she'd had too many cocktails.

For the second time that night, John felt tears stinging his eyes. Pasted inside the lid of the box was a little dog-eared black-and-white photograph of Private Bill Monroe in his uniform. It had been a long time since John had seen the photo and the medal.

"Here," Rose pressed the box into John's hands. "This is for you, for your one year. I want you to remember that your father was a hero. Now you are a hero, too."

"Are you sure?" John knew this was one of his mother's most prized possessions.

"You just take good care of it," she warned sternly.

"I will," he promised. "Thank you."

They shared a warm moment, mother and son smiling at each other, remembering his father in a good way.

"I'll call you tomorrow," promised John.

"Okay, I hope you sleep good and be careful. It's dark out there," she warned him.

"Don't worry, Mom, I'll be careful." He shook his head as he walked out the door. Nine years with the FBI and his mother still thought he couldn't make it three blocks without getting stabbed to death by evil hoodlums. Some things never changed.

****

Dornal could see the faintest glimmer of moonlight reflecting off the water as he finally reached the end of the slime-covered storm drain. He inhaled deeply and the chill air cleansed his lungs after the putrid stench of the tunnel he'd been crawling through for hours. As he climbed out, he found himself on the shore of the Hudson River. Across the water, he could see the Palisades rising up dark and mysterious and to his back lay a tangle of pitch black trees.

This wasn't supposed to be his stop on the pipeline. His employer had arranged for a car, clothing, and money to be waiting for him in one of the alleys off the storm drain. But after setting off the alarm, Dornal knew he needed to get as far away as he could without any risk of being seen. The underground tunnel had provided the cover he needed.

Instinctively, he crouched down as the whir of a helicopter reached his ears and he could see the searchlight sweeping through the trees behind him. It wouldn't be long before the chopper's heat vision cameras picked him up.

The Austrian thief quickly slid into the freezing river. The snow in the Hudson Valley had only begun to melt two weeks ago. Dornal knew, even with his tough physique, he wouldn't survive long in the frigid water, but for the moment, it took care of the heat vision cameras. In this ice bucket, his body temperature was sinking fast.

He scanned the water with his gray shark eyes, spotting a sailboat anchored offshore about a quarter of the way into the river. It was difficult to tell from here if anyone was aboard, but it was that boat or the chopper-infested forest. Still grasping the scalpel he'd picked up in the prison operating room, he began to swim toward the boat.

As he got closer, he could see a dim light coming from the cockpit and the shadow of someone walking around inside. Things were going to get messy.

He didn't like for things to get messy. It was the mark of an amateur, but, then again, this hadn't been his plan in the first place. He'd have to make the best of the situation. Once he had the Hope Diamond in his possession, he'd be back in charge.

Quiet as the mist rising off the water, Dornal swam to the side of the boat and, grasping the anchor line in his iron grip, began to raise himself out of the river.

With the deftness of the professional thief he was, he swung himself over the rail, his powerful arm muscles rippling under the prison jumpsuit before he landed silently on deck.

The helicopter was still cruising around, sweeping the shoreline with its bright beam. Dornal had to get inside the cabin fast.

Peering in the window, he saw a man in a faded blue T-shirt and beat-up jeans sitting in the glow of a hurricane lamp with a guitar on his lap. As far as he could tell, the man was the only person on board. Dornal fingered the scalpel. At least he had a good, clean instrument.

The thief leaped down to the back deck just outside the cabin door, purposely landing with a loud thud. He stepped to the side with the boat's wheel at his back and waited for his prey to emerge.

A square of golden light illuminated the deck as the cabin door opened and the man tentatively stepped out. Before the man could react, Dornal twisted his victim's arm and pulled him back against his own big, barrel chest. The scalpel's blade flashed in the moonlight before it bit flesh and slit clean through the man's jugular.

Without missing a beat, Dornal dragged the body into the cockpit and stripped it bare. He peeled off his own dirty prison jumpsuit and pulled it over the man's lifeless limbs. Then he paused for a moment, paralyzed by the sound of a chopper approaching fast. He held his breath as the white beam spilled in the narrow windows and the roar of the propeller whipped up what sounded like a tornado directly overhead. He could hear the whir of the engine as the electronic bird circled over the sailboat, combing every inch of the vessel with its bright light. Dornal crouched low, waiting.

After one final pass, the helicopter roared down the river and he allowed himself to exhale. He waited a moment to be sure and then slipped back on deck. The chopper was moving farther away now. He could still see the searchlight but the ominous sound of propellers was fading out of earshot. Going below again, the convict picked up the body and carried it to the lower deck.

With only a minor splash, he sent the man into the river and watched as the bright orange jumpsuit disappeared under murky water. He had no illusions that once the body washed ashore it would fool the police for long, but it might slow them down a couple of days and he wouldn't need much more time than that.

Heading back inside, the thief found a suitcase full of clothes. He slipped on a pair of faded jeans much like the ones his predecessor had been wearing and a warm wool sweater. In one of the cupboards of the tiny kitchen, he found a bottle of Remy Martin. He took a couple slugs straight from the bottle and felt the warmth flow back into his frozen flesh.

After a bit more searching, he found the dead

man's wallet with his license, credit cards, and $120 cash. He studied the photograph of the man. With some brown hair dye, Dornal could pass. He took another long, slow pull from the bottle. He'd managed to find himself an identity, a mode of transportation, and a place to crash all in one fell swoop. For the first time in months he smiled. If there was one thing Dornal Zagen enjoyed, it was efficiency.

He relaxed back onto the banquette that served as both sofa and bed in the small boat. Two things were on his mind, the Hope Diamond and revenge. His plan to seize the Hope at the Diamond Ball was already worked out and it was just a question of waiting until the right time. Meanwhile, he had only to discover the whereabouts of John Monroe to take care of his other plan. It was going to be a pleasure to execute the former FBI man.

****

John arrived home to his cramped one bedroom apartment on West End Avenue. The apartment was in one of those 1970s buildings that looked like the projects but wasn't. He had decorated accordingly.

He fidgeted with the little black box in his pocket, finally pulling it out as he sat down in his chair by the window. So much light poured in from the street lamps and the twinkling George Washington Bridge, he could see quite well without switching on the mushroom lamp he had found in an old junk shop. He held the box with his father's medal in his hand, turning it around in his fingers.

The sharp ring of his phone jolted him out of his reverie.

Don't let it be a crazy newcomer, he prayed, remembering the myriad of jonesing heroin addicts, speed freaks, and potty-mouthed alcoholics he'd given his number to in the last month, inviting them to call him any time they needed a friend.

Warily, he picked up the receiver. "Hello?"

It was his old partner from the FBI. "John, it's Quinn. I've been calling you all night."

"Quinn!" said John, relieved. "Sorry, I thought you might be someone from AA."

There was a pause on the line.

"John, have you watched the news or read the paper lately?"

"The Ghost strikes again." John parroted the newspaper headlines.

"We could use your help."

Chapter Three

John passed his hand over his eyes trying to think of how to respond to his ex-partner's invitation. "You know, I just don't think I'm ready to come back. I don't know if I ever will be," he said, trying to be honest.

"That's too bad." Quinn sounded disappointed. "We're so swamped here these days with all this terrorist shit and now they're reorganizing all the computer files and upgrading the systems. I swear to God, my eleven-year-old daughter has a more advanced computer network in her grammar school than we do here."

John shook his head in the dark. "I know, it's ridiculous, but can't you get someone else to help you out over there?"

"Yeah, I can, but not someone who's tracked the Ghost for as long as you have."

"Unsuccessfully tracked him."

"Listen, no one has been able to get anything on the Ghost, not Interpol or Scotland Yard—nobody." Quinn reminded him.

"True," John admitted. "So there's no word from California?"

"Well, Katherine Park had quite a few words to say, but other than that, we got nothing," said Quinn gloomily.

"Well, at least you have the whole thing on film. Every TV crew in the world must have been there."

"Yeah, I've been combing through it frame by frame all day, but Katherine Park didn't take the route up the red carpet she was supposed to. So all I have is a shot of her ass for the most crucial moments when she was hamming it up with her fans in the bleachers. There was one old lady who looks like she could be the Granny, but it's hard to tell from the camera angle. She's also wearing a hat with a veil which clouds things even more."

"Ah, the Granny," said John with a smile. After nine years of chasing down jewel thieves, he had developed a certain amount of affection for some of them and she was one of his favorites. He had first become aware of her when she toddled into Tiffany's and asked to try on a ten carat, $480,000 star sapphire ring. She slipped the ring on her finger and watched it flash blue in the store's perfect lighting.

"I'll take it!" she'd declared continuing to view the ring. "Only...wait...may I please see how it looks in the box?"

The well-trained salesperson had obliged by carefully placing the ring in a box so that it sparkled to its best advantage. Granny had held the box in her hand and examined the ring from all angles. Then snapping the box shut, she'd ordered the salesman to wrap it up! She was just going to step outside and get her checkbook from her driver.

Only later did the unfortunate salesperson discover that, like a magician at a kid's birthday party, Granny had switched the box and taken off with her loot, leaving him with an empty box in his hands and a lot of explaining to do. He had to give her credit, the old lady had guts.

John had eventually tracked Granny down in Stockholm where she had taken the sapphire to be cut and sold. But remarkably, despite mountains of evidence, a jury had found her innocent. Probably because they just didn't have the stomach to send such a sweet old lady up the river in her golden years.

"How is the old broad?" asked John.

"Way too active for a woman of her years."

"Well, it sounds just like her to pull something like this. She has the balls for it, we know that."

"Could be her. We're just not sure yet. The whole Ghost hysteria is really just the press trying to sell papers," admitted Quinn.

"Everyone loves a good Ghost story." John remembered the packs of rabid reporters he'd had to deal with every time the mysterious jewel thief took off with another rare gem. "Besides, there hasn't been any real Ghost activity since we put away Dornal Zagen."

"I can't argue with that," said Quinn, sounding as if he'd like to.

"Maybe he's the Ghost," observed John.

"You still working that angle?"

"I'm not working any angles anymore," John replied matter-of-factly.

"What would you say if I told you Zagen busted out of Sing Sing this evening?"

"You're kidding!"

Quinn sighed. "I wish I freakin' were."

"How did he get out?" John was curious despite himself.

"How's he do a lot of things?" asked Quinn, disgusted. "No one has any idea. The alarm went off and they found his cell empty."

"So he vanished into thin air?"

"That's exactly what he did."

John was silent. He automatically began laying a plan in his head to catch the notorious thief and maybe find out for sure this time if Zagen really was the Ghost.

"Look, here's the thing," said Quinn, interrupting John's thoughts. "I'm using all my resources right now to deal with this Puck Diamond mess. You can imagine with the press and Katherine

Park what a nightmare it is. Now Dornal Zagen breaks out, and, on top of that, the First Lady has decided to throw a big charity event—The Diamond Ball. All the big jewelers, like Cartier and Bulgari, are going to be there with models wearing their loot. The event's being held at the Smithsonian and do you happen to recall what's in the Harry Winston Gallery of the Smithsonian?"

"The Hope Diamond. I just read about it in *The Post*."

"That's right, the fucking Hope Diamond. The most famous jewel in the world. It's like the worst security nightmare since...I don't even know when!"

"I am so glad I don't have your job." John shook his head in the dark.

He could hear Quinn nervously lighting a cigarette. "Are you sure?"

"Oh yeah," said John, emphatically.

Quinn changed his tactics. "But it could be a great time to catch a few thieves, huh? You know they're all out there salivating—old Granny, the Ghost, Maggie the Cat, Nicholas Bezuhov, and now Dornal Zagen is on the loose."

"I feel so out of the loop." John couldn't help the old thrill that was starting to run through him.

"So come back and help me out!" begged Quinn.

John sat back and thought about it.

Quinn exhaled. "You there?"

"I'm thinking," said John, watching a tugboat float down the Hudson. "I wish there was some way I could sort of stick my toe in. I don't want to go back to the FBI and get into it again. I realize it's too soon and feel like I fucked up enough the first time around."

"Well, there actually might be a way for you to do that."

"What are you talking about?" asked John.

"There's this old family friend of the First Lady,

some Park Avenue brat, Veronica Rossmore. She has a treasure trove of jewels and is coming down for the party. Her father asked if we knew of anyone who could drive her and her booty down to DC and watch out for her at the Diamond Ball..."

John cut to the chase. "In other words, she's looking for a bodyguard."

"Exactly. It pays insanely well. I mean, *really* good money, and all you'd have to do is hang out with a beautiful, rich girl and escort her to the ball. I'd have the benefit of knowing someone who had a clue was watching her so I can do my job and not have to worry about it."

John hesitated. "I don't know."

"Listen, you just said you wanted to get your feet wet and you'd be doing me a big favor. There's no one I'd rather have around at this Smithsonian thing than you," urged Quinn. "And who knows...some of our old friends might show up. Maybe we'll finally put the Ghost to rest."

The whole idea gave John a bad feeling in the pit of his stomach, but he did need to make some money. He couldn't put it off any longer.

"How much did you say this pays?"

"Twenty thousand. I'd do it myself, if I weren't so slammed."

"Twenty thousand dollars!" John was certain he had heard wrong.

"That's right."

John was instantly suspicious. "Why so much?"

"They want the best. With people like this, the more money they spend, the better quality they think they're getting," explained Quinn, like he knew the rich.

"Just tell me what I have to do to get this job."

"You just need to call her old man. Buzzy Rossmore, I think the name is." John could hear his old partner routing around looking for the information. "I've got to get a better filing system," Quinn complained.

"Why don't you just call me in the morning with the information?" suggested John, picturing the usual mess of files, photos, old coffee cups, and whatever else had found its way onto Quinn's desk.

"Yeah, I'll do that. My wife's going to kill me if I don't get home soon."

"Say hello to Diane for me."

"Okay, talk to you tomorrow."

"Okay, and thanks. I appreciate your help." John could hear Simon lecturing him in his head about gratitude and remembering to be thankful for the help we receive.

"Sure thing."

****

Dornal set sail at dawn, taking the boat down the Hudson River to New York harbor. Not wanting to answer a lot of questions at the various marinas in town, he anchored offshore and jumped into the yellow rubber dinghy he found tied to the back of the sailboat. The launch sped along the polluted water until he reached the small private dock that serviced The Water Club. The swanky restaurant was located aboard a barge that could be accessed from the highway or the little dock off the East River.

Dornal threw a line to the white-jacketed boat hand, who quickly secured the dinghy and welcomed him to the club. He slipped his sunglasses on as he entered the elegant dining room with its plush booths and magnificent view of the river.

The maitre d' approached. "Are you here for brunch, sir?"

Dornal nodded.

"Will it just be you?" inquired the maitre d' politely.

"Yes." Dornal scanned the room for the most secluded table. "May I have that one?" he asked in his clipped, nearly perfect English, indicating a corner booth.

The maitre d' smiled. "Right this way." He led Dornal to a table with crisp white linen and a small crystal vase filled with black lilies. Dornal couldn't remember the last time he'd eaten a decent meal as he took the menu and began to review its offerings. That pathetic alcoholic from the FBI had made sure of it.

Dornal flashed back to that cold night in Chicago. He could still see the snow floating down outside the posh little jewelry shop, the diamonds glittering like ice in the moonlight. He could smell the scent of pine from the Christmas wreath that hung over the shop door and feel the end of John Monroe's pistol pressed up against his kidney. In that moment, his fifteen-year crime spree had come to an end. That scene was seared into his memory banks more than any other.

The waiter approached. "Good morning, sir. Would you like to start off with something to drink?"

"Black coffee," responded Dornal, "and I'll take the scrambled eggs with crab cakes, too."

"Very good," replied the waiter, with a slight bow before heading into the kitchen.

Dornal pulled the dead man's cell phone out of his pocket and punched in a number. The call connected and his employer answered.

"It's Dornal."

"Where are you?"

"I'm in Manhattan and I need money."

"Didn't you get the envelope I left in the glove compartment?" His employer sounded annoyed.

"I never made it to the car."

There was silence for a long moment. "Go to the Three Brothers' Diner on Eighty-Sixth Street and Columbus at five this afternoon. At the coat-check booth, tell them you left a brown suede jacket there.

If they ask for the check slip, say you misplaced it but that there is a green wallet and a set of keys in the pocket of the jacket. Inside the wallet, you'll find money and your instructions."

"Got it."

"When you arrive in Washington, I'll call you at the number we agreed upon."

"I'll call you," said Dornal.

"That's not the plan…"

But Dornal had hung up; he liked to make his own plans.

After the food arrived, he resisted his urge to wolf it down, eating and then finishing up with hot, black coffee. He paid with the dead man's credit card. He didn't care if the Feds traced it because he'd be out of Manhattan in the next few hours anyway. He left the dinghy tied to the restaurant's dock and exited The Water Club through the main entrance on East Thirtieth Street.

Dornal walked a few blocks north along the river promenade. When no one was watching, he chucked the cell phone into the water where it sank to the bottom with the rest of the trash. He wished it was John Monroe's lifeless body which was slowly sucked under the murky olive waves. He reassured himself that he'd track Monroe down with the same ruthless efficiency he performed all his tasks. Soon, John Monroe would be the only ghost left in town.

****

It was bright and early when John received a call from Buzzy Rossmore. The old man was pleasant on the phone, assuring John he had come so highly recommended he was confident this would all work out beautifully. His voice had the easy charm of old money. Good manners had probably been bred into Buzzy so early in life, he wouldn't know how to behave any other way.

It must be nice, John thought as he listened to

Mr. Rossmore speak. The archeologist asked John to drop by around three o'clock to meet his daughter and go over the details of the assignment. John agreed before hanging up.

He decided to walk through Central Park on his way to the Rossmore's East Side town house. It was a bright, balmy day and the trees were bursting with new, green life, while the magnolias had begun to bloom all around Belvedere Lake.

John passed well-dressed little kids running wild through the playground at the foot of the large, bronze statue of *Alice in Wonderland.* Jamaican nannies chatted together on park benches while keeping one eye glued to their tiny charges. In Sheep's Meadow, private school students lay out on picnic blankets soaking up the first weak sun of the season. They gathered in clusters listening to iPods, drinking diet sodas, and smoking clove cigarettes as they checked each other out from behind dark sunglasses.

He strolled past a patch of earth where Dutch tulips pushed up insistently in beds of red, yellow, and orange. They screamed, "Spring is here! Rejoice!" A little Chihuahua, dressed in a peach angora sweater and matching hat, danced over to the flowers on his tiny feet and christened them, his proud Park Avenue mommy beaming at him, exclaiming, "Good baby! That's a good boy!" in a baby-talk voice that belied her fifty-plus years.

As he turned onto Fifth Avenue and left the park behind, John passed the Metropolitan Museum with its grand, white-columned façade and dancing fountains. Street artists had their easels out and painted bad Manhattan cityscapes for tourists to buy.

John made a right onto Ninety-First Street and scanned the elegant row of town houses. He spotted number 12 about halfway down the block. It was modest-looking compared to some of the wedding cake homes on the block with their carved stone gargoyles and elaborate decorative iron fences and balconies. The Rossmore's house was a three-story brick building with neat, white trim around the windows. Red geraniums spilled out of window boxes and sat cheerfully in large cast iron pots by the front door. John rang the bell and waited.

The door was promptly answered by an Asian woman in a pale blue maid's outfit. She looked sleek and elegant and smiled graciously. "You are Mr. Monroe," she informed him.

"Yes, I am," agreed John.

"Mr. Rossmore is not home yet. He said to tell you he would be a little detained, but Miss Veronica is waiting for you upstairs if you'll follow me," she said, with a polite bow.

John wasn't sure if he should bow back so he just kind of inclined his head a bit. "Thanks."

The maid led him through the small but beautifully decorated entrance. It contained a mahogany hall-tree on which several rumpled tweed jackets and an old trench coat were draped. These were clearly good quality but in desperate need of a pressing, perhaps even retirement. A few stray hats and mufflers left over from the winter and a pile of books on ancient Egypt were also stacked on top of the antique table beside the hall tree. The floor was worn but highly-polished black-and-white marble squares. Poised on a small table across from the doorway, a blue and white porcelain Chinese vase overflowed with an arrangement of fresh cut flowers which filled the room with the scent of roses and springtime lilacs.

They made their way up a narrow staircase to the second floor landing and into an old-fashioned parlor with sliding pocket doors. The room had warm wood paneling and a pale-green stained-glass

Belle Epoque chandelier. Books lay around everywhere in neat piles and a giant periwinkle-blue Victorian sofa was positioned under the bay window that looked out onto the quiet street. Ancient maps, yellowed and fragile looking, lined the walls. The bust of an old Roman bigwig rested on the mantle of the black marble fireplace, which boasted a cheerful blaze though it wasn't the slightest bit chilly out.

"Would you like some jasmine tea?" the maid asked, indicating a beat-up leather club chair for him to sit in.

"Oh, no thanks," said John, trying to get his bearings.

"You might as well," said a low feminine voice as an expensive-looking brunette swept into the room. She was dressed in a white halter dress with a simple, form-fitting cardigan. It was difficult to tell if she was tall or not, because she wore high strappy shoes that showed off her pearly toes with their soft polish. Her hair was pulled back behind one ear to reveal a pair of dark blue eyes, lined with a faint trace of black. Her cheekbones were high but not severe, her skin glowed like an alabaster lamp, and her softly curved lips shone with pale pink gloss. She had a timeless face, a beautiful face, but there was something guarded and unapproachable in her expression. The elegantly old-fashioned scent of *L'Heure Bleue* trailed after her in tantalizing wisps. She barely looked at John as she slid into a chair by the fire. "I'm having some and my father won't be home for a bit."

She didn't seem to want to look at him, but he was sure getting an eyeful of her. It had been a while since he'd felt such a primal physical attraction to a woman.

He barely noticed as the maid slipped discreetly out of the room.

"Well, you must be Veronica," said John.

She looked up, her eyes sweeping over him in a cold, detached appraisal. He flashed his brightest smile, complete with dimples and wickedly sparkling green eyes. She didn't seem impressed.

"Oh, don't *you* tell *me*," she said, with an arch of her perfectly manicured brow. Turning back to the fire, she put her hands out in front of the blaze.

This isn't getting off to a good start.

"I'm John Monroe," John rose to shake her hand.

"You don't have to get up. I know who you are." She picked a bit of invisible lint off her cardigan and tossed it into the fire.

Annoyed, John sank back down. "I'm assuming you're Veronica."

"Mm-hmm."

"I'm sorry, I didn't hear that. Did you say yes?" he asked in the same tone he used to interrogate the crack dealers and two-bit stoolies who used to make his life hell when he still worked for the Feds.

She gave him a look, and sauntered over to his chair. She plastered on a big smile and stuck her hand out like a robot. "I'm Veronica Rossmore. I'm so pleased to make your acquaintance. Thank you so much for coming to see us in our home. We are very appreciative." She shook his hand mechanically, dropped the smile, and went back to her chair.

"Nice brooch," he observed, ignoring her rudeness. "Looks like...," he thought about it for a moment, "Gillot or Cartier, early 1900s."

She swiveled in her chair and looked him up and down again. "So, you can do more than point a gun."

"Where did you get it?" he asked.

She got up again and slid onto the arm of his chair, unpinning the glittering brooch from the breast of her cardigan and handed it to him. He took it gingerly. The piece was exquisitely made up of diamonds and platinum arranged in the shape of a charming little bow with two pear-shaped stones hanging like teardrops from the bottom of each ribbon. The value was not in the quantity of diamonds used, which equaled less than three carats he estimated, but in the incredible craftsmanship. He flipped the brooch around and checked out the maker's mark. Gillot, just as he'd predicted.

"It was my grandmother's," she informed him proudly.

He handed it back to her. "Don't wear it on the subway."

"I don't take the subway," she said rising, all chumminess gone.

"I was kidding."

"Hmm." She settled back into her chair by the fire and picked up a book.

The maid arrived with a modern set of ceramic cups and a squat teapot on a matching tray that looked a little out of place in the old-fashioned parlor.

"Thank you, Iris." Veronica ignored the tea and flipped the page of her book.

"Thank you," mumbled John as Iris once more slipped out of the room.

He sat uneasily in front of the tea set watching Veronica lazily read as if she were completely alone in the room.

"Aren't you going to have some tea?" he asked to break the silence.

"Yes," she said, without moving at all.

John looked at the steaming pot and looked at her. If she was waiting for him to serve her, she could wait forever.

She licked her thumb and flipped another page.

"Can I pour you some?" he asked.

The book was raised up higher now covering most of her face and she had turned even more toward the fire on her swiveling chair.

"No, thanks," she answered after a moment's

pause, as if he had dragged her away from some fascinating sentence and she needed a moment to compute what he had asked her. She waved a hand from behind the big armchair, fluttering fingers toward the tea tray. "Feel free to pour yourself a cup," she advised him.

Grudgingly, he gave into temptation and poured a cup.

Five minutes or so passed and he observed, "I feel like I'm in the waiting room of a really expensive shrink's office, or maybe the dentist."

She smiled in genuine amusement, whether at his wit or the uncomfortable position she was putting him in he couldn't tell, but she put the book down. "I suppose I should be straight with you."

"I would like that." John placed his cup on the table now that they were getting down to business.

"I'm sorry you've gone to the trouble of coming here, but I have no intention of allowing anyone to babysit me. My father insisted I meet you and see how harmless and unobtrusive you would be, but it doesn't matter. I'm a private person." She looked him straight in the eye. "I don't like people hanging around."

"You're kidding?" John snapped sarcastically.

"You can wait for my father, if you like, and we can go through the charade. I promise you, though, after you leave, I will let him know in no uncertain terms that I am not interested in..."

But she stopped mid-sentence at the sound of the door closing downstairs. John and Veronica stood awkwardly as Buzzy Rossmore climbed the steps to the parlor.

The archeologist had a bright, welcoming smile on his face as he entered the room. His manner was warm and jovial. John liked him on sight. Buzzy was clad in an older style, gray flannel suit with a crisp white handkerchief poking out of his breast pocket, which nearly matched the shock of hair that stood out on his head. His sparkling blue eyes radiated intelligence and had a certain childlike innocence to them.

"Well, John, I'm so glad you could make it!" exclaimed Buzzy, as if they'd been buddies for years.

"I'm glad to meet you," said John politely.

Buzzy kissed his daughter on the cheek. "Hello, sweetheart." Veronica lifted her brows and threw herself down on the couch, apparently resigned to the ordeal ahead of her.

"Please make yourself comfortable." Buzzy sunk into the seat by the fire which Veronica had vacated.

John accepted the invitation and sat down.

"So, you've had a chance to meet Veronica." The old man smiled in his daughter's direction.

"Yes," John said, not knowing if he should elaborate.

"Well, Lillian says you're a retired FBI man. Though I must say, you look pretty young to be retired. You must have been doing something right!" He laughed at his own joke and continued. "Anyway, Lillian said before you left the FBI, you specialized in catching jewel thieves."

It took John a moment to figure out who Lillian was, until he caught on that the old man was talking about the First Lady. "Yes, I followed the Ghost around for several years. It didn't get me very far though. He's still at large."

"But you captured several other notorious thieves," Buzzy commented, enthusiastically.

"I did help bring a few people down," admitted John.

"Well then, what we'd like you to do should be child's play for someone with your background. We don't want you to catch any thieves, just make sure no one gets their hands on any of Veronica's treasures."

John looked over at Veronica. She sat tight-lipped with her arms crossed over her breasts, her Gillot brooch shimmering like fairy dust in the late afternoon sunlight.

"I'd like to help you, Mr. Rossmore," John said, trying to be polite. "But your daughter says she doesn't want a bodyguard."

"It's true, Daddy," she said quickly. "If you'd just spoken to me about this before dragging...," she looked at John, obviously trying to remember his name.

He helped her out. "John."

She ignored him. "You know I hate having people around. I'll have no privacy at all."

As John watched her try to convince Buzzy, he remembered something from his doings with the Manhattan blue bloods. During his time tracking jewel thieves, it was inevitable that he would pick up a little Park Avenue gossip. It must have been about three years ago that he had heard about Veronica and her husband who had thrown her down the grand staircase at the Metropolitan Museum's Costume Institute Ball in a jealous rage. There had been lots of pictures of the event floating around the tabloids. That year the ball's theme had been 'Goddesses' and Veronica had come dressed as the Egyptian deity Isis. She had adorned herself in a vintage 1930s beaded gown and piles of the gems her father had given her during their time on archeological trips to the East.

There had been one particular photo of Veronica lying unconscious at the foot of the staircase with her ball dress fanned out all around her, her shapely legs exposed, and her head thrown back showing off a swan's neck encased in an exotic necklace. She had looked like a fancy broken doll flung on the ground by a careless child. Standing over her was her drunk husband, his black bow tie hanging loose around his neck, his jaw dropped open as if he couldn't believe what had just happened. For about a month this picture, and others of Veronica and her husband, had graced the covers of the *New York Post* and *People* magazine. Then it had all blown over and gone away.

John studied her more curiously now.

"I will not have you put yourself in danger, Veronica," insisted her father. Taking a piece of paper from his breast pocket, he handed it to John. "We received this last night."

John unfolded the paper and read the note. It was typewritten on a plain, white piece of paper.

"Stay away from the Diamond Ball, Miss Rossmore, or you could find yourself an unwilling character in the latest Ghost story, to which there will not be a happy ending."

"Have you notified anyone yet? The police or the FBI?" asked John.

"We don't want any publicity, and really, I'm not afraid of ghosts," insisted Veronica.

"Miss Rossmore, you really ought to take this seriously. Why don't you let me take this down to the lab? They could test it for fingerprints, DNA, all kinds of things."

"I really think this whole thing is silly," she said with a cold smile. "I'm a big girl and I don't want a high profile police investigation *or* a bodyguard."

"Will you at least promise to be more careful with your jewels?" pleaded Buzzy. Clearly his little girl had him wrapped around her finger.

"What's careful?" she asked.

"She won't be," exclaimed the old man, now turning to John. "She flaunts her diamonds all over the place, even wears them on the subway or walking through Central Park alone—at night, for God's sake!"

So she did take the subway. What else was she

lying about? John raised his brows at Veronica, but she wasn't looking at him. She had fire in her eyes and all her attention went to her father.

"I can take care of myself and you know it."

Her father shook his head and collapsed back into his chair looking as if his daughter would be the death of him. "You understand, Veronica, that I have a very important lecture to give on Saturday night. I cannot accompany you to this affair."

"I'm not asking you to!" she said, exasperated.

"Veronica, I will not be able to sleep at night worrying about you and those jewels. Not with this Ghost on the loose and every other thief worth their salt probably lining up to take turns stealing from the people attending this ball!"

Veronica shook her head and a curtain of dark hair fell over one eye. Annoyed, she pushed it back behind her ear.

"All right," said Buzzy with a sigh, "I'll cancel my lecture."

John almost smiled. So he and his mother weren't the only people who went through this.

"You will *not* cancel your lecture," declared Veronica.

Buzzy was about to reply, when he turned to look at John and, taking a deep breath, remembered himself. "John, I'm so sorry. Perhaps I can call you tomorrow when my daughter and I have straightened this thing out."

"That sounds like a good idea." John rose and handed back the note. He paused a moment, not wanting to interfere but feeling it his duty to say something. "You know, you really should call the cops about this note. The person who wrote it might be dangerous."

Buzzy nodded his head. "Thank you, John. Veronica and I will discuss the matter and decide what we think is best."

John shrugged; it really wasn't any of his business.

Buzzy rose. "I'll walk you out."

"Don't worry about it."

"Well, here," the old man pulled a beat-up leather checkbook out of his jacket pocket, "let me at least compensate you for your wasted time."

John shook his head. "It's okay."

"It would make me feel better." Buzzy's pen was poised over a blank check.

John felt Veronica's cool eyes on him, watching to see if he'd take the money.

"Seriously, Mr. Rossmore, I had a great walk through the park on my way over here. It was a pleasure meeting you and your daughter. You don't owe me anything." John couldn't help but wonder just how much the old man would have given him.

"Well...all right." Veronica's father slipped his checkbook back into his jacket. "Thank you for coming by; I'll be in touch."

John nodded to Veronica, who sat stone-faced tapping her heel on the ground. She inclined her head a fraction of an inch in his direction.

"It was a pleasure meeting you, Veronica." He flashed a smile in her direction. "Maybe I'll catch you on the A train sometime."

She smiled back with hard eyes. "Don't count on it."

Chapter Four

The next morning, John sat quietly reading a passage out of the *Big Book of Alcoholics Anonymous* as he'd done every morning for the past year. This morning he'd been reading about Step Two: "*Came to believe that a Power greater than ourselves could restore us to sanity.*"

He drank his coffee and thought about this concept. He still had trouble with the idea of a Higher Power. If there was one, why had his father's liver burst one day? Why had he watched his old man vomit blood all over the immaculate floor his mother had spent hours scrubbing before she left to run the day's errands? Why should any seven-year-old be left alone with his father crumpled against the refrigerator, the older man's eyes bugged out with fear, his face a waxy yellow? John could go back there in a heartbeat and see his father coughing up noxious poisons, unable to speak or move until his system was so polluted it shut down completely. Then he had just been a dead man with a little boy shaking his beefy blood-drenched shoulder. The little boy had cried and screamed but there had been no one to help.

John closed his eyes and whispered, "God, grant me the serenity to accept the things I cannot change, the courage to change the things I can, and the wisdom to know the difference. God, grant me the serenity to accept the things I cannot change..."

That's when the phone rang. It was Veronica.

"I'm downstairs in my car," she said, in her cool,

low voice. "I'll give you ten minutes to get down here. If you have a tuxedo, bring it. Otherwise, we'll be gone four days, so pack accordingly."

He was in a bad mood and a lot of not-so-nice comebacks sprang to mind, but instead he said, "I haven't brushed my teeth yet."

"Okay, eleven minutes." She hung up.

He was used to having to pack on the double from his days at the FBI. When a jewel thief struck, whether it was in Lisbon or Los Angeles, he had to be on the first plane out before the trail got cold.

When John came out of his apartment building, he found Veronica waiting in a platinum convertible. Her hair was covered by an iris print scarf and she wore big bug-eyed, Jackie-O sunglasses, a perfectly pressed sleeveless button-down shirt, and a preppy floral skirt. But what caught his eye was the shimmer of diamonds dancing around her wrists as she clutched the steering wheel and another white hot sparkle peeping out from beneath her collar.

"Showing off your collection?" John asked, tossing his suitcase into the back seat and sliding in next to her.

She smiled and shook her glittering wrist in front of him so the diamonds danced in the sunlight. "This is nothing."

Then she reached into her purse and pulled out an envelope with his name scrawled across it. "My father asked me to give this to you." She presented it to him with a pearly white smile that seemed a little too much like a smirk.

"What is it?"

"Probably money." She shifted the car into gear and tore away from the curb. "I'm sure you'll have expenses and things and my dad, being the sucker he is, probably threw in a nice advance, too."

John slipped the envelope in his pocket. He sure wasn't going to give Veronica Rossmore the satisfaction of watching his eyes light up at the sight of a few greenbacks or a fat bank check.

She pulled onto the West Side Highway and quickly shot ahead of a cab driver who was vying for the same crack in the traffic flow to get into the fast lane. She appeared to be in a good mood today. Something about getting out on the open road with the wind whipping around them seemed to appeal to her.

John watched the Hudson River flash by in a blur. "Of course, it would have been better to hire a limo with bulletproof glass and tinted windows."

"I detest limousines," she scoffed. "I think they're the most vulgar cars. Any wannabe rap star or pimply seventeen-year-old on a prom date can drive around in one."

She had a point.

"Still, if you want security…"

"But I don't want security, or rather, I'm not worried about it. It's my father who's the big worry-wart."

"I take it he's not coming to the ball?" remarked John.

"No, he hates these big social things."

"What about you?"

"I hate them, too, but Lillian Spencer was a friend of my mother's. They went to Vassar together and she specifically asked me to come and, of course, I *am* curious to see all the beautiful jewels. I won't be able to stand most of the ladies wearing them, but that doesn't matter. Just seeing this collection of gems all in one place will be something."

He could imagine her eyes lighting up behind the Jackie O's. "It'll be a security nightmare is what it'll be."

"But there will be secret service and the museum's security and, of course, I'll have you," she said with a slight condescending lilt to her voice, which John did not appreciate.

"Listen, I'm telling you, it's a security nightmare. You're lucky your father had the foresight to hire someone to watch over your stuff," he insisted.

She shrugged and they rode in silence after that all the way through the state of New Jersey.

Somewhere around Trenton, Veronica reached over and flipped open the glove compartment. She pulled out a CD and slid it into the built-in player on the dashboard. The velvety voice of Lena Horn purred out of the speakers with a swanky band arrangement to back her up.

Veronica sang along with Lena as she flew past the other cars on the highway. John liked the way she drove. She was sure of herself and had quick reflexes. She didn't tailgate, choosing instead to jump ahead of any slowpokes on the road. He stretched back in the leather seats and watched the world fly by with the sun on his face and the music soothing his spirit. This might not be such a bad job after all.

They were speeding through Pennsylvania when Veronica said, "So tell me some exciting stories about your days at the FBI chasing jewel thieves."

"Well, let's see." He thought about it. "The man who gave me the most trouble is your friend the Ghost."

"The one who wrote the note."

John nodded.

"I read about him in the newspapers," said Veronica. "He took Katherine Park's diamond ring."

"It's possible. I've tracked him all through Europe, down to Charleston, and over to Los Angeles, among other places. The thing about him is...he doesn't leave any trace—nothing." John bit his thumb and shook his head. "Every other thief leaves some kind of telltale sign. Some of them are just glorified thugs who pull off jewelry store robberies like they were hitting a local gas station. Some of them are so caught up in their own crazy game they get arrogant and leave calling cards."

"Actual calling cards?" asked Veronica, unable to keep the interest from her voice.

John smiled. "One guy does. He calls himself the White Russian because he claims his family goes back to the aristocracy of the Russian Empire, though it's more likely he's a descendant of the craftsman from the House of Fabergé. He seems to have inherited some of their skill with jewels."

"What has he stolen?" she asked.

"His biggest heist was about five years ago. He grabbed a Burmese ruby the size of an egg out of the hotel room of a Saudi Arabian sheikh."

"Did you catch him?"

"Well, yes and no," said John. "We knew it was him. He left his card for Christ's sake. He was staying in the same hotel, but we had no proof and we couldn't find the ruby on him."

"Was the stone ever recovered?"

"No, the thing about the White Russian is since he's a jeweler, he cuts all the stones himself, which makes it more difficult to track him down. Normally, you get your guy when they try to sell the stones or get them cut," John informed her.

"If most thieves get caught cutting their stones, why don't more of them do it themselves?" she asked, revving the engine and speeding up to pass a big rig truck.

"It's no easy thing to cut a gem," he explained. "That's a serious craft, often passed down through generations. There are only a few places in the world you can even get it done."

"The White Russian, he's a trained gem cutter as well as a master craftsman?"

"The official name for it is a lapidary, but yes,

that's his deal," said John.

"What about the Ghost?" she asked. "Why can't you track him when he gets his stones cut, or do you think he knows how to do it, too?"

"There's something about him," said John, drifting back into the past. "You go to the scene of the crime where the Ghost has struck and there's nothing. No fingerprints, no broken locks, nothing disturbed in any way, and there's no word on the street either. Not a peep. The stones don't show up on the black market." He shrugged. "I've never seen anything like it."

"What about my note?"

John frowned. "I've never known him to do something like that before."

"You don't think he wrote it?"

"It's possible."

"But why would someone pretend to be the Ghost?" she asked, puzzled.

John shook his head. "I don't know."

"Well, whoever the real Ghost is, he must be pretty smart." Veronica had a hint of approval in her voice.

"He's more than smart, he's a genius." John sat wrapped in thought for a moment. "There is a guy...Dornal Zagen. He was doing thirty years to life until he busted out of Sing Sing two nights ago. He might have somehow written the note."

Veronica was silent for a moment and then asked, "Are you the man who originally put him behind bars?"

"I was."

"Are you afraid he's going to come after you now?"

John hadn't thought of that. He sighed. "One more thing to worry about, huh?"

"I'm sorry, I didn't mean to frighten you."

"You didn't," said John. "I'm sure the Feds'll

catch up with him soon enough."

"How did *you* catch him?"

"Well, it was about three years ago in Chicago. I had tracked him that far on a lead from one of our favorite stool pigeons who'd heard there was a lot of ice floating around town. Even though it was the middle of winter, he wasn't talking about frozen water, I can tell you that."

Veronica smiled at John indulgently.

"Anyway, it was a little after one in the morning," John continued. "I had just flown in, when the local police called about an ongoing theft at a fancy Gold Coast jewelry store. It was about a week before Christmas, so the owner had put all his most expensive trinkets on display hoping to sell them to people looking for some eye-popping holiday gifts. When I arrived on the scene, the alarm was going off like crazy, but there was no sign of a break-in and nothing was missing. Everyone figured the system had just freaked out. They got another call about a homicide a few blocks away, so the police took off. I had a strange feeling about the whole thing and decided to hang out and wait."

He winced as Veronica suddenly swerved to avoid a biker who darted dangerously in front of them, before continuing his story. "I turned off all the lights and pretended to leave the shop, but instead I slipped into the bathroom and just sat there for a while. I waited for about twenty minutes. I was just beginning to think I was wasting my time when I heard something in the main room. I cracked the door open and saw one of the decorative ceiling panels slip aside. A pair of legs soon appeared from a cavity where the thief had been hiding. I held my breath and didn't move until he was standing in the middle of the room with a diamond necklace dripping through his fingers. Then I hit the lights, and before he knew it, I had my gun against his back, catching him red-handed."

"Very impressive," said Veronica.

He couldn't tell if she was actually impressed or just making fun of him.

"And he got thirty years to life for that one robbery?" she asked.

"Oh no," said John. "Dornal Zagen must have stolen about fifty million dollars worth of stuff over the years. There were also rumors that he worked as a hit man for hire, though I was never able to dig up any real evidence on that one."

"Sounds like a charming person."

"Yeah, well, he's not someone you'd be likely to run into at one of your garden parties."

She just gave him a cool smile.

"So tell me about this Diamond Ball. What's it for?" John asked, changing the subject.

"Oh, it's something Mrs. Spencer and her daughter, Cynthia, are doing. It's a charity event to raise money for a library," she said, all the excitement gone from her voice.

"What's the price of admission?"

"Twenty-five thousand a plate." She said it like that was no big deal.

John whistled. "For that price, people should get to take the Hope Diamond home with them!"

"Personally, I wouldn't *want* the Hope." A little shudder ran through Veronica's slim frame.

"No?"

"No!"

"Afraid of the curse?" he asked, studying her more closely. He hadn't pegged her for superstitious. She seemed too calm and controlled, too in charge of herself for nonsense like that.

"I sure am," she admitted.

"Huh, I'm surprised." It was nice to find she had some vulnerable chink in her armor.

"I'm the daughter of an archeologist," she

reminded him. "I've been with my father when he's dug up Egyptian mummies, raided tombs in Ecuador. There are certain things you shouldn't touch because they have a life of their own. Jewels, in particular, have their own life, their own energy. You can feel it when you wear them. Some of them are lucky. In ancient India, it was said that diamonds gave a person virtue and purity and would protect them from evil. I think that's generally true, but not *all* diamonds and *especially* not the Hope."

"Now you sound like those New Age crystal freaks," John laughed.

"Laugh all you like, but look at what happened to Tavernier," she said.

"Tavernier?" he asked, baffled.

She turned to him and smiled. "I thought you knew about jewels."

"I know who makes what and how to recognize it. I can tell if a rock is real and if it's good quality. That's my job, or was my job," he corrected himself. "But all the airy, fairy stuff, the legends and hearsay, I never bothered with it."

"Well then," she was enjoying telling him something he didn't know. "Tavernier was the original jewel thief. In 1661, he went to India and stole the Hope Diamond, which at that time was not known as the Hope. He called it the French Blue Stone because he sold it to King Louis XIV. But get this, he stole it from a very sacred temple. He plucked the diamond right out of the Goddess Sita's third eye—or at least a statue of her. She's very revered in India, even to this day. Anyway, he brought the diamond back to France. Then he tried to go back to India to plunder more jewels, but he never made it past Russia. He was torn to bits by wild dogs in the streets of Moscow." She raised her brows triumphantly now that she'd proven the curse.

"That's it?" asked John, just to wipe that smug

look off her face.

Veronica was enjoying herself too much to get mad. She turned an eager, conspiratorial face toward him as if she were sharing a dark secret. "That's *not* it. There's much more."

"Oh, yeah? Like what?" he asked, trying not to sound interested.

She got a funny little Mona Lisa smile on her face and turned her attention back to the road. "I don't think I'll tell you."

"We still have a good hour left."

"Why don't you pull out another CD," she motioned toward the glove compartment, her diamond bracelet catching the light and his eye.

He fished through her CDs. There were several of classical music which he didn't know at all and one Dean Martin album. Bingo. He slid the CD in and turned up the volume. The catchy opening riff of "That's Amore" started up.

She raised her eyebrows. "You're a big cornball, aren't you?"

He smiled. "Maybe I am." John wasn't afraid to like Dino.

For the rest of the trip they didn't speak. They just listened to CDs and the radio. A cozy feeling continued to grow between them and John couldn't help wondering if they'd have adjoining hotel rooms.

Chapter Five

The Puck Diamond burned like electric ice in Delores Pigeon's wrinkled hand. How she wished she could go out into the living room and show her nephew Larry the lovely ring, but of course she didn't want to get him into any trouble.

She would never have dared to come to his Chestnut Hill home, but she had traveled under the false passport her antique dealer friend in Amsterdam had acquired for her and she felt quite certain about not being followed. That Antoine was such a useful fellow, always able to make the right connections when she needed them, finding the perfect buyer for her wares, and he was always so polite and respectful, too.

They know how to treat their elders in Europe, she thought, remembering the shocking treatment she had received at the Academy Awards four days ago when a teenage girl had tried to push her out of her place near the red carpet.

But that nice Antoine, she must remember to knit him an afghan before flying back to the continent. Delores frowned. She didn't have much more time. Her flight to Amsterdam's Schiphol airport was in only—she counted on her wrinkled but still quite dexterous fingers—one, two, three, four days away.

Goodness!

And of course, she'd be busy all day Friday preparing for the Diamond Ball the following evening. After all, making off with the Puck

Diamond, magnificent as it was, had just been a warm-up. Use it or lose it, she always said.

She certainly had to admit, though, it *was* exciting to see Katherine Park in person. Why, she had even gotten to shake hands with the star! She couldn't wait to have a nice pot of that lovely bittersweet Belgian cocoa with Antoine and tell him all about it.

She'd have to make that stop in Washington first, but after that, with the Puck and the Hope in her possession, she could cash in her bingo chips and retire to that lovely little cottage in Wales she'd always dreamed of. Yes, she'd just do that little bit of business in Washington and then wouldn't everything be just lovely!

Delores Pigeon took one last look at the glittering 33-carat diamond in her pruny, blue-veined hand before firmly sticking a piece of tape to the end of the pale pink yarn she'd been using to knit booties for her niece's baby girl. She attached the yarn to the diamond and began wrapping it around and around, until the stone was hidden under a soft cloud of angora.

****

Veronica drove through the historic cobblestone streets of Capitol Hill until she reached the circular driveway of the Monticello Hotel. As the platinum convertible slid to a stop in front of the Greek revival building with its white marble columns and gracious veranda, a team of porters in spotless gray uniforms and caps swarmed to help Veronica out and attend to their luggage. John had to stop himself from snatching his bag away from a fresh-faced bellhop. Instead, with the ghost of Simon haunting him from the dark reaches of his brain, he said, "Thank you, but I can get that myself," as he picked up his shabby suitcase and gave the kid five bucks.

Veronica pranced ahead, giving him a nice view

of her shapely derrière. Waltzing through the gleaming brass revolving door into the airy lobby with its sparkling chandeliers and antique Persian carpets was as natural to her as it was for him to slip into the bleachers at Shea Stadium. Though he tried to act natural, he couldn't help but watch her red alligator jewel case as she swung it back and forth with her graceful gait.

After they had checked in, a team of porters led them to room 147 and opened the door. As they were about to head in, John suddenly envisioned Veronica plopping her jewelry case on the bed and opening it up for all to see. He knew already, just from the few hours he'd spent with her, it was the kind of thing she would do.

He jumped in front of the entourage before they could enter the suite. "Thanks, guys, I'll take it from here." After he peeled bills out of his wallet and handed them out like candy at a playground, the porters wasted no time in disappearing.

Inside the room, Veronica stood with her arms crossed. "Why did you do that?"

"Because this is not a secure situation for your jewelry," John said quietly. He tried to step into the room. But before he had a chance, she shoved her hand hard against his chest, blocking him.

He tried to reason with her. "Listen, why don't you let me take your stuff down to the hotel safe?"

"Why don't you mind your own business?" she snapped and closed the door in his face.

He stood there for a moment with his Irish rising hot and fast. Then he closed his eyes and prayed silently. He took a deep breath and pushed the doorbell.

She didn't answer.

This time he put his finger on the bell and didn't take it off. He could hear the melodious little chimes repeating themselves over and over and over again.

The door sprang open. She had taken her scarf off and her hair fell lose around her shoulders. She had removed her sunglasses, too, and her eyes crackled like the blue flames at the hottest part of a fire. "Well?"

"I was going to say, your father is not paying me to mind my own business."

Their eyes locked in a battle of wills until she took a breath and said, "What if I double his rate and you leave me alone?"

John raised his eyebrows in surprise. *Forty-thousand dollars for doing nothing?* Of course, that would be wrong, and he didn't do wrong things anymore. Sober members of Alcoholics Anonymous did not do wrong things if they wanted to stay sober members of Alcoholics Anonymous. He closed his mind to the temptation before he did something he shouldn't. "I'm sorry, Veronica, we both know I can't do that."

"Well, I'm not handing my jewelry over to anyone else," she said stubbornly.

"It's a hotel vault where it will be safe," he reminded her.

"You don't get it," she snapped. "This is my mother's jewelry. It belonged to her and I'm not giving it to you, or a hotel vault, or anyone else. It's nonnegotiable."

Annoyed, John paced up and down the hall, his steps muffled by the expensive carpet. He finally turned back to her. "All right...but if those rocks get stolen..."

"They won't," she said, firmly.

"But if they do..." he jabbed an index finger her way accusingly.

"They won't," she said, gritting her teeth and once again the door was closed in his face.

When he reached his own room, John was still mad. He opened the minibar and it was lined with little jewel-colored bottles of poison—Russian vodka, Kentucky bourbon, French cognac. He marched over to the phone and dialed the operator. He told them his room number and asked them to clean out the minibar.

"Would you like to replace that with anything else?" asked the obsequious desk clerk.

"Sure, how 'bout seltzer and pretzels—lots of them?"

There was a slight pause on the line and then, "We'll take care of it, sir."

After they hung up, John stood there for a moment before he picked up the receiver again. He dialed a number ingrained in his memory.

Quinn answered. He sounded stressed out without even knowing who was on the line. "Hello?"

"It's me," said John. "What's wrong?"

Quinn exhaled. "You don't even want to know."

"Well, I took the Rossmore gig. I'm in DC staying at the Monticello."

"Nice." Quinn sounded impressed. "I'm in DC, too. Did Miss Rossmore tell you about the rehearsal tomorrow at the Smithsonian?"

"What is this, a wedding?" asked John, annoyed that Veronica had *not* informed him about it.

"They're doing a fashion show for jewels. It's an excuse for every rich dame in town to show off her rocks and have everyone applaud."

"Must be nice," said John.

"Anyway, I'll try and make it over there. I've already got your security clearance and all that malarkey, but listen—no gun."

"What!" exclaimed John, outraged.

"They don't want you carrying a gun. I'm sorry, you're not officially back yet and you've had your drug problems..."

"Alcohol—I had an alcohol problem and let's not pretend that half the force isn't hopped up on something."

"Listen," said Quinn, trying to calm his friend. "This isn't me, okay? It's not even about you. I shouldn't have said that. They don't want *anyone* carrying guns, except a few of the secret service guys watching the First Lady and her daughter."

There was a pause.

"John, are you there?"

"Yeah, okay," muttered John.

"Listen," his old partner reassured him, "I'm really glad you're going to be there. We've already gotten word that Nicholas Bezuhov is in town, we lost sight of the Granny last week, and still no word on Dornal Zagen."

"He'll surface one of these days."

"No kidding. I just don't want it to be at the freakin' Diamond Ball. It's going to be like a jewel thief convention, so anything you can do to help us out..."

"That goes without saying."

"Okay, well, I gotta go." The exhaustion in Quinn's voice fed through the phone line.

"Don't let the bastards get you." It was the old line they always fed each other when things got tough. He could picture his ex-partner's smile.

"I won't, buddy."

****

Veronica slumped in the corner of her hotel room's damask loveseat staring moodily at the jewel case which had caused so much drama between her and John this afternoon. He had only been doing his job. Her father was paying him to watch her jewels and she had not been very helpful. She must have appeared completely irrational. Of course, he didn't understand. How could anyone really know what these diamonds meant to her?

She went to the jewel case, unlocking it and pulling out a finely crafted diamond bracelet. She held it tenderly as she struggled to retrieve memories that were harder and harder to recall, like dog-eared photographs which had begun to disintegrate from being handled too much.

An image of her mother came, dressed in cool, white linen against the Egyptian heat, as she held out a cup of mint tea sweetened with honey. Her mother helped little Veronica hold the cup with both hands and take a sip, her diamond bracelet, brilliant in the bright sunlight, dancing before Veronica's eyes.

Her mother smiled warmly. "Taste good, baby?"

The sunlight, and shimmering diamonds, and her mother's perfect love all fused and glowed around her like a magic spell.

The bracelet now in her hand became a blur as her eyes welled up. Gently, she returned the treasure to its case. She brushed the tears from her lashes and quickly snapped the case shut. When a person died what was left of them? The love she felt for her mother would never fade, but she couldn't physically hold onto that love with her own two hands when she needed so much to hold onto something. She couldn't wear that love like an amulet against her heart for courage when she was afraid the way she could a shimmering jeweled pendant. Diamonds were the only indestructible thing she could count on to always be beautiful, always perfect, always survive...

The knock on her door snapped Veronica out of her reverie.

"Veronica," John's voice sounded muffled through the door. "It's me. Are you in there?"

She hesitated. Despite their earlier argument, she had to admit now that the sound of his voice was comforting. There was something warm and good about him that she liked, despite her annoyance at his professional duties.

She started toward the door when she heard him strike up a whistled tune on the other side. She stopped and stood there smiling as the sound of his little melody floated into her room. Leaning back against the door, she crossed her arms, thinking. What was she going to do with John Monroe?

****

Marguerite Gateaux longed for the feel of dice in her hands the moment she arrived aboard the French financier's yacht *La Sirène.* A casino had been set up this evening as a diversion for the billionaire's international guests. Tonight, Marguerite was a hired hand. She was to perform on the web of fishing nets which hung from the ceiling decorated with gauzy draped seaweed, shimmering giant oyster shells, and ropes of black Tahitian pearls. The ship's grand salon had been designed for the party to look like a scene out of Davy Jones' Locker complete with a treasure chest overflowing with fabulous goodies to be presented to the highest roller of the evening. Marguerite had dressed for the occasion by ordering a designer minidress.

She had been afforded a sumptuous stateroom, which her considerate employer had stocked with dozens of white iceberg roses overflowing their elegant vases and a box of lavender-scented chocolates from Maggie's favorite Paris confiseur. The real attraction, however, was the fact that the yacht was anchored just off Oyster Bay in Long Island Sound, less than three hours' drive from the nation's capitol, and after all, that was the true reason she had come to the U.S. this time around. The Diamond Ball was only a few nights away, and Maggie the Cat was itching to see how the Hope would catch the light and explode with brilliance against her naked flesh.

René escorted Marguerite down to the casino and everyone turned to look as the glamorous redhead entered the room. She made straight for the craps table where a few of her colleagues from the Ballet de l'Aire had already congregated. She could tell from their joyful faces and applause that the table was so hot she might just get burned if she wasn't careful.

Marguerite placed ten $1,000 bills on the green felt. Her heart sped up as the croupier handed her back a pile of golden chips minted for the occasion to look like sea-salvaged Spanish doubloons. She pushed a few coins René's way and began to lay her own across the pass line. Her stage manager, Marcel, handed her the dice. It wasn't Maggie's turn, but everyone at the table knew she had infallible luck and they wanted in on it.

She shook up the dice and tossed them across the felt. They rebounded against the table wall and then came to a halt in the center.

Seven!

The table exploded with delight as the croupier handed out chips and doubled the pass line bets for everyone.

She picked up the dice again and tossed them hard across the table. Everyone held their breath, waiting to see if Maggie could work her magic a second time. But the dice turned against her and a pair of snake eyes stared up at them. She frowned as the croupier swept the gold doubloons from the table.

Concentrating harder this time, she carefully placed a stack of coins on the table. She turned to René and gave him an encouraging wink, then once more shook the dice and tossed them across the table. Everyone cheered and clapped as they bounced along but went silent when they turned up a now very unwelcome seven.

Some of the guests began to drift towards the roulette table or the bar as Marguerite passed the dice to an ageing British pop star. She brought one of the gold coins to her mouth and chewed on it absentmindedly, trying to decide whether to continue or walk away.

Marguerite placed her attention back on René who had begun to pout. "Come along, René. I need you to help me into my costume."

An hour later, as she sat before her dressing table expertly applying makeup for her performance, Marguerite pondered her misfortune at the craps table. As an experienced gambler, and jewel thief, she had learned over the years that one of the biggest elements of luck was knowing when to walk away and she could feel the tide strongly against her. Should she forget the Hope and return to France? Her gut told her it was the right thing to do, but desire gripped her so intensely it could never be filled with the rugged lustful thrusts of young René. She yearned for the famous blue diamond as she had not for any other jewel.

Marguerite powdered her face absentmindedly. Perhaps she could find a way to petition the gods for a little luck—or maybe she would just have to steal it.

She turned to René who lay naked on the bed, his glorious tanned body resting comfortably, his cheeks flushed and covered with the sweaty glow of lovemaking.

"Can you do me a favor, *cher*?" she asked.

He pulled a few pillows behind his head and propped himself up. "What is it?"

"I need a very fast car."

René smiled; he knew she was up to something and he loved it. "What for?"

"I'm going to pick up a little good luck charm," she replied mysteriously.

"How little?"

Maggie furrowed her brow as she calculated in

her head. "About 215 carats."

"*Mon Dieu!*" exclaimed René, sitting up.

Maggie calmly turned back to her reflection and met a pair of jade green eyes lined in theatrical black liner. "*Exactement.*"

Chapter Six

The following afternoon, John and Veronica made their way into the Smithsonian's Hall of Geology, Gems and Minerals with a cool distance between them. She was playing ice princess and he was letting her. Veronica was dressed for the occasion in a chiffon dress that fluttered around her slim figure, making her look as demure and ladylike as any Sweetbriar undergrad. She had on the same rocks as yesterday, except today she sported a pair of matching earrings and a big, shimmering, pink diamond ring surrounded by bright white brilliants set in platinum. John thought the flashy ring looked like something out of the most elegant bubblegum machine in the world. She had pale pink lips and nails, and her dark hair was pulled back from her face, revealing the perfect structure of her cheekbones and those incredible eyes.

John wore his best suit, which he had picked up at an old vintage store in upstate New York during one of his reparation outings with his mother. He looked snappy and he knew it. He had seen it by the flicker in Veronica's eyes when she met him in the hotel lobby, just before she slipped on her Jackie O's and made a big show of ignoring him.

Maybe Veronica was playing it cool. The ash-blond ladies in their buttoned-up Washington DC lunch suits and demure pearls, however, looked him over like a big shiny lollipop they couldn't wait to get their collagen-infused lips around. He flashed the ladies a bright smile as they entered the dark gallery.

The room was almost black with big light-up display windows giving John the odd feeling of being in an aquarium. Inside the cases, piles of famous, glittering jewels flickered in the spotlights like the geological superstars they were. Marie Antoinette's icy teardrop diamond earrings sat next to the flaming orange cushion-cut Pumpkin Diamond, so named because the House of Winston had acquired it one day before Halloween. The mystical Star of Bombay, a 182-carat sapphire bequeathed to the museum by Mary Pickford, glowed like a view from outer space—a ghostly six-pointed star glimmering across the milky way of its blue cloudy world. Under the spotlights next to the Star nestled Queen Nefertiti's elaborate rose-gold necklace with over five hundred finely crafted turquoise beads. These were just the tip of the iceberg. The obscene piles of rubies, emeralds, and amethysts, exquisitely cut and crafted into some of the most beautiful jewelry ever made, was almost too much to take in at once.

The ladies chatted amongst themselves as they entered the room. Some of the younger, more press-worthy socialites compared notes on which designers were lending them gowns for the ball and what their stylist envisioned for them. Only Veronica, who wore her own gowns and wouldn't dream of allowing someone else to dress her, stepped away from the crowd to check out the gems. Hidden in the corners of the room, security guards stood in dark suits, purposely fading into the scenery. More museum security watched the room through hidden cameras on black-and-white grainy TV screens in a control room at the back of the museum.

A woman in an ivory pants suit with gray-streaked hair spoke up and thanked the ladies for coming. She was Kay Hopkins, the museum's social director. A polite ruffle of applause ran through the room and she smiled graciously.

"Well now," she said, peering through the dimly lit room, "I think we're all here, except for Cynthia Spencer. Has anyone seen Cynthia?"

The DC matrons twisted their necks around and scanned the room, but there was no sign of the president's daughter.

"Hmm, well, we'll just start without her and I'm sure she'll be here any minute." Kay exhibited the smooth manner of an accomplished hostess. "Georgette, my assistant, is going to pass out numbers to you all. They will be your marching order, so to speak, for the jewelry show. If you're number one, you'll be the first one to come out and walk down the red carpet. Two will be second and so on. Are there any questions?"

The ladies nodded their ash-blond heads.

"Good!" said Kay with her gracious smile. "Now, you all are going to walk along this red carpet. Of course, for the ball, we'll be downstairs in the rotunda, but for now you can just practice." She displayed the path into the room marked by a red carpet which had been laid for the occasion. "When you come to the end of the carpet," she stomped her feet deliberately as she reached the edge, "you will stand and smile as pretty as you can and the press will take your picture with all your lovely jewels. Then you will turn around and walk back the way you came. Do y'all get that?"

The ladies' heads bobbed in unison.

"Great. Now, most of y'all will be wearing your own beautiful gems, but there are a few of you who will be modeling some of our very own Smithsonian treasures..." She paused midsentence as a team of secret servicemen slid into the room, along with a sullen teenager with limp blond hair and dark purple circles under her eyes. The girl wore a blue Izod shirt, pink bell-bottom corduroys, and faded white sneakers. Her sunburned skin was starting to peel at the tip of her nose while two braided cornrows adorned with colored beads hung against her cheek, looking out of place on the "WASPy" president's daughter.

John watched the awkward teen enter the room. *Someone just returned from a nice sunny spring break in the tropics.*

Everyone turned to stare at Cynthia, and an expression crossed her face like she wanted to sink into the core of the earth and never be heard from again.

Kay plastered on a smile that looked fake, even for her. "Cynthia, I'm so glad you made it."

"Sorry I'm late." The teenager dropped her dishwater gray eyes to the floor and combed back one of the braided cornrows with her chubby fingers.

"That's all right; you're just in time," said Kay brightly.

As the social director babbled on about who would be wearing what, Cynthia spotted Veronica at the edge of the crowd and shuffled over to her. "Hi, Veronica," she said quietly under Kay's speech.

Veronica turned and looked down at the girl who was a good six inches shorter than her. "Hello, Cynthia."

The disapproval and dislike in Veronica's voice took John by surprise, and though he hated to admit it, it made him feel a little bit better. She might not be crazy about him, but he'd yet to get that particular tone of disgust directed his way.

"How are you enjoying Yale?" she asked the sulking girl.

Cynthia gave an awkward shrug. "It's okay."

"Hmm," Veronica turned away.

"I guess you talked to my mom." The teenager sounded discouraged.

"Yes, I have," replied Veronica shortly.

A blush crept into Cynthia's wan cheeks and tears welled up in her dull gray eyes. When Veronica saw this, she tightened her jaw and did her best to ignore the girl. Eventually, she cracked and laid the hand with that bubblegum pink diamond on the teenager's shoulder. She whispered in a kind but exasperated voice, "Don't worry…"

Veronica caught John staring at her. Closing her mouth, she patted the girl's shoulder a few times and turned her back to him to listen to Kay blab on about how *wonderful* it was of the ladies to come down, how *ecstatic* the Smithsonian was to have them, and what a *spectacular* event this was going to be.

When Kay finished her spiel, Veronica broke away from the pack and drifted into the Harry Winston Gallery. The room was a circular shape lined with displays of dimly lit crystals, rock formations, and meteorites. In the center stood what looked like a small Greek temple with a domed ceiling and marble floors. A single display case stood inside the structure; it was lit up like Time's Square on New Year's Eve.

Veronica stepped past the bronze bust of old Harry standing guard over the temple's treasure. She stopped in front of the display case and gazed in fascination at the magnificent dark blue diamond glittering on a platinum chain of forty-six white-hot rocks. She appeared to be hypnotized by the explosion of violet light that was the Hope Diamond.

John couldn't help noticing as he approached Veronica that the jewel perfectly matched the color of her eyes.

"Still sure you don't want it?" he asked, almost in a whisper because he understood that for her this place was church.

"This diamond wasn't meant to be worn," she said, unable to lift her eyes from the play of light dancing in its depths like a cold blue fire.

"What do you think it was meant for?"

"Worship." She breathed out the word like a prayer.

"I don't know about that."

"Don't you?" she asked, and turned to him, smiling playfully. "Do you want me to tell you the rest of the gem's history, now that it's here in front of you and you can really see what I'm talking about?"

He looked at her quizzically and wondered if maybe it wasn't coyness or perversity that had stopped her from reciting the full story of the diamond yesterday in the car. Was it possible she had purposely been waiting until now? Did she really care that much about giving him the experience?

He decided she didn't. She would have grabbed a bum off the street, or Cynthia Spencer for that matter, and given them the same treatment, just for the pleasure of sharing her enthusiasm with another human being. She'd make the story real for them, so it could be real for her again.

"Well, you remember about Tavernier and the wild dogs?" she began.

He nodded.

"Anyway, before he was killed, Tavernier took the Blue Stone, as it was known at the French court, and sold it to King Louis XIV." Her face glowed with the delight of a child reciting a favorite bedtime fairytale. "Well, King Louis wore the diamond one time and immediately contracted smallpox and dropped dead. His heir was smarter than his father. He knew where the jewel had come from and that it was cursed. So he never wore it; but guess who did?" She stood there waiting for him to guess.

"Uh, I don't know."

"His son and daughter-in-law, none other than

Louis XVI and Marie Antoinette and we know what happened to them!"

John drew a finger across his throat and whistled.

"Correct." She nodded like an approving grade school teacher. Only she was much more beautiful than any teacher he'd ever had. "The diamond disappeared from the scene after the French revolution, but in 1830..."

"You know your dates." John was impressed.

"Yes, I do," she agreed. "Anyway, in 1830, it reappeared in London and was bought by a British banker named Mr. Henry Thomas...can you guess his last name?"

"Hope?" he ventured.

"Yes, and not much is known about him, *but* in 1890..."

"You mean no terrible, cursed thing happened to him?" John teased her.

"Not that we know of," she said, making it clear from her tone he was ruining the story. "In 1890, the diamond was inherited by the Duke of Newcastle, Lord Francis Hope. He was married to an American actress, and as soon as Lord Hope got his hands on the diamond, she ran off with another man."

"Well, what did he expect, marrying an actress?" asked John. "You don't need a cursed diamond to tell you an actress is going to..."

"Don't interrupt me, John," she said, interrupting him. It was the first time she had called him by name and he liked the way it sounded coming from her. The word struck a chord somewhere inside his chest, maybe a chord that had no business sounding when an employer was speaking to you, but it throbbed and hummed just the same.

"As I was saying, before I was so rudely interrupted," she continued, her eyes dancing, "Lady

77

Hope, the actress, ran off to Boston where she ended up dying penniless. Of course, she had worn the diamond. Lord Hope, who had possessed a massive fortune, went inexplicably bankrupt. Next an Eastern European prince, what's his name?" She wracked her brain and rubbed her hands together trying to spark her memory, but it was no use. "I can't remember. This prince was in love with a dancer from the Folies Bergère, but he *mistakenly* believed she was in love with another man and shot her. Next, a Greek gem dealer got ahold of it and he drove his car, with his wife and children in it, off a cliff! After that, a Turkish Sultan named Abdul-something took hold of it and was almost immediately overthrown by his own army officers."

"Okay, I believe you," said John smiling.

"I'm not done," she snapped. "After that, in 1911, Evelyn Walsh McLean, who was married to the owner of *The Washington Post*, got her hands on the diamond and her son was killed in a car accident, her daughter overdosed on sleeping pills, and her husband ended up in an insane asylum. *Finally,* after she died, Harry Winston bought the Hope and was smart enough to donate it to the Smithsonian, which put it right here, safe and sound." She smiled at him, satisfied at last. "*Now* do you understand why you couldn't pay me to take ownership of this necklace?"

John stared at her beautiful face, her dark blue eyes glowing and alive. "Maybe you're right," he conceded.

She nodded as if to say, "damn right I am," but knew she didn't need to say it.

"Next you'll be telling me you believe in astrology, too," he joked.

"Well, as a Capricorn I'm not supposed to, but I do anyway," she admitted. "Don't you believe there must be a bit of truth in something so ancient?"

John laughed. "I never did, but then I kept dating Gemini women—with disastrous results. Everywhere I went I seemed to fall for one. After a while, I started to think there might be something to it and swore off future Geminis."

Then she surprised him.

"Well, since I'm not a Gemini, what are you doing tonight, John?" she asked, tilting her face up to his with a flirtatiousness he hadn't seen from her before.

"I...I don't know," he stammered, like a school kid caught unprepared.

"You must know DC a little."

"Sure, I used to come down here a lot for work."

"Well," she bit her juicy lower lip, "maybe you know some quiet little place you could take me to dinner?"

"It'll help me keep an eye on those diamonds of yours since you insist on wearing them around," he joked.

"Do you like to mix business with pleasure?"

"I normally don't," he said, trying to be honest.

"I do," she said, suggestively.

"But you're not doing any business down here. Just going to a party and showing off your rocks."

She smiled that same Mona Lisa smile she had smiled in the car yesterday when she refused to tell him about the Hope.

"I'll make a reservation at a little Italian place I know for eight o'clock—but it isn't fancy," he warned her.

"That's okay."

They started moving out of the Hall of Geology, timing their feet to walk in a slow, mutual pace so they could talk.

"What are you up to now?" he asked.

"I'm going to a dress fitting for Saturday night."

"I better go with you since you're wearing a

79

king's ransom," he cautioned her.

She stopped walking and turned to look him straight in the eye. "Let's get one thing straight." She jabbed a surprisingly sharp fingernail into his chest. "My overprotective father is paying you to watch out for me at the Diamond Ball. Okay, I've agreed to that, but that's it. If I want to walk stark naked all by myself through the worst ghetto in Washington with nothing on but my diamonds, that's my business."

John would have liked to see that, but he only said, "Point taken."

She thrust out her hand and he took it. Her skin was soft and cool, her fingers wrapped around his palm and it felt right. He forced himself to let go after the appropriate two pumps.

"What are you going to do now?" she asked.

"Maybe I'll..." he was going to say hit an AA meeting, but instead replied, "Maybe I'll stick around here. It looks like there's a great exhibit of WWI flying ace planes from the banners I saw in the lobby."

"You do that."

He realized he had been dismissed for the rest of the afternoon, which he didn't like one bit.

He watched her float down the corridor in her fluttery chiffon dress. When she was gone, he wandered back into the mineral gallery and poked around. There were brightly lit slabs of natural amethyst quartz from the Rio Grande, shining lemon yellow sulfur from Yellowstone National Park, and opals of shifting colors from the Cyclades. Rocks, crystals, and boulders filled every corner of wall space in the dim room.

"ROCKS TELL STORIES," declared one museum sign. "ROCKS REMEMBER" and "ROCKS INFORM," said some others.

John stepped up to a big, brightly lit replica of

the earth's core. It looked like a giant orange with a section cut out. The sign by the display read:

Inside Earth, beneath its familiar surface and thin crust, lie a rocky mantle and iron core. The inner earth is hot. Its core is hotter than the surface of the sun. The inner earth flows and churns. In the outer core, a churning dynamic liquid iron generates Earth's magnetic field.

John thought about Veronica as he looked at the model of the world with its cold rocky surface and the hot inferno within. She had surprised him with the come-on. Every time he thought he had her pegged, she changed. He wondered what lay beneath her surface, how many different sides of Veronica Rossmore there were and how he'd know when he'd seen them all.

Chapter Seven

Oscar Kelly, the superintendent at the John Adams Apartments in Georgetown, watched in amazement as the old woman in front of him raced up the steps, as chipper as a puppy in a fresh green field, while he dragged his ass up after her.

"I just can't wait to see my Army!" chirped the old bird as she reached the third floor of the converted townhouse.

"You're sure he said he left the key with me?" asked Oscar, as he reached the landing.

She turned big, watering eyes on him. "Oh yes, that's what he said. He told me he would be at work baking all day for that fancy caterer he works for."

Oscar looked her over again. "Okay, he must have just forgotten to let me know on the way out this morning. Sometimes he gets busy and he forgets things...like the rent!" Oscar let out a big laugh like a whale blowing its spout.

"Oh, I hope poor Army isn't having money problems." She looked troubled.

"He does pretty well for himself with all those cookbooks he writes." The superintendent's words reassured Delores as he unlocked the door and held it open for her to shuffle past into the apartment.

"Well, thank you so much for your help, Oscar," said the lady, and with a friendly little wave, she closed the apartment door.

What a sweet old lady. Oscar headed back downstairs.

Inside the apartment, Delores Pigeon looked

around and nodded in approval as she entered the kitchen. The room was big and airy with a nice window overlooking the C & O Canal. Pots of fresh rosemary, lavender, and mint grew in the sunlight that streamed onto the windowsill. Shiny copper pans hung above the Viking range and the white tile walls gleamed with cleanliness. From a successful chef, she expected nothing less, but one never knew what one would find when one entered a house unexpectedly.

Now for the chamomile tea.

With her prim white gloves on, she opened the kitchen cabinets until she found a pretty orange tea tin. Chef Armand never failed to mention on his television specials that his very favorite accompaniment to the delicious desserts he whipped up was a nice cup of chamomile tea. In fact, he swore he never went a day without drinking a pot.

The Granny hummed slightly off-key as she opened up her black alligator purse and took out a packet of fine cinnamon-colored powder. Carefully, she removed the lid to the tin of loose tea and sprinkled the powder over the crushed chamomile leaves.

Hmm...

She threw in a good pinch more. Satisfied, she closed the tin, replacing it on the shelf. Returning the packet of powder to her bag, she snapped the purse shut and stepped into the living room. She peered out at the fire escape just outside the living room window. It seemed to be in good repair. Without a second look, the Granny slid open the window and crept down the fire escape to the alley below.

As her sensible black shoes touched pavement, she decided to head back to that lovely furnished apartment she had rented. It would be delightful to see all the sights of the nation's capitol but, she remembered with a sigh, she did have those brownies to bake...

****

John met Veronica in the hotel lobby at a quarter to eight. He was there first, nervously drumming his fingers against a fluted column, craving a cigarette, craving a shot of Maker's Mark, but just drumming his fingers instead and watching the posh crowd mill around.

The elevator doors opened and there was Veronica. She wore a dark red strapless dress that clung to her curves. Her lips and nails were red, too, and her dark hair fell loose around her shoulders. A massive diamond-and-ruby necklace lay propped against the tops of her breasts, which swelled out of her dress provocatively. The necklace was the only jewelry she wore, but it was enough. It looked like the kind of piece you would see on Queen Victoria at an important royal event. Strands of glittering icy diamonds laced around her throat like a sparkling spider's web, and the eye-popping, pear-cut ruby glittered devilishly, a perfect pigeon's blood red. If Veronica had attached a roaring police siren around her neck she couldn't have attracted more attention. She smiled when she caught John staring.

But he wasn't the only one.

Veronica's eyes flickered over to a tall, thin man in a tuxedo; his dark hair was greased back and he wore a white flower in his lapel and a blonde DC debutante on his arm. John narrowed his eyes as he realized who the man was. There was no mistaking Nicholas Bezuhov, also known on the jewel thief circuit as the White Russian.

Nicholas must have seen him, too, and he would certainly know John after all the years of cat-and-mouse they had played together. Of course, it was also possible Nicholas was just getting an eyeful of Veronica and her big ruby necklace. Either way,

John didn't like it.

Neither did the blond debutant. "Come on, Nicky," she said in her cool, boarding-school voice. "We'll be late for dinner."

With a polite nod, Nicholas moved on. The debutante gave Veronica an icy stare as they passed her on the way into the elegant dining room, which was already full of senators, foreign diplomats, and the occasional well-heeled tourist who came to see where the Washington power brokers broke their bread.

Veronica sized up the blonde and dismissed her in the blink of an eye. Then she walked to John who was still staring after Nicholas Bezuhov.

"Do you know that man?" she asked, following his gaze.

"He calls himself Prince Bezuhov," said John, disgust seeping into his voice. "Fancies himself some kind of Russian aristocrat, but according to our records, he's pure peasant masquerading as the great-grandson of the Grand Duchess Anastasia like all the rest of the Euro-trash he runs with."

She raised a manicured brow. "I get the impression you don't like him."

"I don't like phonies and he's one of the worst. I didn't like the way he was eyeing your rocks either."

She patted his arm. "Well, that's what I have you for—to protect me and my rocks." She was making fun of him, but he didn't care. She looked so beautiful that she could make all the fun she wanted.

Still, he was concerned about her diamond stash upstairs. "You sure you don't want me to put your jewels in the hotel safe? You have to understand, with this guy on the premises, you're very likely to come home tonight and find it all missing."

"Don't worry," she said confidently. "They're in a very safe place."

John shook his head. He didn't like it, but he couldn't force her to lock up her valuables if she didn't want to. "I hope you have good insurance."

Veronica wanted to take her convertible, but John wasn't letting a woman drive him around if they were on a date. Since the elevator doors slid open to reveal Veronica at her bombshell best, it was clear this truly was a full-fledged date.

He held out his arm and she slid her hand through the crook of his elbow as a team of capped bellhops rushed to open the door for them. The night was soft and warm with a hint of summer in it.

"By the way, you're overdressed," he informed her as they slid into one of the taxis that stood in line outside the hotel.

"I know." She settled in next to him as the cab pulled away.

****

Across the street, Dornal Zagen's dead, gray eyes followed the red taillights of the taxi as it disappeared down the avenue.

So Veronica Rossmore and John Monroe were together. The Austrian thief smiled. That made things simple. With the two people he most wanted access to right under his nose, it was as if the stars had aligned to assist him in his plan. Or perhaps, his employer had arranged it.

As he struck a match and watched the flame sizzle and burn for a moment before lighting his cigarette, he pondered what exactly the two of them wanted from each other. Surely, Monroe was there in some sort of professional capacity—probably as a bodyguard. It had looked, however, from Veronica's red-hot dress and the even hotter look in their eyes when they stared at each other, as if there were more to it than that.

Dornal smirked. Veronica wasn't exactly known for fraternizing with the help, let alone sleeping with them. She was rumored, in certain circles, to have other, more intense, obsessions.

Dornal flicked his half-smoked cigarette into the gutter and turned to go. In the end, it didn't really matter why John Monroe and Veronica Rossmore were shacking up. Before this was all over, Monroe would be dead and Veronica…

Well, he'd just have to think about what he could do with the lovely Veronica Rossmore.

****

John had picked out a cozy Italian place with dark red walls covered in grainy black-and-white photographs of the old country. Big mirrors reflected the glow of softly lit lamps, which were set out on tables draped in checkered cloths. Wine bottles hung from the ceiling and the tender voice of Corelli crooning a Puccini aria played in the background.

Veronica smiled as the short, stout maitre d' escorted them to a black leather booth and dramatically fluffed a napkin in the air to lie on her lap. Their waiter recited every dish on the menu with the passion of an ardent young lover pontificating on the curve of his lady's derrière. Veronica ordered the eggplant parmesan and a glass of merlot. John got the lasagna and a soda.

She looked around the room. "I was right. You're a complete cornball."

"Why? Because I'm not too cynical and jaded to enjoy a blatantly romantic atmosphere?"

"Are you calling me cynical and jaded?" she asked.

"I don't know, you tell me."

"I can respond to a romantic atmosphere as well as the next girl—if I'm with the right man," she said, her eyes sparkling wickedly.

The waiter set their drinks down on the table and disappeared into the kitchen.

"Don't drink?" she observed, looking him up and

down like she was trying to figure him out.

He held her stare. "No, I don't."

"Why not?" she asked, running a finger around the rim of her wine glass.

"The Irish really shouldn't," John replied with a smile.

She smiled, too. "I hope you don't have any objections to my..." She pointed to her glass.

"On the contrary, I think you should get good and soused. It'll give me an advantage over you."

"You'll need it," she replied, with a self-satisfied smile.

"Don't be too sure."

"You know, it's probably not right for me to have asked you out," she said. "It probably would make my father angry."

"Is that why you did it?"

"No." She took a sip of wine.

"Then why did you?" he asked seriously.

She gave him her Mona Lisa smile. "Maybe I wanted to get to know you a little better."

"Why?"

"Because I think I might like you," she admitted. "I think you're a nice, honest guy. There aren't many of those around."

"You don't really know me," he said, dropping his eyes. All the terrible, low, cowardly things he'd done in the past flashed before him; the lies he'd told, the money he'd borrowed, the people he'd let down before he got sober.

"Why don't you drink?" she asked him for the second time.

He looked up and saw sincere interest in her eyes. She wasn't playing games. She really wanted to know.

"Because I'm an alcoholic."

"Why?" she asked, and now there was intense interest written all over her face.

"Why?" he asked confused.

She leaned in closer to him. "Yes, why?"

"I don't know," he said, fiddling with the breadbasket. "It's just one of those things. You either are or you aren't."

"So nothing happened to you? Nothing made you like that?" She seemed cagey and desperately curious all at the same time.

He looked at her more closely, but he still didn't get why she was asking. "My father was an alcoholic and they say it runs in families. He died when I was seven."

She sat back and nodded her head slightly, like she had found what she'd been looking for. Then she said quietly, "My mother died when I was twelve. I don't like to talk about it."

"I don't like to talk about my dad, either," he said, and their eyes met. They understood each other perfectly. They both knew what it was like, that hopeless grief and the lost feeling of things no longer being okay in the world—that they never would be again. They both had the raw wound still open, like it was only yesterday when their childish worlds had shattered. In just one glance, they understood that about each other.

She took a sip of wine. "Tell me a joke."

John searched his mind. He knew a million of them. That's all they did at AA meetings, stand around smoking cigarettes and telling jokes like it was one big cocktail party—minus the cocktails.

"Okay," said John. "A panda walks into a bar, sits down, and orders a sandwich. He eats the sandwich, pulls out a gun, and shoots the waiter dead. As the panda stands to go, the bartender yells, 'Hey, where the hell do you think you're going? You just shot my waiter and you didn't pay for your sandwich!' And the panda yells back, 'Hey man, I'm a panda! Look it up!' and storms out of the bar. Well, the bartender grabs his dictionary and looks up 'panda' and it says: *A tree-dwelling marsupial of Asian origin, characterized by distinct black and white coloring. Eats, shoots and leaves."*

It was the first time he had ever seen her really laugh, and he decided he liked the look of her eyes crinkling up and the sound of her low voice rising like a musical scale. For a moment she looked truly happy, and he was glad to be the cause of it, if only for a moment. She arched her brow and said, "Eats, shoots and leaves, ha? That how you like to do it?"

John grinned. "Not always."

The food arrived, delicious and steaming hot. They ate in silence, and just as it had been in the car on the ride down to DC, it was a chummy, comfortable silence. They ordered cannoli and cappuccinos for dessert. Veronica took a bite of the Italian pastry and sighed like she was in heaven, licking the extra cream around her lips. John was torn between watching her movements and staring once more at the fiery red ruby between her breasts. She fingered the necklace provocatively and looked at him through her lashes.

"Those rocks real?" he asked.

"Maybe after dinner you'd like to examine them more closely and decide for yourself," she purred in her low voice.

"I'm no expert."

"Oh," she dangled the jewel along her décolletage, "maybe I could help you out."

He looked up into her face and her eyes smoldered under his gaze.

John flagged down the waiter. "Check, please!"

John and Veronica walked arm in arm through the Mall admiring the national monuments lit up all around them. Feeling a slight chill in the air, Veronica put her hand in John's pocket.

"Is that a gun in your pocket or do you just have

a thing for tall, pointy monuments?" she asked.

They were standing in front of the Washington Monument, which seemed to reach up to the stars from the dark park below.

"That necklace has got to be worth a couple million dollars and we're walking through a dangerous park at night. I better have a gun on me."

"Oh." She stopped and looked down, her voice low and breathy. "I was hoping you'd say it wasn't a gun *or* a building; maybe you'd say it was me."

John lifted her chin and looked deep into her eyes but couldn't see what lay in their depths in the darkness. Was she playing with him?

He didn't care.

He lowered his mouth to hers and gently kissed her. The tenderness and shivering passion he felt coming from Veronica hit him like an electric current. He pulled her closer. The burning ruby pressed against his heart and his hands were in her soft dark hair. He could still taste a hint of dessert on her sweet mouth and the scent of *L'Heure Bleue* filled his nostrils.

It had been a while since he'd kissed a woman like this. Since it had felt the way it did now. He didn't want to let go. If he were still drinking, he would have dragged her into the bushes and had his way with her here and now. But he wasn't drinking any more and she wasn't quite like any woman he had ever kissed before.

Veronica pulled back. From this angle, the light of the Washington Monument lit up her beautiful face. Her eyes blazed with desire.

"Let's get a cab back to the hotel," she whispered.

He nodded and, wrapping his arm around her waist, led her quickly to Independence Avenue to hail a taxi.

When they entered Veronica's hotel room,

without a word, she reached for him.

John grabbed her hips and held her firmly back for a moment. "Are you sure you want to do this?"

He knew it was stupid to ask. What if she said no? But somehow he found himself feeling protective of her. This couldn't be just some one-night stand. Or could it? His brain wasn't working right. There was too much testosterone raging through his system, confusing him, muddling his mind. The specter of Simon rose up and then disintegrated. When she pulled him in tight with a soul kiss that reached down to the very root of him and then wrapped a long leg around his hips, he knew it was over.

They pulled at each other's clothes as they fell down on the bed, the heat between them making their actions almost violent. All the reserve John had been forced to employ since he'd met Veronica slipped away as he consumed every tender morsel of her pampered flesh. His almost brutal passion seemed to awaken a fire that had burned in Veronica behind her mask of cool beauty. She struggled out of the tight dress and a low moan of pleasure escaped her lips as John inched down the red lace bra to reveal her swelling breasts and slipped his fingers beneath her matching panties. The feel of his sensitive fingers probing her seemed to drive Veronica wild; she pulled at his shirt, his pants—anything that came between his flesh and hers.

At last, he felt the velvet warmth of naked skin on skin and it seemed as if neither of them could wait a moment longer. Taking charge, John pushed her down on the bed, feeling her arch up under him as they melted together. She moaned and pulled him close, wrapping her arms and long legs around his muscular back. His hands were in her hair pulling her head back; her pink lips parted, her eyes squeezed shut in pleasure, and the ruby necklace blazed like a supernova against her sweaty flesh. He'd never seen anything so beautiful.

She squeezed and pulled him deeper, moaning and crying out with each violent thrust. There was nothing left of the lofty ice princess he had met three days ago. Veronica Rossmore had melted into a boiling wet cauldron of fire.

John felt a surge of lightning run up his spine. He was reaching his peak. "Open your eyes," he commanded and relaxed into a slow burn.

Veronica obeyed and looked up at him, helpless with desire. He kissed her lips and cradled her flushed face in his hands, their bodies moving like the slow powerful rise and fall of waves. He looked deep into her eyes; beyond the lust, underneath they were naked with emotion. The same feeling he had experienced at the restaurant returned now as their gazes fused and they understood the depths of each other. Only this time the moment had an otherworldly feeling about it. As if now that all the barriers had been torn down they gazed upon each other's souls, as if they'd reached up and captured a bit of eternity.

The spell was broken as Veronica cried out and shivered in her final moment. Accelerating their rhythm, they both surged together in a blinding climax that closed his eyes and all he could see were the fireworks going off in his head.

****

The next morning when John awoke, Veronica lay sleeping at the other side of the bed, a little frown creasing her brow, her dark hair tangled around her pale face. All the rosy glow from the night before was gone. Now that the smoke had cleared, John didn't know what to do. His usual MO was to run like hell the minute he woke up in a woman's bed, but he didn't feel like running this morning. Still, he didn't know how she would react to what had happened. He figured he'd handle anything she had up her sleeve better after his morning prayers and a few passages from the *AA Big Book*.

John slipped out of bed and quietly into his clothes. He tiptoed to the door, but as he was pulling it open, someone twisted the knob from the outside. He opened the door to see who it was and came face to face with the notorious jewel thief, Nicholas Bezuhov.

Chapter Eight

The White Russian stood in Veronica's doorway looking well-rested and like he had just come from the posh barbershop downstairs. He wore cream-colored pants and a light blue, button-down shirt. John almost rolled his eyes when he noticed the ascot tied neatly around the thief's neck.

"Well, good morning," said Nicholas Bezuhov, his Russian accent making him sound just a little bit like Dracula. "I thought you'd retired. What brings you here?"

"I wish I could ask you the same question," growled John.

Nicholas smiled brightly. "Why, I'm here for the Diamond Ball, of course."

"I bet you are," said John. "What are you doing outside Veronica Rossmore's room?"

"I don't know," said the White Russian, looking John up and down with an amused smirk. "What are *you* doing sneaking out of her room in last night's suit?"

John took a step forward, forcing Nicholas to back away from the door. "That's none of your fucking business," he said, his temper rising. "And if you know what's good for you, you'll walk away and not come back around."

The White Russian laughed. "I'm sorry, but it is not a crime to pay a visit to an old friend, now is it?"

That took the wind out of John's sails. That changed everything.

"If you don't mind," said the thief stepping

forward and reaching for the door. But John's hand shot out and grabbed Nicholas's wrist in a tight grip.

The White Russian's dark eyes glittered dangerously. "You are beginning to annoy me."

"Miss Rossmore is asleep right now," said John. "I don't think she would appreciate you busting in on her."

They stared each other down for a moment, but a maid pushing a breakfast cart rounded the corner, leaving it parked in front of a room two doors away. John and Nicholas turned to look at her and she nodded politely.

"Well," said Nicholas, pulling his hand away and straightening his cravat, "I'll come see Veronica later on." He started to walk away.

"What happened to the blonde?" John called after him.

The thief turned with an amused grin. "You mean Jessica? Do you know her?"

John didn't answer. He just watched his man.

"What am I saying? Of course you don't." The White Russian's grin broadened. "I'll see you later, Mr. Monroe."

"We'll be watching you," warned John.

Nicholas didn't look worried. "It was my understanding you are no longer a member of the FBI—something about a drinking problem." He smiled nastily.

"Still, there's nothing to stop me from making a citizen's arrest if anything disappears from this hotel."

All mock innocence, the White Russian threw up his hands. "I don't know what you're talking about. As I said, I'm just here to attend the Diamond Ball— charity, you know." His smile deepened and he turned away.

John watched the jewel thief as he walked down the hall, careless and arrogant. After the elevator doors closed behind him, John turned back to Veronica's door. There were a few things he'd like to ask her, but he was too angry. He decided to head back to his room, take a shower, order some eggs, and cool off.

****

When John returned to his room there was a message waiting from Quinn.

"Call me back," barked his ex-partner on the hotel voicemail.

John went to the minibar and opened it. He had to smile. It was jammed full of seltzer and pretzels. He pulled out a seltzer. The bubbles burned his throat, but the cold burst first thing in the morning felt good. He stripped off his wrinkled clothes and jumped in the shower. It was nice to take a shower in such a blindingly clean, white bathroom. There was plenty of room to move around, good lighting, and good-smelling bath products lined up along the marble sink. He closed his eyes as the explosion of cool water jets washed away last night's sweat and this morning's anger. He let it all go down the drain. Pulling a fluffy towel from the rack, he rubbed it through his hair and all over his body and then donned the white terry robe hanging on the bathroom door.

He headed into his room and sat down in a patch of sunlight on the floor. He crossed his legs Indian style, the way Bethany, an ex-pothead in his Thursday night AA meeting, had shown him.

He took a breath in and then exhaled long and slowly. His mind went back to Bethany. He remembered how she had taught him one night at two a.m. to stop the thoughts whirling in his mind from looping over and over on the same old bad news. John had come to her after not sleeping for three days straight, and he knew that if he didn't get some rest soon, he would go crazy. Simon had made the call to Bethany. Mercifully, she hadn't seemed to care about the late hour.

Bethany had sat John down in her yoga-den living room with its honey-toned candles. The floor had been covered in old flea-market Persian rugs and the room smelled like incense. Bethany had seemed to glow with an inner light, her soft brown eyes reassuring. Her tanned hands, covered in silver rings, were gentle as she ran her palm along his spine, showing him how to sit straight and relax at the same time. She had touched his third eye with her finger and told him to focus. She taught him how to breathe deep and let everything go with a long exhale.

Before sobriety John would have stayed away from Bethany and her meditation room like it was a den of ghetto-raised pit bulls, but that night he learned how to meditate and he finally slept.

Since then, whenever the world spun off its axis, he had learned to sit down and pretend he was in Bethany's apartment with the incense swirling and Indian chants playing in the background. If he was lucky, he experienced a fleeting moment of peace.

He sat now with his eyes closed and felt the sunlight warm on him. He slowed his breathing down and let his mind go blank like a television screen without a channel, all white fuzz. But out of the fuzz Veronica emerged, her eyes glowing dark blue, her naked breasts swelling up against him, the ruby around her neck crackling like a fire...

Frustrated, he opened his eyes. His room was peaceful and orderly except for his wrinkled suit which he had thrown on the floor. He couldn't meditate right now. So he switched positions and climbed onto his knees. Squeezing his eyes closed again, he whispered, "God, help me to do your will today and to stay out of trouble. Thank you, Amen."

He stood up, pulling his robe tighter around

him, and punched Quinn's number on the phone.

"Special Agent Quinn Brown."

"It's John."

No one was bothering with the niceties this morning.

"Maggie the Cat's booked herself a little show on a private yacht floating off Long Island," announced Quinn, sounding like he'd been up all night.

"I can top that," said John. "I saw Nicholas Bezuhov this morning outside Veronica Rossmore's room. Said they were old friends."

"The White Russian?" asked Quinn.

"Your friend and mine."

"He knows Veronica Rossmore?"

"That's what he says," replied John.

Quinn exhaled a world of worry and stress into the phone. "I don't like that at all."

"Me neither, makes my job tougher, but why's it so bad for you? It gives you more information on him."

"It's b-bad for me," Quinn stuttered the way he sometimes did when he was mad, "it's bad because I have my hands full! We still don't have a clue about what happened to the Puck Diamond and Katherine Park is like a goddamn dog with a bone over the whole thing. Half my people have gone off to Houston where the president is meeting with the entire Arab world's leaders to try and straighten out that mess. The last thing I need to worry about is Nicholas Bezuhov running off with Veronica Rossmore's jewelry collection!"

"Listen, partner, you don't have to worry about that," John tried to reassure his friend. "That's what I'm here for, right?"

There was a pause on the other end. "Yeah, yeah, you're right. You know what you're doing. So I'm not going to worry about it. I'm crossing that one off my list."

"Good."

"All right, I'll see you at the Diamond Ball," said Quinn wearily.

"I'll see you there."

"I can't wait till this friggin' thing is over," barked Quinn right before he hung up.

John was thoughtful as he put down the receiver. Had Quinn always been this stressed out and John just hadn't noticed because he'd been too lost in his own vodka-drenched haze? Then again, dealing with Katherine Park, the First Lady, the Hope Diamond, and a bunch of jewel thieves circling the Smithsonian like sharks would be enough to give anyone a good bloody ulcer.

****

Pandemonium reigned at the normally well-run Fabulous Food catering company. Nancy Malone, the owner of Fabulous Food, had just hung up the phone with her pastry chef, Armand. One way or another, he'd spent the entire morning on the toilet with gut-wrenching cramps and nausea that left him as green and limp as a piece of overcooked asparagus. With the Diamond Ball only a little more than twenty-four hours away, this was a major catastrophe.

As every caterer and restaurateur in DC was aware, the First Lady had a serious sweet tooth and was notoriously fussy about her pastries. Since this was the biggest event of the year for Lillian Spencer, failure to provide anything but absolute perfection could mean losing out to her archrival, Le Grand Gourmet Catering, for all future White House parties.

Mentally Nancy ran through the list of suitable pastry chefs in the area. Almost all were either already employed at one of the city's major hotels or restaurants, impossible to deal with, or out of town. Nancy put her head in her hands. She was on the verge of stamping her feet and screaming her head off, the staff in the kitchen behind her tasteful little gourmet shop be damned!

The tinkle of the bells attached to the shop's front door made her look up. A sweet-faced, little old lady in a beautifully tailored dress and a plaid shawl made her way past the neatly lined shelves of champagne vinegar and tins of beluga.

"Good morning," said the old lady cheerfully.

Years of plastering on smiles in impossible situations served Nancy well. In a flash, her pearly whites were on display as she greeted her customer. "Good morning. How may I help you, ma'am?"

"Well, I've just moved here from Philadelphia and was told by many people that you are the very best caterer in town."

"That's very kind of you." Nancy wondered how much money it would take to steal famed pastry chef Casper Dupres from the Willard Room for one night.

"Well, I'm no gourmet," said the old lady with a warm smile, "but I've been told I make the best cookies and brownies in the universe and I was wondering if you might be interested in carrying them in your lovely shop?"

Nancy didn't have time for this. "You know, we bake all our own..."

But now the old lady lifted the napkin that lay over her basket to reveal an array of beautifully arranged dark chocolate brownies dripping with fudge sauce, golden cookies dusted with powdered sugar, and light fluffy meringues smelling sweetly of lemon and orange oil.

"Oh," was all Nancy could say, staring at the pile of homemade goodies.

"Maybe you'd like to try something, dear?" asked the old lady kindly, handing Nancy a chocolate chip cookie.

"Well, why...thank you," said Nancy, accepting the cookie.

The caterer took one bite and her eyes popped out of their sockets. Being in the gourmet food business, Nancy had had the opportunity to eat a lot of tasty desserts, but she had never in her life tasted such a perfectly scrumptious chocolate chip cookie.

"Now try the brownie," urged the old woman, eagerly shoving a rich fudge brownie at the caterer.

Nancy swallowed her cookie and took a bite of brownie.

Chocolate heaven!

When Nancy had recovered from the divine experience, she grabbed the basket and said, "Wait one moment, would you please?" and whisked the goodies back to her kitchen staff.

Everyone from the head chef to the dishwashers sampled the homemade yummies and it was unanimous—they were the best damn desserts anyone there had ever eaten.

"Like my Nana used to make," declared the sous chef with tears in his eyes as he crunched on a lemon cookie glazed with a light sugar coating.

Nancy rushed back to the front of the store where the old lady waited patiently. "Did they like them?" she asked sweetly.

"Your desserts are incredible," declared the caterer. "Where did you learn to bake like that?"

"Oh, from my own dear grandmother when I was a little girl on the farm," said the old lady with a wistful smile.

"Look," said Nancy, unable to stop herself from snagging a sugar snap, "I think the good Lord sent you to me today. Our pastry chef is sick with a stomach flu and we've got a huge, I mean a *really* important event tomorrow night. Could you, I mean, I know this is ridiculously short notice, but is there any way you could make enough of these desserts for 350 people by tomorrow night?" Nancy knew she had desperation written all over her face.

"Why, I'd be just thrilled to help you out," said the old woman, clapping her hands in delight, but then a little frown formed a mass of wrinkles along her blue-veined forehead, "only..."

"Only what?" Nancy began to panic. "We'll do anything. Just please help us!"

"Oh, it's only that I'm very particular about how my sweets are arranged," the old lady smiled modestly. "You see, I put so much love into the things I bake. I just like to personally make sure they get the showing they deserve."

"Oh, that's fine!" said Nancy, relieved. "You can come to the event and lay everything out as you like."

The old lady beamed. "Oh now, isn't that nice of you?"

"Then you'll do it?"

"I'd be very pleased to help you; just tell me what time and where you need me."

After getting the information for the next evening, she left Fabulous Food with a smile on her face. *Delores Pigeon, you did beautifully.* Of course she did feel badly about spiking poor chef Armand's tea. She just hated to think of how he must be feeling right now, but she consoled herself with the knowledge that his colon was getting a good thorough cleaning and that would keep him healthy for years to come. With a sigh, she pulled her plaid shawl a little closer around her and headed down Prospect Street.

****

By the time lunch rolled around, John couldn't take the suspense any longer. He headed for Veronica's room. Maybe she'd want to get a bite to eat.

As he rounded the corner, she was just stepping out. She wore a beautifully cut, pale blue suit with a short skirt that showed off her long legs. A white

103

scarf was tied around her hair and the Jackie O's were perched on her WASPy little nose. Diamonds shimmered at her throat and wrists.

John was about to call out to her, when something in her manner made him pause and then duck back around the corner. He'd seen that body language before. It was stealthy and secretive. She was going somewhere she didn't want it to be known she was going. He could feel it in his gut, the way you got to feeling things when you'd chased criminals around for most of your adult life. You learned to trust that inner radar because very often your life depended on it.

He heard the soft sound of expensive shoe leather crinkling as she quickly made her way down the hall. When he felt the moment was right, he stepped out just in time to see her disappear into the stairwell. He hurried to the door and, quietly pushing it open, listened to her footsteps echo on the cement stairs. She went down two stories and then swung open the door to enter the second floor.

John took off his shoes and bolted down the stairs after her. When he reached the second floor, he pushed the door ajar, just enough to see Veronica slip into room 211.

John went down to the first floor, slipping his shoes back on before he entered the elegant lobby. He made his way to the polished wood concierge desk. An older gentleman in a neat gray uniform with a good-natured fat face smiled at John as he approached.

"Can I help you, sir?" asked the concierge.

"Yes," said John. "I wonder if you could tell me if a Nicholas Bezuhov is staying here? I thought I saw him in the lobby last night and I didn't get a chance to say hi." John flashed a bright smile.

"Oh, do you mean the prince?" asked the concierge.

John suppressed a smirk. "Yes, that's him."

"We're not supposed to give out room numbers, but…" The concierge stood waiting expectantly.

John shook his head. Could the guy be any more obvious? He pulled out his wallet and slid a twenty dollar bill across the front desk

The concierge's chubby fingers closed around the cash. "The prince is in room…let me see," he punched a few buttons on his computer, "room 211. Would you like me to call up and let him know you're here?"

"No, that's all right," said John, "I'll stop and see him later. Thank you."

The concierge smiled. "You're welcome, sir."

Now what? John headed toward the elevator bank. Elaborate schemes of commandeering the room above the White Russian's and bugging his suite, or a dozen other crazy things he might have done if he were still in the FBI danced in John's head. But he wasn't in the FBI anymore and Veronica Rossmore wasn't a criminal. At least, he didn't think she was.

He decided to go back to his room, pick up his sunglasses, and go for a walk. But when he got on the elevator, his finger pushed *two* as if it had a will of its own. When the doors slid open on the second floor, he stepped out and walked to room 211.

He put his ear to the door and listened.

All he could hear were Veronica's cries of pleasure.

Chapter Nine

The warm, honey tones of Veronica's thrilled gasp were a familiar sound. John had heard it the night before when he'd traced her throbbing flesh with the tip of his tongue.

His face flushed and he had to squeeze his hand into a fist to keep from grabbing the doorknob and busting in on them. He exhaled long and deep, and before he did something stupid, bolted up the stairs to his own room.

As soon as the door closed behind him, he went straight for the phone and dialed. He paced the room as the phone rang. It seemed to ring on into eternity until at last Simon picked up.

"Hello?" John could hear the ball game on TV in the background.

"It's John."

"Well, good to hear from you, John," said his sponsor, turning down the television.

"I'm fucking furious, Simon, and I don't know what to do."

Simon chuckled. "Congratulations, you're an alcoholic."

Smug old bastard. "Listen, I'm in a situation and I don't know how to handle it. I got a job as a bodyguard for this rich woman. She has a lot of expensive jewels and I'm supposed to be watching out for them. We're down in DC for this big charity ball. Anyway, I slept with her last night…"

"That was your first mistake."

Here we go.

"Never ever shit where you eat, John."

"I know it's not a good idea," John admitted. "But I'm only working for her for a few days and *she* came onto me..."

"I see, so you had no choice in the matter. She tied you to the bed and forced you."

John just shook his head. "Can I tell you the part that's screwing me up?"

"Go ahead."

John took a deep breath and tried to calm down. "The part I'm having trouble dealing with is...well, you remember how I used to track jewel thieves?"

"Yeah."

"Okay, well one of the thieves, this jerk called the White Russian, is staying here in the same hotel and I caught him trying to get into Veronica's room this morning..."

"He was breaking in?" asked the old man.

"Well, no," said John. "He was just walking in. He said he was a friend of hers."

"Uh-huh."

"Well, later on today, I caught her sneaking into his room and then I heard her having sex with him."

"You want to tell me what's wrong with what you just told me?" asked the old man like he was talking to a five-year-old.

"Yeah, she's running around with a notorious jewel thief behind my back. She's not being honest, she's..."

"I'm not interested in what *she's* doing," interrupted Simon. "Let's take a look at what *you're* doing. First, you sleep with your employer. Then you stalk her and listen at the door. What's this woman's name again?"

"Veronica."

"Okay, I want you to get this and get it good. Veronica is an adult and she gets to do what she wants. You were hired to do a job and you need to start showing up for it like a professional person. What Veronica does is Veronica's business and nobody else's."

"No, but seriously, Simon," objected John. "Last night she's coming onto me and today she's sleeping with this jerk."

"I don't care if she screws every inmate in Sing Sing, she's not the one trying to stay sober. *You* are. Now, listen to me," ordered Simon. "Tell me what Step Two is."

John sighed heavily. "Came to believe a Power greater than ourselves could restore us to sanity."

"Right! You get that you are insane right now?"

John hesitated. "You know, I don't know that, I mean anyone..."

"I see." Simon was amused. "You're a serene picture of contentment and balanced thinking."

"Fine, I get your point," John conceded.

"The good news is that we can be restored to sanity if we're willing to ask God for help and take a few right actions."

Here come the instructions.

"I want you to go to a meeting of Alcoholics Anonymous and find the most hopeless-looking case in the room. Take him out for coffee and try to help him. Then when you see this Veronica, you are to be polite and professional."

"Okay," John bounced his fist against his thigh, "okay, Simon."

"Call me tomorrow and let me know how it goes," advised the old man.

"I will," said John. "Thanks."

After hanging up, but before he could think himself out of it, John picked up the phone again and called the central office for Alcoholics Anonymous. He got the location of a meeting starting in half an hour and dashed out the door.

****

Dornal Zagen slid a little lower in the seat of the stolen BMW as he watched John Monroe enter St. Peter's Cathedral. He glanced over at the UMP submachine gun lying on the floor next to him. He was tempted to pick the ex-fed off right there on the steps of the church, but Dornal prided himself on doing things just right. Even though his gun had a silencer and he had a fast getaway car, the conditions were not quite perfect.

With the Hope in sight he didn't want to make a single mistake. Before the weekend was through, he'd have his revenge *and* the most coveted jewel in the world. It was worth the wait. He pulled a pack of cigarettes out of the glove compartment and settled in.

****

As John entered the meeting, which was held in the vestry room of St. Peter's, the fluorescent lights and circle of chatting people seated on metal folding chairs informed him he was in the right place. It was the usual crowd. Bankers in suits on lunch break, crack whores in tube tops with wild hair and wilder eyes, trust fund babies in their designer duds, tattooed convicts in jeans and wife-beaters, punk rockers with dyed hair and clothes pinned together with safety pins, wholesome-looking blonde trophy wives with perfect bodies encased in expensive casual clothing all sharing the same space. The speaker was a frail-looking woman with long, black hair and pale skin, who spoke passionately about her relationship with God and how AA had changed her life.

God came easily to some alcoholics once they made the decision to open themselves up to divine intervention, but John still had his doubts. He believed this fiery young woman had all kinds of guardian angels watching over her at any given moment, leading her to the right career, the right man, the most primo parking spot. But he couldn't quite believe he was getting the same treatment from the Almighty.

When the meeting ended, John scanned the room for the most messed-up-looking newcomer he could find. He saw a kid in faded jeans and a dirty *Linkin Park* T-shirt with limp hair hanging in his face and dark, haunted eyes. He had chipped black nail polish and a skull ring on his index finger. He was two sizes too thin and his skin had a yellowish cast to it. He would have been a good-looking guy if it weren't for the inner decay that had worked its way out to the surface.

John headed the kid's way and smiled. "Hey, I'm John. Are you new?"

"Yeah," mumbled the kid shyly. "I have two days."

"Congratulations," said John, trying to sound encouraging.

"It's not much," said the kid to his scuffed-up sneakers.

"Hey, this is where it starts," said John. "I remember when I had two days. I never thought I could make it to one year."

"Yeah?" The boy looked up, hope, despair, and a world of doubt in his dark eyes. "How did you do it?"

"If you want to go get a cup of coffee, I could tell you about it," offered John.

But the kid shook his greasy head and looked down again. "No thanks, man. I gotta be somewhere."

"Okay," said John unperturbed, "but if you need someone to talk to, here's my number." He fished a pen out of his pocket and scribbled awkwardly on a receipt from the Monticello drug store where he had stopped to pick up a pack of gum before his date with Veronica.

The kid took the number without even looking

at it and slipped it into his jeans' pocket. "Thanks, man."

"Seriously, call me if you need me."

"I will," said the kid, looking antsy.

John knew he wouldn't. As he walked out of the vestry, his heart sank. Before the day was out, the kid would probably drink or light up a pipe, snort something or shoot up—whatever it was he was into. That was the sad fact of the disease they shared.

John left the church feeling almost as discouraged as when he had entered. The sun was beginning to set, sending warm rays over the charming street with its Revolutionary War townhouses and the bright little gardens packed with blooming, spring perennials.

Slowly he walked along the cobblestones until he reached the church garden halfway down the block. It was enclosed in black wrought-iron gates. At the garden's center stood a stone statue of Mary wearing a crown, with the baby Jesus cradled in her arms. She looked disappointed and downhearted, too, but behind her stood a beautiful weeping willow. Its bows arched protectively over the Virgin's head, its strong trunk at her back and the setting sun shone through, silhouetting her. At her feet bloomed lavender, white roses, orange day lilies, and deep magenta hydrangeas.

John shuffled to a stop and turned to face Mary in her serene garden. Unexpectedly, he felt a gentle wave of peace warm him as he gazed at the statue. Maybe things weren't as bad as he thought.

Though he felt slightly foolish there on the public street, he bowed his head to offer up a silent prayer.

It took less than a second for John's adrenaline to surge as he heard the bullet whistle over his shoulder and knick the black iron gate where his head had been only a moment before. He was flat on the ground as a second bullet whizzed over him. He had his hand on his Glock 27 before he could think about it. He spotted the BMW across the street with a man sporting dark glasses and shocking, white-blond hair behind the wheel. John pulled the trigger, sending a loud popping noise echoing off the cobblestones. It had been a long time since he'd fired a gun, but like riding a bike, all his training came back in a flash and he fired again, shattering the rearview mirror on the Beemer before it took off with a squeal of tires down the street.

John's brain started to work now, along with his adrenaline-hopped reflexes. He knew it was Dornal Zagen speeding away.

Mad as hell, John ran hard after the car. He knew he didn't stand a chance of catching the Austrian thief, but he would damn well try anyway. Pausing for a moment to aim his gun, he shot out the back left tire of the sports car as it swung around the corner.

Behind him, John could hear the doors of the sedate townhouses opening and feel the glare of worried eyes upon his retreating figure as he flew down the street. He hit Pennsylvania Avenue and discovered he was in luck. The BMW was stuck in the gridlocked mess created by an accident between a small sports car and a motorcycle, fortunately harming no one, but creating the traffic jam from hell. Vehicles had almost come to a complete standstill as everyone waited for a traffic cop to wave cars past the accident one at a time.

As John advanced on the BMW, Dornal jumped out and took off running into a nearby alley. John was on his tail as they raced down the pavement.

The Austrian thief ran fast, but John ran faster. He reached out and his fingers grazed the back of Dornal's coat, but with a sharp turn, the convict swerved into a doorway and they found themselves in the middle of the giant barn-like space which held the Eastern Market. The building was filled with vendors selling fresh produce, colorful cut flowers, and kosher meat.

The thief burst through a stall, overturning a display of Granny Smith apples and ripe Georgia peaches. The people in the crowded market panicked and screamed as Dornal turned and pinched off another shot in John's direction, missing him by a fraction of an inch, before leaping over a counter bursting with dyed hot pink and orange carnations.

Pushing an ancient Korean fishmonger out of the way, John leapt forward and caught the Austrian's sleeve, knocking the UMP submachine gun across the floor. John shoved his own pistol in the thief's ribs.

"Stop right there, Zagen! You're under arrest," John puffed, as sweat ran down his flushed cheeks.

Dornal's free hand closed around the handle of a toddler's stroller that a frantic mother had not been able to pull away in time. Quick as lightning, the scalpel was at the little girl's rosy throat. The child burst into tears, as her hysterical mother screeched, grabbing at John's arm and trying to pull him away.

"Drop the gun," said the convict curtly, his dead shark eyes nailing John's.

There was a ninety-nine percent chance John could pull the trigger before Zagen hurt the kid, but John knew if something went wrong, he'd have the image of the little brown-eyed girl in her denim overalls and the feral cries of her grief-stricken mother burned into him for life.

"Please, please drop your gun!" whimpered the mother as her fingers dug into his arm.

Anger pumping through every cell in his body, John replaced the safety and slid the Glock 27 across the floor away from the Austrian.

The frantic mother screamed again as Dornal

backed away with the toddler's stroller.

"Let the girl go!" yelled John, squeezing his fists tight in impotent rage.

As Dornal reached the exit, he gave the stroller a hard push and it went flying in John's direction. Cursing, John caught the toddler before the stroller slammed into the corner of a stainless-steel meat counter. Shoving the kid into her sobbing mother's arms, he ran after Dornal, but as he burst onto Seventh Street, he saw no evidence of the thief.

Coming to a halt, his breath flowing in ragged bursts from his lungs, John turned and swung his head from left to right. He looked up at the trees and the roofline of the Eastern Market. With a sick feeling in his gut, John knew he'd lost Dornal Zagen. He collapsed onto a bench out front as the wail of sirens heralded the arrival of the DC police.

John's head shot up. He wasn't a federal agent anymore and carrying a concealed weapon and getting involved in a shootout was no longer an officially sanctioned activity for him. Sure, Quinn could probably get him out of any trouble with the police, but he didn't need an incident like this to go on his record if he ever hoped to rejoin the FBI.

Before he knew it, John was on his feet and back inside the market. The Glock still lay on the floor in the corner of the room. Without breaking his stride, he snatched up the pistol and ran back through the alley. He'd decide what to do once he was back in the quiet of his hotel room and could think straight again.

It was dark by the time John returned to the Monticello. He grabbed a cold seltzer out of the minibar, kicked off his shoes and lay back on the king-sized bed. It had been a while since anyone had taken a shot at him. It was no mystery why Dornal Zagen was trying to kill him or what he was doing in DC. If John were not very much mistaken, he'd see the notorious thief again at the Diamond Ball tomorrow night. He wasn't afraid for himself. He'd been dodging bullets for most of his adult life, but he was concerned for Veronica. What if the Austrian thief had penned the letter warning her to stay away from the ball? If only she'd listen to reason.

Then again, maybe she knew how to take care of herself better than John expected. After all, if she was friends with Nicholas Bezuhov, she might not be as innocent as he had originally believed.

What really troubled him was whether to tell Quinn about his encounter with Zagen. His ex-partner had enough on his plate to overwhelm ten men. Besides, over the years John had come to feel that Dornal was his bone to pick. The fact that the Austrian convict had just tried to blow his brains out only made this more clear. If he had not stopped to pray...

John grew thoughtful as he pondered this. The only reason he was alive now was because he had bowed his head in reverence. Was it a sign? Was God watching out for him after all?

Why now? Why did God seem to be around sometimes and not others? And why were so many messed-up things allowed to go on if there was a God? There were so many things he couldn't come to terms with. His father's death, Veronica and the White Russian, the junkie kid who wouldn't get sober. John wondered why he was given the gift of sobriety but that poor kid was stuck in his own private hell. None of it made sense. He felt like he would never understand God and His plan. Simon had told him he didn't need to understand, but John had spent his entire adult life trying to use his agile mind to uncover the mysteries, figure out the crime. It was hard to just throw up your hands and trust.

He let out a long, deep breath and a fleeting sense of the peace he'd felt in Mary's garden came back to him. Maybe he didn't have all the answers, but he was at least willing to admit his life had been saved by a prayer today—even if it was just a coincidence.

He rolled his eyes up toward the ceiling and whispered, "Thank you."

He sat quietly for a moment and then picked up the remote, turning on a sports channel. It was time to give his brain a rest. If he couldn't drink and he couldn't smoke, well, at least there was college basketball. Forget Zagen, Veronica Rossmore, the White Russian, Simon, the sad junky kid, and the true nature of God and the universe. He would anesthetize himself in the fascination of March Madness.

About forty-five minutes into the game, there was a knock at the door.

He jumped up and opened it before he had a chance to think.

Veronica stood there looking as beautiful as he'd ever seen her. She was dressed for dinner in a black evening gown. Her hair was coiled in an elegant chignon at the nape of her neck. The usual blast of white rocks shimmered at her earlobes, wrists, and throat. She seemed poised and calm.

"I hope I'm not intruding," she said in her low voice, the scent of *L'Heure Bleue* faintly wafting into the room.

John marched over to the TV and snapped it off. "No, that's fine." He sounded cold even though he could feel his neck and face catch fire and his body tense up on red alert.

A bit of the sparkle died out of her eyes. "I thought I'd just say hello and let you know I'm going out for the evening."

"You shouldn't be going out alone. It's dangerous," growled John.

"John, I really can't..."

But he cut her off. "And by the way, why didn't you tell me you're friends with the White Russian?" John sounded more hostile than he wanted to.

Now it was her turn to a go a little red, the color washing becomingly into her cheeks as she crossed her arms over her breasts. "It's none of your business who my friends are."

"It is when they're notorious jewel thieves and I'm being paid to guard your rocks." He couldn't help adding, "Besides, I mean, Veronica, the guy's like a bad character in a *Pink Panther* movie. How could you possibly be friends with him?"

She shook her head and came toward him so that she stood in all her overwhelming beauty just an arm's length away. "I've known Nicholas for a long time. I met him in Switzerland when I was at school. We both share a passion for jewels, which a lot of other people don't fully understand. We've had the similar experience of living all over the world, never being in one place for more than a year or two."

"I see, and do you have any other criminals among your acquaintances?"

"Nobody has any proof he's the White Russian." Her dark blue eyes flashed in defensive loyalty for her friend.

"There's proof and there's proof, Veronica," said John, sounding cynical and bitter. "Is he here for the Hope Diamond?"

She looked him square in the eye. "No."

"How do you know?"

"Because I asked him."

"And you believe him?" asked John incredulous.

"Yes, I do!" She was furious. "Nicky knows as well as anybody that the diamond is cursed. He wouldn't go near it with a ten-foot pole!"

"So he's Nicky now," said John mockingly.

"I told you, he's an old friend and, I might add, a

117

true artist," she said indignantly.

"He's an artist all right—a con artist!"

"He happens to be one of the most talented jewelers in the world," Veronica informed him haughtily. "He's created exquisite pieces for everyone from Princess Diana to Nicole Kidman!"

"Really. Is that why you snuck into his room this afternoon without letting me know?"

Veronica opened her mouth to say something, but instead pressed her lips tight and her eyes turned as hard and cold as the icy diamonds that shimmered in teardrops around her throat. "Have you been spying on me?"

"What were you doing sneaking into a known jewel thief's room?" he demanded, nailing her to the wall with his eyes.

"He just acquired some new stones and he was showing me his jewels."

"I bet he was," sneered John.

Then she took a step back and shook her head, recognition coming into her eyes. She'd been through this too many times before. "You don't give a damn if Nicholas is a thief. You're just jealous." She shook her head in disgust. "Well, let me tell you something, John, I don't like jealous men."

His mind flashed once more to the photograph of her on the front page of the *New York Post* after her ex-husband, Derrick Chapin, had thrown her down the stairs. It was like a slap in the face. She was right. He was so jealous and angry he could barely speak. He knew he should apologize, but he was too mad.

"I'm going now to have dinner with the wife of the President of the United States. As I told you before, I am also old friends with her. Hopefully you won't have any objections to that!" She turned sharply, fury written into every tense line of her body as she marched out of the room.

Just before she left, he called out, "For such an antisocial girl, you're friends with just about everybody!"

It was childish of him. She didn't respond, of course. The door slammed and she was gone.

****

The black sports car came to a silent stop on the street in front of Senator Hayes' Capitol Hill townhouse. Maggie the Cat, clad all in black, slid out of the passenger seat and shut the door behind her. She winked at René, who sat behind the wheel with the motor still purring quietly. Maggie motioned for him to cut the lights and he quickly obeyed.

With a silent leap, she sprang up and grabbed the bottom branch of the stately old magnolia which graced the small garden in front of Senator Hayes' home. In seconds, she had reached the top of the tree. Uncoiling a slim metal cord from her belt, she tossed the rubber-coated grappling hook attached to the cord and it hit its mark. The rubber muffled the sound of the hook catching on the open window of an upstairs bedroom. Securing the other end of the cord around the tree's trunk, Maggie put one foot on the rope, testing it to make sure it could handle her weight. As gracefully as the cat she was named for, she tiptoed across the wire and stood just outside the window peering in.

She smiled. It was the master bedroom, the room where people almost always kept their valuables when they were not securely locked up in bank safe-deposit boxes. The old gray-haired senator lay in his striped pajamas with his back to his wife, who from the look of the prescription bottle of sleeping pills by her bedside, was down for the count.

A low growling came from the foot of the bed and a cranky-looking bulldog raised his head.

Looks as though you need a nice sleeping pill like

your mommy. The fat, slobbering mess of a dog jumped off the bed with a thud, and growling louder, came toward her.

"*Bonsoir,*" Maggie whispered, as she waved a little doggie treat laced with a harmless, but extremely effective, sedative through the window.

The bulldog put his two front paws on the window ledge and sniffed the treat. It must have checked out, because with a phlegmy snort, he accepted the gift and waddled back to a corner of the room to enjoy his feast.

The minutes ticked by, but Marguerite knew better than to enter the room before the dog was fully sedated. Patience had never been her forte, but she was able to recognize when it was a necessity.

On the street below, the flash of headlights spilled across the cobblestones as a car turned onto the block. Catching her breath, Marguerite leaned as close to the building as she could, hoping the shadow of the magnolia hid her from view. A midnight blue Mercedes came to a stop across the street and an older-looking gentleman got out. He walked around to the passenger side of the car and opened it for a pretty blonde in a low-cut dress.

Maggie smirked. These Americans were not so very different from the French after all. She stopped smirking when the older man frowned and looked at the black Lotus with René still sitting in the driver's seat, but relaxed as the blonde slid her arm in his, and the gentleman quickly led her into his house.

Maggie exhaled. The young blonde would keep that old man busy and out of her hair, but it would still be a good idea to get in and out as quickly as possible. She peered in the window and now the old bulldog was snoring nearly as loudly as his master. No wonder the lady of the house needed sleeping pills.

Carefully, Maggie slid the window open a touch

more. After all, she wanted a nice wide exit on her way out—especially if something went wrong. Open windows like this were the reason spring and fall were her favorite times of year to commit thefts. In the winter and summer, people kept their windows locked to keep out the elements, but at the turn of the seasons, who could resist inviting the fresh air into their home?

Maggie's foot silently touched the carpet and she was in the room. There'd be no alarms to contend with here in the bedroom while the owners of the house slept in it. If she'd tried to break in downstairs through the back door, it would have been an entirely different story. Maggie knew better than to pull an amateurish move like that.

Now, if her friend Thomas at the Inter-Vac company, who had installed the senator's safe, was on the money then what she sought lay behind that atrocious fake Renoir hanging above the vanity table. It would have been a fun test of her abilities to crack the safe, but since Thomas had already supplied the code, that would not be necessary. Soundlessly, she pulled the offending painting off the wall and placed it on the floor.

Viola! The safe was just where it was supposed to be.

She considered switching on the penlight she had brought with her for the occasion, but excellent night vision was one of her strengths and she could just make out the letters on the dial.

Not wanting to fuss with papers in the dark, she had committed the code to memory which had not been difficult. She put her hand on the dial. Her fingers were sensitive even encased in gardening gloves with surgical gloves beneath those to prevent that naughty DNA-holding sweat from getting out onto the dial. She tried the code—J-E-F-F-E-R-S-O-N.

The metal door swung open and she caught her breath. This was always the most intoxicating moment.

Apparently the senator and his wife were a pair of packrats, because the safe was crammed with all sorts of bonds and papers. Without touching anything, she examined the contents with her eyes until she noticed a velvet jewel box in the corner. Maggie slid it out and gently lifted the lid.

The Mogul Emerald glittered up at her from the silk-lined box. It was a massive 217 carats and had once been the centerpiece of an Indian maharaja's turban pin. More recently, Islamic prayers had been etched into the face of the stone and it was rumored to have spectacular, protective magical powers. Gleefully Maggie shut the box and began to tiptoe back across the room just as the old senator stirred.

With those famous cat instincts, Maggie was plastered against the wall of the tiny hallway between the bedroom and the bath in the blink of an eye. She stood there, not breathing, as the senator sat up and rubbed his eyes for a moment.

Merde.

The old man raised his creaky body from the bed and began to head toward the bathroom—and Maggie.

Thinking fast, Maggie shoved the velvet box down her body-hugging shirt. She noiselessly gave a little jump and grasped the top of the molding above the doorway leading to the bathroom. With a slight kick of her legs, she lifted her body up into a handstand and balanced precariously upside down above the doorway, thanking God the place had high ceilings!

She closed her eyes and prayed to St. Nicholas, the patron saint of thieves, as the old senator walked though the doorway just below her and into the bathroom. He shut the door behind him and it was only pure luck that the old man had not noticed his safe hanging wide open on the wall in the darkness. On his way back to bed, he might be more alert. She couldn't take the chance.

Swift as lightning, she sprang down from the doorway and was out the window and taking a flying leap from the treetop before René had time to look up. She jumped into the passenger seat, and giving him a wicked grin, commanded, "DRIVE!"

René put his foot on the gas. The car went from zero to a hundred and sped off into the night.

Not bad for a warm-up. Maggie clutched her new good-luck charm. She rolled the window down so she could feel the wind whipping through her flame-colored hair. Now she would be invincible at the Diamond Ball.

Upstairs the senator stood gaping at the open safe.

"Louise, wake up!" he bellowed at his wife. "Wake up, goddamn it!" But Louise Hayes, still under the influence of her pills, lay peacefully asleep.

"Goddamn it!" swore the old man, looking around the room for his dog. "Where's Jefferson?"

As he looked around, he heard the bulldog snoring in the corner. Infuriated, he went to Jefferson and shook him. "Where the hell were you when this happened?"

Jefferson just whined in his sleep and farted.

"That's about the size of it," said the old man shaking his head in disgust before he picked up the phone to notify the authorities.

Chapter Ten

John was fast asleep when his phone rang. Blindly reaching out his hand in the darkness, he fumbled for it. His fingers closed around the receiver. "Hello?"

"John..." It was Veronica. She paused and he was surprised to hear the badly suppressed sound of her sobs across the line. "My jewels are gone. They've been stolen!"

"I'll be right there." John slammed down the phone. He *knew* this was going to happen.

Veronica had dried her eyes by the time he pulled on some clothes and raced down to her bedroom. Her eyes were red and puffy and she was paler than her bedsheets. She hadn't yet changed out of the black evening gown, but that was all she wore. Her diamonds were noticeably missing. She looked naked without her sparkling jewels and he realized it was the first time he had ever seen her unadorned.

"They're all gone," she said, wiping her runny nose with her hand. She sounded as heartbroken as a mother whose baby had just been kidnapped.

John scanned the room. "Have you touched anything?"

She shook her head. "Nothing, there was nothing to touch. The door to my room was locked from the inside and so are all the windows."

John walked to the windows and inspected the locks. It was all as she said. Next he checked the air conditioning vent, but the screws holding it in were perfectly in place. There was no other way into the room. "Tell me what happened."

Veronica sank into a chair and ran her naked fingers through her hair. "I came home from dinner at about ten-thirty. I sat down on the loveseat over there by the windows and I guess I was so tired I fell asleep. When I woke up, I knew something was wrong. I raised my hand to touch my necklace and it wasn't there. Then I looked down and my bracelets were gone, too. Someone slipped the jewelry right off my body while I was sleeping! How on earth could they do that without waking me up?"

"I don't know. What happened after that?"

Her dark blue eyes welled up and she pointed to the jewelry case resting on her vanity table. "Well, I went straight to my jewelry case, which I found locked by the way, and everything inside it was gone."

John narrowed his eyes. "The case was locked when you left for dinner?"

She nodded her head.

"And when you went to look for your jewelry, it was still locked? You had to unlock it to look inside?"

"That's right."

He kneeled in front of the jewel case being careful not to touch it. "Where's the key for this?"

"It's in my purse. I'll get it," she said, rising.

She pulled a deep burgundy alligator purse out of the closet and produced the key.

"It's exactly where I always keep it," she said, bringing the bag over to him and pointing to a little zippered compartment inside the purse. "You see?" She shook her head. "I just don't understand how all this could have happened while I was asleep in the room. How did the thief know where my key was? It's as if..." her voice trailed off.

"A ghost came and took them." John finished her sentence and added, "Or maybe *the Ghost*."

"Oh God." She sank down on the bed and put her head in her hands. "That's what I was afraid of. Have you ever recovered anything he's stolen?"

"I'm not so sure it is the Ghost." Though he had to admit it sure as hell seemed like it from everything he'd ever seen of the elusive jewel thief. "What about Nicholas Bezuhov? He didn't pay you a visit tonight, did he?"

She raised her chin, a little life coming back into her face. "No, he wasn't here and he didn't do this. He's my good friend, John. He would never in a million years steal from me. He knows what my jewelry means to me."

"All the same," said John, "I'd like to find out where he was this evening."

Veronica looked annoyed. "Don't you think we should be busy trying to track the real thief instead of wasting time with Nicholas? Besides, even if it was the thief you call the White Russian, didn't you say he always leaves a calling card? There's no card in this room that I can see."

She had a point there, but John was beginning to think maybe Nicholas only left calling cards when he wanted to confuse the authorities. What better way to portray your innocence than by throwing everyone on the scent of a supposedly different thief?

"Listen," said John, "in a minute I'm going to call someone at the FBI and get him down here. I promise you he's going to want to talk to your Russian friend—calling card or no calling card. Now, we can let him take your pal in for questioning or we can go ask him ourselves right now. What do you want to do?"

Veronica looked miserable. He knew she didn't like either option but finally said, "All right, let's go."

They didn't say a word as they made their way down to room 211. He was too busy thinking and she was still too upset. When they reached the White

Russian's room, John stood aside and motioned toward the door. "Go ahead. He's your buddy."

Glaring at John, she raised her hand and knocked on the door, calling softly, "Nicky, it's Veronica."

There was no answer.

"Try again," said John.

She did, but there was still no answer.

"He's not here," she said. "I'm going back to my room and call the police."

"Wait a moment," said John thinking. "You go downstairs to the lobby and ask the concierge if he's seen Nicholas tonight. I'm going to wait right here until you come back and tell me what they say."

"This is ridiculous, John. You're chasing the wrong man!"

John turned and looked straight into those teary eyes. "Listen, Veronica, do you want your stuff back or not? You may not think much of me, but I did have a pretty good track record in my years with the FBI. I've caught more thieves and recovered more stolen jewelry than anyone else in the department—then or now."

"But you never recovered anything stolen by the Ghost, and that's who took my jewels. I know it and you know it!" Veronica shot back, her temper obviously starting to rise.

"Maybe it was the Ghost," admitted John, "but maybe it wasn't. Either way, you have to believe that there is no one else who offers you a better shot of recovering your things than me. So I need you to help me, and I need you to help me now, before the trail gets too cold."

They stared each other down for a tense moment, but at last, Veronica nodded. "All right, I'll meet you back up here in a minute."

When the elevator doors had safely closed behind her, John scanned the hallway. All was quiet.

He took a "Do Not Disturb" sign off the knob of a nearby room and carefully slid it between the crack of the door to room 211 and the molding. He shifted the sign around until the lock clicked. Slowly, he pushed the door open to reveal the White Russian standing in the entrance. The thief was wearing a navy silk dressing gown and an antique ebony cigarette holder was stuck in his mouth. His black eyes were cold and unamused.

"Can I help you?" he asked, in his thick Russian accent.

"Can I come in?" asked John curtly.

"No, I'm afraid you cannot. I have a guest with me."

"Why didn't you answer the door when Veronica knocked just now?"

The White Russian exhaled a stream of smoke through his nostrils like a dragon. "I just told you, I have a visitor and do not wish to be disturbed."

"Listen, Bezuhov," John said in his best tough cop voice, "Veronica Rossmore's entire jewelry collection was stolen tonight, and as far as I'm concerned, you're the number one suspect."

The White Russian narrowed his black eyes and didn't say anything for a moment. Then he surprised John by asking, "Is she terribly upset?"

"You're damn right she's upset. Maybe you can tell me where you were this evening?"

"Jessica and I went to the Kennedy Center for the ballet. We just got back to the hotel about twenty minutes ago," replied Nicholas.

"Did the concierge see you come in?"

"Yes, in fact, I picked up a note from him on my way in," said the White Russian smoothly.

"Who's the note from?" asked John.

"None of your business," snapped Nicholas.

"What ballet did you see?"

"Giselle, my favorite. I still have the tickets if

you'd like to see them," he sneered in mock helpfulness.

"Jessica in there, too?" asked John.

Nicholas turned his head and called, "*Moheta*, could you come here a moment please?"

The debutante stepped out of the shadows, clutching a pale pink satin robe across her naked breasts. Her hair was disheveled and John could just make out a purple bruise under her left ear, which she tried to cover by wrapping her hand around her throat. "What is it, Nikoli?" she asked in her well-bred voice.

"I'm sorry to disturb you, miss," said John, "but can you tell me what you did this evening?"

Jessica blushed clear to the roots of her blonde hair and looked at Nicholas confused.

"He means where did we go tonight," explained the White Russian.

"Oh," said the debutant. "Well, we went to dinner at the Willard Room and then to the ballet." She looked John up and down trying to figure out what he was doing there.

"I'm sorry, miss. My name is John Monroe. I'm working as a bodyguard here in the hotel and my client's jewels have just been stolen."

"But what has that got to do with us?" asked Jessica, mystification written across her baby-soft face and innocent pale-blue eyes.

"It has nothing to do with us," said Nicholas. "So if you don't mind, Mr. Monroe, we'd like to go back to bed."

I bet you would, John watched the dishy debutante turn away and disappear back into the dark room.

"Veronica know about her?" asked John.

"Good night," said the White Russian and shut the door in his face, just missing John's nose by a fraction of an inch.

A few moments later, the elevator doors opened and Veronica stepped out. John made his way down the hall to her. "What did they have to say downstairs?" he asked.

"They told me Nicholas was out all evening but came in about twenty minutes ago with that same blonde girl he was with last night."

"All right," said John. "I just spoke to him and he gave me the same story."

"You see? I told you he had nothing to do with this," said Veronica, annoyed.

"We'll see about that." John jabbed the elevator button with his finger. "In the meantime, we better officially report the theft."

"Yes, we should," she agreed.

The elevator arrived and they stepped in. John leaned back against the wall and inspected Veronica. She looked miserable. Her dark hair hung in lose clumps where she had clawed it from its pins, a faint line of black mascara streaked her pale cheek. She was a far cry from the immaculately dressed, poised woman he had become used to over the past few days. He felt a swell of sympathy for her and squeezed her arm reassuringly. "Don't worry, Veronica. We'll get your jewels back."

She looked at him and smiled wanly. It was clear she didn't believe him.

The elevator doors slid open, but John put his hand on the HOLD button. "Listen, why don't you let me take care of this? You go upstairs, wash your face, change into something else, maybe have a glass of wine. I'll be up in a moment. It could be a long night once the authorities get here. You may want to camp out in my room while they dust yours for prints." He didn't tell her he was beginning to get the feeling they wouldn't find any.

She nodded and looked relieved. "Thank you, John."

He gave her a wink. "Don't worry." He stepped out of the elevator and the doors whispered shut behind him.

****

Half an hour later, Veronica's hotel suite had turned into the three-ring circus John had known it would. Downstairs the press was already clogging up the lobby, waiting for their first scoop on the latest installation of the Ghost chronicles.

When Quinn arrived, John realized it had been a long time since he'd laid eyes on his old partner. Quinn's little paunch had turned into a full-fledged potbelly and his hair seemed to have thinned dramatically. He wore a gray slicker against the rain that had begun to pour down outside and his wet, mouse-brown hair was plastered against his skull.

"I'm sorry it took me so long," he announced to the room full of cops. "I had to fight my way through the vultures downstairs." He shook his head like it was all too much.

"Sorry to bring you out at this hour," said John, walking his ex-partner over to Veronica, who had slipped into a pair of jeans and a black cashmere sweater. "This is Miss Rossmore."

"Nice to meet you," said Quinn, distractedly sticking out a chubby hand for her to shake.

She nodded and murmured, "Nice to meet you."

She had sunk into a morose depression so deep John was almost shocked by it. Where had the feisty, confident woman gone? He studied her as she quietly moved into a corner of the room and sat with her head propped up on one elbow watching the police check out the room.

Quinn frowned. "She okay?"

"She's taking this pretty hard."

"Well then, maybe she should have kept her freakin' jewels in the hotel safe," whispered Quinn irritably. "I cannot believe this night. I really can't.

Do you know where I just came from? Guess! Why don't you guess?"

"I don't know."

"I'll tell you." Quinn stuffed a cigarette in his mouth and flicked the lighter repeatedly in short sharp jerks until it finally produced a flame. "Senator Hayes' house. And do you know why I was there? Because friggin' Maggie the Cat, or at least I'm pretty sure that's who it was, hit the place and took off with the Mogul Emerald."

"The Mogul Emerald?" John mentally tried to place the stone.

"You've been out of the game too long," observed Quinn with his first grin of the evening. "It's a massive square-cut emerald. It used to belong to the maharajas of India. About a hundred years ago, someone got the idea to etch Islamic prayers into it. The senator's wife, who's a nut about New Age stuff, bought the thing last year during their peace-making trip to the Middle East. She thinks it will protect her and her family from terrorist attacks. She's fucking freaking out."

"Maggie the Cat does love her high-profile jewels," said John, remembering some of her past suspected heists.

"Yeah, God forbid she hit up a jewelry store and steal a few engagement rings," grumbled Quinn.

"So what makes you think it's her?"

Quinn started counting off the reasons on his chubby fingers. "One—she's in the area. Two—this is her kind of rock. Three—my men found a, a...what do you call it? A sparkle? No. A sequin, they found a friggin' sequin on the floor of Senator Hayes' bedroom."

John shook his head. "That's pretty flimsy evidence, but I see what you're saying. Once again, you know who did it but can't prove it."

"Isn't that always the game," complained Quinn,

looking discouraged.

"Well, it looks like it's been a busy night," said John, patting his friend on the shoulder.

"You said it. Anyway," Quinn scanned the room, "what about this? What have you got?"

"I hate to say it, but it looks to me like the Ghost," admitted John.

"Are you sure? It's been a long time since the Ghost's been in action."

"But the Puck Diamond—"

"Turned out to be the Granny who pulled that one off. I managed to identify her in the crowd after watching that damn video frame by frame for about twelve hours straight. Now we just have to catch the old broad so I can get Katherine Park off my ass." He put his palms together and turned his eyes toward heaven. "Please, dear God." He took a long drag off his cigarette and snatched up a crystal ashtray from the bedside table to flick his ash into before it dropped onto the expensive carpet. "And you know what? I'm beginning to have a theory about the Ghost."

"Oh yeah, what's that?"

"What if there is no Ghost?" said Quinn, raising his eyebrows dramatically.

"What do you mean?" asked John, confused.

"I'm saying," said Quinn, stabbing his cigarette into the air, "what if there never was any Ghost? What if we've just been attributing any well-executed jewel theft to the Ghost? Think about it. We find a clean robbery with no break-in and no fingerprints and we say, 'Aw Christ, it must be the Ghost.' But it could be all kinds of different thieves at different times."

John shook his head. It didn't seem right, though logically it would explain why they had never been able to find this almost mythical jewel thief. "I don't know," said John skeptically.

Quinn shrugged. "It's just a theory. Anyway, what about the White Russian? Any chance he could have pulled this off?"

"Well," said John, "no calling card and he has an alibi that, at least superficially, checks out. Still, I don't trust him as far as I could throw him."

Quinn nodded his head in agreement. "What about Maggie the Cat? We know she hit the senator's tonight. It's not like her to rob more than one place in an evening, but then again, how often are you going to have this many prize jewels all in the same town at the same time. We gotta to thank this fucking Diamond Ball."

"Not her style." John remembered the flamboyant red-haired acrobat who had gracefully somersaulted her way through some of the most exclusive private vaults and safe-deposit boxes in Europe. "I'll tell you what I think. I think it's Zagen."

"Dornal Zagen? You think he's dumb enough to show his face here in DC when there's so much heat on him?" asked Quinn skeptically.

"I'm almost sure of it."

"What makes you so sure?"

"Well, for one thing, all the Ghostly activity stopped when we sent him to jail three years ago. Now he's broken out and suddenly Veronica's stuff gets stolen in just the same way as past Ghost thefts."

"It's possible," nodded Quinn, his brow darkening.

"And...there's another reason I think it was him," said John quietly.

"What's that?"

"Well, let's just say, I saw him today."

Quinn turned slightly purple. "What? Why didn't you tell me this before?"

"I should have. I just thought you had enough on your plate," John explained.

"Where the hell did you see him? Was it here at the hotel?"

"No, it was out in the street. He was driving a white BMW, but I'm afraid I didn't get the license plate number."

Quinn exhaled a long stream of smoke. "Jesus H. Christ, this is all just a mother-fucking mess."

"What are you going to do?" asked John.

His old partner mopped the sweat off his forehead with his shirtsleeve. "Well, I guess I'm gonna look for the Granny for Katherine Park, Maggie the Cat for Senator Hayes' wife, and then try and find Zagen *and* figure out, once and for all, if he is, in fact, the Ghost."

John patted his shoulder. "Don't worry, partner. After tomorrow night, I have a feeling a lot's going to come clear."

"It better." Quinn sighed and looked over at Veronica sulking in the corner with a glass of white wine in her hands. "Anything more she can tell me that you didn't over the phone?"

"I don't think so," said John, an unconscious frown of worry creasing his brow as he, too, turned his attention to Veronica.

"She sure is a knockout," said Quinn.

"She's exhausted and very upset. You think we could clear everyone out of here for now? There's nothing to find, I swear."

Quinn thought about it for a moment and nodded his head. "Okay...the fucking Ghost, huh?"

John shrugged.

"All right, I'll have a little chat with the hotel manager downstairs. Then I've got to catch a flight to Islip where the freakin' Ballet de l'Aire are performing aboard some jerk's private yacht and I can listen to those French fucks BS me about how Maggie's been with them all night long. Then I have to get on another plane and be back here by tomorrow afternoon in time to get ready for the goddamn Diamond Ball," griped Quinn.

"I hope you have a trip to the Caribbean lined up after this one's over," said John sympathetically.

Quinn grinned. "Hey, at least I got you to help me out over here—unofficially, of course."

"You know I'll help you in any way I can."

Quinn slapped John on the back. "That's my partner." Then raising his voice, he called out to everyone in the room, "Okay, folks, let's take this party downstairs. The lady needs some sleep."

When they had all gone, Veronica still sat pensively swirling her wine. John squatted beside her and she raised her head. "They're not going to be able to find my jewels, are they?" She looked like a kid asking him for the truth about Santa.

He gently brushed her hair away from her face and tucked it behind her ear. "They're just a bunch of rocks, Veronica. You have insurance, don't you?"

The hurt in her eyes hit him in his heart. "It's just..." She trailed off and looked down at her drink.

"Well," he patted her shoulder, "I promise I'll do everything in my power to help you."

He rose and was about to leave, when she spoke his name so quietly he almost thought he'd imagined it. He turned around and she stood up, placed her drink on the side table and twisted her fingers together. "I just want to say that I'm sorry we've had so many arguments and that I've been difficult." She bit her lip. "I know you're a good person, John."

He shook his head. "No, listen, I'm not the easiest guy to get along with. Lord knows I have my faults and..." There were so many things he wanted to explain, but all he said was, "I'm sorry, too."

She nodded her head in acceptance.

He was about to leave again, but on impulse he walked back and kissed her tenderly on the forehead. She smiled up at him and their eyes met.

The gentle pattering of rain against the window and the subtle scent of anise and orange blossoms rising up from her perfume were the background notes of a moment that stretched on and on.

The heat was still there between them, and standing alone with her in the room where she had writhed under him screaming his name only twenty-four hours ago wasn't easy. He thought of slipping his hands under her sweater to the soft skin around her hips and then pulling her against him so he could feel her breasts beneath the thin cashmere press against his chest. Then he would kiss her with all the hunger and violence he had kissed her with the night before. It would be so easy…

But as she cast her eyes down, he came back to earth. He knew it was the wrong time. So he just said, "Try to get some sleep."

"You too." She walked him to the door, stepping aside as he made his way out.

He heard the lock click behind him a moment later. She could lock the door all she liked, he thought, it wouldn't keep the Ghost out. Of course, she didn't have anything the thief wanted anymore. The only person who wanted what Veronica Rossmore had locked away in her bedroom was him.

****

At a quarter to six the next morning the parking garage under the Monticello was deserted. The first blue light of dawn had just begun to erase the dark corners of Nicholas Buzuhov's suite when he'd tiptoed out, leaving Jessica fast asleep in the bed they'd torn apart the night before. The practiced thief hadn't forgotten to slip her car keys in his pocket before slinking out. Now in the parking garage, he wandered through the levels looking for her Cadillac. He spotted it in between a black Range Rover and an acid green Volkswagen Bug.

Glancing around to make sure no one was

watching, he hit a button on the key chain, and with a cheerful blip, the Cadillac's locks sprung open. Nicholas slid into the backseat, closing the door behind him. Even though he knew the place was empty, he looked around again for security cameras, or any sign of life, before opening the black valise he'd brought with him.

Certain he was unobserved, he slid the little key into the case's lock and popped it open. Nicholas smiled at the blaze of shimmering stones that glittered up at him in the dim light of the garage.

"Quite a collection, Veronica," he whispered, as he let his fingers roam through the piles of star-bright diamonds and the deeper tones of the rare colored jewels. It was a shame he would have to sell it all. The connoisseur in him appreciated what a spectacular array of gems he had in his possession, but the grim reality of money could not be overlooked. No matter how exquisite the design of an art deco bracelet or how magnificently a ruby necklace pulsated with red fire under his gaze, business was business. That was something he had to keep in mind if he wanted to continue with the lifestyle he'd become accustomed to ever since picking up his lucrative little sideline. Nicholas snapped the case shut and locked it again.

"Now, Jessie, if you'll just be good enough to hold this for me for a little while," whispered Nicholas as he slipped the valise under the passenger seat in front of him. It was not the safest place in the world. He usually preferred a nice Swiss bank vault, but it would only need to stay there for the next twenty-four hours. He felt quite confident that by this time tomorrow morning, the most daring jewel theft in history would be complete and the Hope Diamond would leave its home in the Smithsonian forever.

When Nicholas returned to his room, he came

bearing a tray of fresh raspberries and whipped cream scented with the faintest whiff of vanilla. He laid the tray on the bed next to Jessica as she opened her eyes.

"Good morning, *slatkaya*," he said, murmuring the endearment in his Russian accent.

Jessica smiled sleepily. "Good morning."

Nicholas dipped a ripe red raspberry in the cream and held it dangling just above her mouth. "I brought you breakfast."

"Mmm, so I see," she raised her head a touch to catch the berry between her lips, but Nicholas pulled it away and used it to spread a line of cream down between her naked breasts and across her ticklish belly. She moaned softly as he rubbed the ripe berry against the tender folds between her legs, and it burst apart, its sweet juice spilling down the inside of her thighs. He lapped up the juice with his warm tongue for a few exquisite moments. Her fingers curled in his black hair as his mouth moved to the swell of her nipple and his gentle bite arched her back. Wrapping his arms around her waist, he pulled her against him, spilling fresh berries and cream across the white bed linen. All in all, the morning was starting out very well, thought Nicholas, before he crushed the society girl's mouth under his own.

Chapter Eleven

At a quarter to eight, John was roused by the insistent sound of the phone ringing next to his ear. His first instinct was to pull a pillow over his head and ignore it until it stopped, but it could be Veronica. Reluctantly, he answered the phone.

"It's Quinn."

John glanced at the clock. "What's up?"

"Listen, John, we've had some developments." Quinn sounded nervous.

"What? Did you find Maggie the Cat?"

"Yeah, yeah, we found her here aboard ship with her troop. She has all kinds of alibis, but I don't believe any of them. I'm convinced half the fucking Ballet de l'Aire is in on it and they're all covering for her."

"Don't worry, you'll find a hole in their story somewhere," reassured John.

"I damn well hope so, but in the meantime, I'm more concerned about the Ghost." Quinn sure did sound worried. "Or maybe I should rephrase that. The First Lady is very concerned about the Ghost and she's come up with a truly cockamamie plan. Her and Veronica Rossmore. I spent the last hour trying to talk them out of it, but in the end, she pulled rank."

"What do you mean?"

"Veronica Rossmore has lost her mind over the theft of her jewels and the First Lady is freaked out that the Ghost is going to make an appearance at the ball tonight. So they got this idea." Quinn paused for a moment. "It's so insane, I don't even want to tell you."

"Just tell me," said John, rubbing the sleep out of his eyes.

"Well, they've decided the best way to catch the Ghost is to lay out some bait and set a trap."

"Oh no," moaned John, shaking his head.

"Yeah, you know how a lot of the women attending the ball are going to be wearing the Smithsonian jewels? Well, they've decided to let Veronica prance around in the fucking Hope Diamond all night."

"No!" John sat straight up in bed, fully awake now.

"Yes," said Quinn, "and they're going to lie in wait for the Ghost and try to catch him in the act."

John was speechless for a moment. "Did you tell them it won't work and they are putting Veronica in serious danger? Dornal Zagen is on the loose, for God's sake."

"You know, I even put the boss on the line. I don't know what he said to them, but you know how women are. Veronica's crying and Lillian Spencer is in there giving orders." Quinn had the tone of a beaten-down man who has been henpecked his entire life.

John shook his head. "There's something not right about this."

"EVERYTHING is not right about this!" exclaimed Quinn.

"This isn't safe for Veronica. The Ghost may not be the only thief likely to show up tonight. What if Dornal Zagen gets there first with his automatic rifle going off? She wouldn't stand a chance."

"Hey, you don't have to tell me."

"I'm going to find Veronica and talk some sense into her."

"Please do." Quinn sounded like a wet rag being

wrung.

"Okay, I'll check in with you later." John hung up.

He quickly dressed and, bypassing his usual morning routine, headed straight to Veronica's room.

He knocked on the door, but there was no answer. He called her name and knocked some more, but he got nothing.

He went downstairs and his friend, the chubby concierge, was there on duty. "Good morning, sir," he said with a cheerful smile.

"Good morning," said John. "Did you happen to see Veronica Rossmore from room 47 go out this morning?"

The concierge shook his head. "I'm sorry, sir, but I just came on duty a few minutes ago."

"Well, thanks anyway," said John, disappointed, but then he had a thought. "Could you check my box? Room 22."

"Certainly, sir." The concierge ran his fingers over the mahogany mailboxes until he came to 22. Beaming, he pulled out a note. "Here you go."

John gave the man a tip and, unfolding the note, leaned against the desk as he read. It was written in Veronica's elegant hand on the hotel stationery.

John,

I'm going out for the day. I'll meet you in the lobby at 7 p.m. You're my date for the Diamond Ball tonight, so please make sure you're in a tux. You can charge one to the room in case you don't have one with you.

V

John refolded the note and slipped it in his back pocket. What the hell was she up to?

He turned back to the concierge. "Is there a good greasy spoon diner around here?"

The concierge thought about it for a moment. "The closest place I can think of is Spanky's. It's a bit far away, though. Would you like me to call you a cab?"

John shook his head. "No thanks, I could use a nice long walk."

****

It was chilly outside. The fickle March weather had snatched spring from the air and John shivered as he walked down Independence Avenue. He didn't mind the cold; it woke him up and enlivened him which was exactly what he needed right now—to wake the hell up. He rubbed his hands together and across his face. He could feel his brain springing to life. The cobwebs on the deductive cogs, which used to run like a well-greased cuckoo clock during his FBI days, were clearing away and the wheels were starting to turn again.

He thought about Quinn's theory that the Ghost was a true phantom of their imaginations; something he and the press had dreamed up to explain any perfect jewel theft. He knew it wasn't true. He could feel it when he was near the Ghost, the same way people claimed to be able to feel real spirits hovering around them, even if they couldn't quite make them out with their eyes. Maybe you couldn't always see an apparition, but your spine tingled and you sensed something elusive and mysterious in the air around you. That was how he had felt last night in Veronica Rossmore's room.

He wished he could pin it all on the White Russian, because he didn't like phonies and because he was jealous of his relationship with Veronica. It might not be Bezuhov, and yet John felt somehow the man was mixed up in all this. Maybe that dishy blonde, Jessica, too.

He reached the diner with its bright pink neon sign and metal rail car exterior. He stepped inside gratefully, feeling the warm blast of heat against his chilled cheeks and hands. *God bless diners*; he took in the familiar surroundings though he had never visited this particular establishment before. The metal walls, the orange 1950's leather booths and matching stools at the counter, the buzz of everyday Joes grabbing a cup of coffee or plate of bacon and eggs, the eighty-year-old hostess with too much war paint reeking of cheap perfume—for a sober alcoholic, a diner was Mecca.

The hostess led him to a booth by the window and slipped the plastic menu on the table. "Coffee?"

"Yes, please," John smiled warmly.

His smile didn't register on her and she shuffled away in her sneakers and pantyhose toward the counter. The last customer had left *The Washington Post* in the booth's corner and John picked it up.

The headlines screamed: *"GHOST STRIKES AGAIN!"*

John quickly scanned the article. It said everything he already knew, which wasn't much. The waitress plopped his coffee on the table, and he ordered the *Sammy's Special*, which was two eggs, two pancakes, two sausages, and a pile of hash browns. He didn't know who Sammy was, but he liked his choice in breakfast food.

John flipped through the rest of the paper until he hit the entertainment section. There on the front page was a big picture of the Hope Diamond, glittering its blue fire, along with a feature article on tonight's ball.

"Fast work," he muttered to himself as he let the paper drop. They must have had to stop the press to get this one out so quickly. He picked up the paper again and finished reading the article. It read like an infomercial for the Hope as well as some of the other Smithsonian treasures.

He put the news aside when his breakfast arrived and gave his full attention to *Sammy's Special*. When he was finished, he tossed his crumpled napkin on the empty plate and let the waitress give him a refill on his coffee. The Ghost headline caught his eye again. He asked the waitress if he could borrow a pen.

She frowned like this was an unreasonable request, but said, "Sure," pulling a black ballpoint from behind her ear. "Just give it back when you're done."

"I will," he promised as she shuffled away.

He pulled a napkin out of the dispenser and began to list all the Ghost's past heists. It read like an underground resume:

1988—New Year's Eve, Alexandria, pasha's yacht, Winged Isis necklace stolen from pasha's wife.

1989—New Year's Eve, NYC, Pierre Hotel, diamond bracelet stolen from Trina Surma, wealthy widow from Buenos Aires.

1990—New Year's Eve, Vienna, Victorian diamond tiara stolen from Princess Charlotte of Malstonia.

1991—New Year's Eve, Scotland, diamond and emerald necklace, bracelets, and earrings stolen from Duchess Fiona Malachi of Glamis.

1992—New Year's Eve, Palm Beach, canary diamond ring stolen from Suzy Eaton, an American plastics heiress.

1992—August 5th, Lake Como, Italy, Fire of the Maharaja ruby ring stolen from Italian businessman Giovanni Freni.

That was where the pattern changed. 1992 was the year the Ghost was no longer content to steal exclusively on New Year's Eve but had begun to branch out to other times of year.

Why?

It made sense from a practical standpoint to steal on the one night of the year when people dressed to the nines and pulled all their most valuable jewels from their bank vaults.

It also made sense that the Ghost stole mostly diamonds. Diamonds were easier to fence than emeralds or rubies, which often had distinctive inclusions or coloring which made them unique and easy to trace. When it came to trading a stone in for cold hard cash, diamonds were always the best bet. The thing was, the Ghost's booty never showed up on the black market and he did upon occasion pick up some very famous, distinctive pieces of jewelry, which would be impossible to sell anonymously and difficult to hide. Apparently the Ghost didn't like to play by the rules—even his own.

John continued scribbling down every theft attributed to the elusive thief until the year 2000 when John had captured Dornal Zagen and the thefts had abruptly stopped.

Until now—maybe.

He sat staring down at the Ghost's resume. John had always worked under the assumption that he was dealing with some kind of off-the-charts genius. Someone who could do what all the other notorious thieves combined could do. Someone with the acrobatic skills of Maggie the Cat, the balls of the Granny, and the elegant taste and knowledge of gems the White Russian possessed.

Dornal Zagen had all of these qualities. He could outwit complicated computer alarm systems, crack uncrackable safes, and climb up a three-story building like a trained monkey. During his years with the FBI, John had let the theory circle around in his head like a swarm of birds swooping and diving until he picked up a drink and things quieted down. At least for a little while.

He knew logically it made sense that the ruthless Austrian was the Ghost, but something inside him just wasn't buying it. Not even after Zagen hit Sing Sing and the thefts stopped. Now as he looked at the evidence in front of him, another thought crossed his mind.

What if he'd been looking at this the wrong way the entire time? Maybe the Ghost didn't need to have any of these super-criminal qualities. Maybe all he really needed was access.

John pulled his cell phone out of his pocket and started dialing.

Buzzy Rossmore answered the phone in his usual good-humored tone.

He has no idea what happened. John's heart sank. "Good morning, Mr. Rossmore. It's John Monroe."

"Oh hello, John. How are you?"

"I'm fine, but I'm afraid we've got a little problem down here." John rubbed his forehead as he plunged ahead. "Veronica hasn't called you?"

"No," said Buzzy, sounding concerned. "Is she all right?"

"She's fine, but...unfortunately, all of her jewelry was stolen last night."

"All of it?" The old man sounded shocked.

"Yes, all of it. People around here seem to think it's the Ghost.

"I see," said Buzzy soberly. "He managed to get into the hotel safe?"

John swallowed hard. "She wouldn't keep her stuff there. I begged her but she refused."

"That's just like her, headstrong..." but the old man stopped himself from finishing the sentence and paused. "Well," he said finally, "I don't blame you. I'm sure you did everything you could."

"Oh, don't throw in the towel yet. I'm going to track down the Ghost and find out what happened to those jewels. That's a promise."

There was a long silence on the other end of the line and then the old man said, "Do that, John, and I'll double your money. I just hope...the last thing we want is a lot of press or scandal. My daughter had an incident several years back with her ex-husband and...well, I hope you can be discreet."

"I'll do whatever I can, but you might want to pick up the newspaper. I don't know what the New York papers are carrying, but down here the latest Ghost story is all over the front page."

Buzzy sighed. "I better call Veronica."

"Before you do, Mr. Rossmore, do you mind if I ask you a few questions?"

"Not at all," said the old man politely.

"Was your daughter with you in Egypt in 1988?"

"Yes, she was."

"And what about Vienna in 1990? Or Italy in the summer of 1992?"

"She was at school in Switzerland during those years and she always liked to jump on the Eurail and travel around the continent on vacations. Why do you ask?" inquired Buzzy.

"I'm trying to put together the pieces of a jigsaw puzzle, Mr. Rossmore."

"Well, you let me know how the picture comes out."

"I give you my word, you'll be the first person I go to," said John. "And once again, I'm very sorry about your daughter's jewels."

Buzzy sighed again. "Well, you know they're all insured. It's just...some of them belonged to my late wife and Veronica was very attached to those particular pieces. I think I better call her and see how she's doing."

"All right, I'll let you know the minute I have any news," promised John.

"Thank you."

But before he could hang up, John asked, "Mr. Rossmore, one last thing before you go. Does New Year's Eve hold any special significance for you?"

The line went quiet for a moment. "It's Veronica's birthday."

Chapter Twelve

After John hung up with Buzzy Rossmore, the waitress slipped the bill on a plastic tray under his nose. John spaced out on the tray without seeing it. He held his cell phone in his hand debating. He didn't know if he should call Quinn, or his AA sponsor Simon, or just get on the next train back to New York and forget the whole thing.

He picked up the list scrawled out on the paper napkin and studied the Ghost's resume. New Year's Eve was Veronica's birthday. It was entirely possible that she had been at the scene for every theft. John would have to do a lot more research to be sure. He hadn't been working for the FBI during the two incidents in Alexandria and New York. Vienna had been his first Ghost hunting experience.

The *Fasching* Season, Austria's carnival period, had just kicked off with the famous New Year's Eve Kaiser Ball at the Hofburg Imperial Palace. The Baroness Hull had invited several distinguished individuals to attend the ball with her and then vacation at her family's 17th century *Schloss* just a few miles outside the city.

Dressed in old-fashioned ball gowns and white tie and tails, the baroness and her guests had waltzed their hearts out to the romantic strains of Strauss's famous melodies in the candlelit palace halls until, donning their silk-lined furs, they had ventured out through the sugar-coated city of picturesque baroque buildings. The ladies' diamonds glittered like ice in the frozen moonlight as they awaited the New Year with the rest of Vienna in the square outside of St. Stephan's Cathedral. The holiday revelers had laughed and cheered with the gathered crowds as the massive bell struck its yearly toll and rang in 1990. At last they had brought the party back to the *Schloss*, inviting several people they met during the course of the evening to join them.

The festivities whirled madly on until dawn, but not everyone had stayed up for the fun. Some of the elderly guests had retired to bed as soon as they returned to the *Schloss* and during the night someone had made their way into the ninety-seven-year-old Princess Charlotte's room and nabbed her diamond tiara. The old lady hadn't even realized the treasure was missing from its case until her maid checked the following day as part of her usual packing ritual. True to form, the Ghost had left no clues.

It was Interpol who had first noticed the pattern of New Year's Eve jewel heists. They linked the theft to the same person who had struck in Alexandria and New York the two previous years. As a result, John and Quinn had been called in to see what they could add to the equation. Unfortunately for the Malstonian princess, John and his partner had not been able to find out much more than the European authorities.

Considering the princess had been a known Nazi sympathizer, John hadn't felt too badly for her. It was really Lloyds of London, who had insured the tiara, who had been jacked. But then again, John wasn't exactly in love with big insurance companies either. Still, if there was one thing he hated, it was an unsolved mystery and his obsession with the elusive jewel thief had begun on that first trip to Vienna.

This had also been the period when the

European press really began to run with the story. In no time, the Ghost was front-page news all over the continent. The publicity hadn't exactly made John and Quinn look like brilliant agents and that had been a problem, too.

John looked at the list scrawled out on the napkin in front of him and thought about the dates. If Veronica was twenty-seven now, in 1988 when the first theft occurred in Alexandria, she would have been... He wrote on the napkin working it out— twelve.

He put down the pen. Could the notorious jewel thief who had eluded the FBI, Interpol, and Scotland Yard for over a decade really have been a twelve-year-old girl?

He shook his head and laughed softly to himself, but then he grew serious. After all, this was serious business. The jail time for all the thefts the Ghost had committed was enough to send her away for life. He better have his facts straight.

Assuming she was the thief, what had she done with the jewels? It would be too risky trying to carry them through customs as often as she and her father traveled. She couldn't have sold them unless she'd had them cut first and how would a prepubescent girl even know about something like that?

Of course, she *was* friends with Nicolas Bezuhov. He could have cut the stones and sold them for her, but he hadn't gotten into the jewel thief game until the early 1990s and he had never been in the same location at the time of a Ghost theft. John wondered again about Veronica's relationship with the White Russian. He wondered if Nicholas really had just been showing her some jewelry in his room the other day, or if they were lovers after all.

But then he remembered the dishy, blonde Jessica. Spoiled debutantes like that weren't usually too keen on sharing.

Another thing, if Veronica was the Ghost, then who had stolen her jewels? She could have staged the whole thing herself, but why would she fake having her own stuff stolen? What purpose would it serve?

He remembered Veronica's expression when she looked at him and told him her jewels were missing. Either she deserved an Academy Award or she was truly heartbroken. He remembered her eyes filled with hurt and that brought other images to his mind. Images of Veronica zipping through traffic in her platinum convertible, cool and confident; of the way she looked when she had come down to the lobby in her red dress with that enormous ruby around her neck, glowing and alive with the promise of their night to come; and the almost unearthly beauty of her asleep, mahogany hair framing a pale, troubled face. What had she been dreaming about to pucker her brow and lock up her jaw like that?

Were any of those images of Veronica the real one? Or were they all fakes to hide what lay beneath the pretty wrapping paper?

The old waitress broke his train of thought as she blurted out, "You all finished here, honey? I got a line of people waiting for the table."

John smiled, and slapping a couple bills down, stood up and let the old lady do her thing.

He stopped off at the Southeast branch of the public library on his way back to the Monticello. He trotted up the steps of the weathered, old brick building, which, like everything else in this town, was fronted by a neoclassical portico complete with four white fluted columns. He passed through the doors and made his way to the information desk.

After waiting in line for what seemed like forever behind a gaggle of eager-looking Capitol Hill interns, he finally reached the reference librarian.

He was a middle-aged hippy guy with salt-and-pepper shoulder-length hair and round John Lennon glasses. "Can I help you?" he asked in a soft voice.

John asked him if they kept old copies of the *New York Post* around.

The hippy librarian said they did and pointed him toward a small room in the back of the building with the word *PERIODICALS* engraved in gold letters over the door.

John plowed through the dusty shelves of plastic-bound newspapers until he found what he was looking for. There in the society pages of the April 29 issue, Veronica Rossmore lay splayed out on the floor of the Metropolitan Museum. The headline read: *Park Avenue Princess Takes A Fall At Costume Institute Ball.*

He read the accompanying article, but it didn't tell him anything he didn't already know. Her drunk, art dealer husband, Derrick Chapin, had pushed Veronica in a jealous rage. As a result, she had tumbled down the grand marble steps of the Metropolitan's Great Hall to the astonishment of the well-heeled guests.

John felt bad looking at Veronica lying there with her dress up practically around her waist, her head thrown back to one side exposing her long throat and the fabulous necklace she wore. He wished suddenly that he had been there to pull her dress down and to look reassuringly into her eyes when she came to. Maybe give old Derrick Chapin a square right hook to the chin and see how he liked having his lights knocked out.

Suddenly he saw himself as if from a distance. This was an unnerving occurrence, which sometimes happened to him now that he was sober. He observed himself getting way too emotionally caught up in something that really was no longer any of his business. Next thing you know, he'd be searching through Veronica's underwear drawer, looking desperately for signs of her guilt or innocence.

If he'd learned anything in the past year, it was that pursuing one of his obsessions usually wasn't good for him or anyone else. Granted, it was his obsessive nature that had made him a good detective for the FBI. He'd loop on a case night and day until he figured out the vital clue and landed his man. Maybe he'd gotten his man, but he also ended up at the bottom of a discount vodka bottle. He never wanted to end up there again.

He put the paper down and took a deep breath. He needed to go back to the hotel, get his tux pressed, and relax. Maybe he'd do a little meditation, maybe watch ESPN on the satellite TV. If Veronica Rossmore was the Ghost, it was none of his damn business. It was time for him to back off.

But despite his resolution, he couldn't stop himself from dropping a dime in the library Xerox machine and running off a quick copy of the *Post* article before leaving the building.

****

Veronica lay soaking in the large whirlpool tub surrounded by lightly foaming bubbles. She inhaled the scent of relaxing lavender, but it did little to dispel the tension that still kept her body as tightly wound as a metal spring. On the side of the tub, the note rested next to a flickering candle and a bar of Italian milled soap. She had found it slipped under her door when she returned to the Monticello late that afternoon. Just like the first one she'd received at her father's townhouse in Manhattan, the note was a simple, white piece of paper with a typewritten message:

Veronica, unless you wish to participate in an exorcism, stay away from the Diamond Ball tonight.

There was no signature, of course. Veronica frowned as she tried to figure out who could possibly be sending these messages. She was already nervous about the plan she and Lillian Spencer had cooked up for Veronica to wear the Hope tonight. This warning only increased her apprehension.

Still, she firmly believed it was time for these Ghost stories to come to an end. If that involved a bit of risk, so be it. The note had told her to stay away unless she wished to participate in an exorcism. Well, an exorcism was just exactly why she was going in the first place.

She watched her perfectly manicured big toe as it poked through the suds. The cherry-red nail polish stood out against the white porcelain and silvery bubbles. She wondered if she should show the note to John.

She didn't want to worry him and he already had enough to keep him busy with the disappearance of her jewelry the night before. She chewed on her lower lip. She liked John Monroe. She liked him more than she had liked any man in a long time. Maybe after this whole thing was over, and the Ghost was finally laid to rest, just maybe something real could happen between them. She was suddenly glad he would be there tonight. She didn't like to admit it, even to herself, but maybe she could use a little protection—just this once.

Deciding she wouldn't worry him with the note, she picked up the paper in her dripping fingers and laid it flat across the water line. The black ink began to fan out and dissolve across the page until the typewritten words were nothing but a blur.

Veronica sighed. If only she could stay in this soothing tub of warm water all night long.

****

Dornal Zagen stood at the phone booth in the crowded Metro station and punched in the number of his employer. The phone rang for a long time until finally a voice came on the line. "You haven't been behaving yourself, Zagen."

"I'm all ready for tonight," said the Austrian, ignoring his employer's displeasure.

"You'd better be. We can't afford any mistakes."

"There won't be any."

"Good, now remember, the lights will only be out for three minutes, but that should be more than enough time for you to slip the Hope off Veronica Rossmore's neck and get out of there before the security lamps go on."

"Three minutes will be sufficient."

"And don't forget, I'll be watching you, Zagen."

"I won't fuck up my end," said Dornal coldly. "Don't fuck up yours."

His employer hung up and the line went dead.

Three minutes. That would be more than enough time to slit Monroe's throat and then take off with Veronica Rossmore *and* her precious diamond. The girl's father was worth millions and he'd be willing to part with every last penny to save his only child's life. Besides, it would be a pleasure to hide out with the beautiful heiress for a few days. He hadn't been with a woman in three years and the thought of wiping the proud expression off her face sent a perverse thrill up his cock.

And she wasn't the only woman who would get what was coming to her.

Dornal knew there'd be competition among the thieves for the fabled Hope Diamond, but Marguerite Gateaux was the only one who posed any real threat to him. Tonight he would execute his plan to get that red-haired bitch permanently out of his way. He smiled his wintery smile. He'd find out if cats really do always land on their feet.

A train roared into the station and Dornal hustled through the rush-hour crowd to get aboard. With the Diamond Ball starting in less than two hours, he had no time to waste. The doors slid shut behind him and the train lurched forward.

Dornal clutched the metal pole and watched the dark tunnel flash by as he mentally reviewed his plans for the evening. His employer wanted a new Ghost story. He'd teach everyone at the Diamond Ball that restless spirits don't always play nice.

****

When John came downstairs, the platinum convertible sat humming in front of the Monticello with Veronica in the passenger seat. She wore a simple, floor-length gown in a shade of deep blue that matched her eyes. Her dark hair hung loose and fell over one eye in glamour girl waves. A white fur wrap was draped carelessly off her shoulders and she sat drumming glossy pale pink nails against the dashboard, evidently impatient for him to slide in and take the wheel.

John smiled politely as he opened the car door and adjusted the seat to fit his 6'2" frame before getting in. He could feel the Glock 27 pistol concealed in its holster beneath his tuxedo jacket. Quinn had told him not to bring a gun, but with Dornal Zagen on the loose, John wasn't taking any chances.

"So I get to drive tonight," he observed pleasantly.

She flashed a nervous smile. "I think it would be better."

He had never seen her nervous before and it only confirmed his suspicions. As he pulled away from the hotel, John reminded himself of his resolve to be professional and courteous. No jealous scenes, no wild accusations or questions about where she had been today. It was none of his business, but when he felt her soft hand rest on his shoulder, he realized it might not be quite that easy.

"John?" she asked, her voice fluttery as a hummingbird.

"Yes?"

"They told you about tonight, about how I'm going to wear the Hope Diamond?"

"Yes, they told me," he said, squeezing the steering wheel a little bit tighter to hold his tongue in check.

She took her hand away and began fiddling with the corner of her fur wrap. "You think it's a bad idea. I know that. But if we can just catch the Ghost and everything gets resolved," she said, now sounding almost exasperated, "it will have been worth it. I just want you to know, the reason I feel safe enough to do this is because you'll be with me."

Surprised, he turned away from the rush-hour traffic clogging up Maryland Avenue and looked at her. But she was leaning her elbow on the door and gazed out in the opposite direction.

"I didn't do such a great job watching over your stuff last night. What makes you think I'll do any better at the ball?" he asked, not quite able to keep the bitterness out of his voice.

"But that was different. You were only supposed to watch my jewelry. Tonight you're watching over me and I don't think you'd let anything happen to me."

"I don't know, Veronica. You've put yourself in a very bad position."

"Why?" she asked. "What could happen? We'll be in a room with hundreds of people including a security staff and I'll have you by my side."

John pulled over to the curb and stopped the car. He cut the motor and turned to face her head on. "Listen, I don't know what kind of fucked-up little game you're playing, but I want no part of it."

She opened her mouth to speak, but he didn't give her the chance. "You want to be the self-sufficient woman who doesn't need any help—fine, but don't turn around and suddenly transform into some whimpering little kitten who needs my protection. I don't buy it and I think you're full of shit."

Amazed, she stared at him with big eyes and then throwing up her hands she turned stone-faced and looked straight ahead.

John felt the anger flowing out of him now that he'd had his say, but he suddenly had a bad feeling that he'd been way off. In profile, Veronica looked like a beautiful marble statue, her skin was so white and she sat so deadly still. Then she said quietly, "Please get out of my car."

He just sat there frozen for a moment, feeling like the biggest jerk in the world. Finally, he swung open the door and stepped out.

Not looking at him, Veronica slid into the driver's seat. She turned the key in the ignition and the convertible came to life.

John just stood there with his hands still on the car door. She reached out to grab the handle and slam it shut, but he gripped the door harder and wouldn't let it budge.

"Veronica, wait."

She looked up at him with fury in her eyes and said through clenched teeth, "*Let go of my door.*"

His fingers loosened and she slammed the door shut between them, but he wasn't going to have it. She was always slamming doors between them, retreating and disappearing into her ivory tower world and he was sick of it.

"Listen, I was wrong," he said. "I was wrong to yell at you and spy on you and all of it! I have a short fuse and I'm suspicious and I get jealous. I admit all of it. But I'm not Derrick Chapin and I would never do anything to hurt you. I want to help. I can't be just your hired gun anymore, the guy you can dictate everything to and open up to when you feel like it, and then disappear when you feel like it because your father's signing my paycheck. If I'm just some guy your father hired and you fucked me just for fun, I'll go back to New York and we'll forget the money. We'll call it even. But if there's more than that, please admit it and tell me what's going on here. I want to know the truth."

She had been staring pointedly down at the steering wheel throughout his speech and she still sat there in the same position now. He opened the car door and knelt down next to her. Taking her chin in his hands, he turned her face to his. Her dark lashes were wet with brimming tears and she bit her bottom lip hard, but her eyes were open and filled with the same hunger he had seen in them when he had held her in his arms and kissed her for the first time.

"Trust me," he said.

They held each other's gaze for a long moment. He could see a struggle going on in her by the way she clenched and unclenched her jaw and the way she searched his eyes like she was looking for the answer to something. Then she took his hand and he could feel the gentle pressure of her palm against his. "I'll trust you, if you'll trust me."

He thought about it and realized he hadn't really trusted Veronica since he'd met her. Or maybe it wasn't that he couldn't trust her exactly, but that he couldn't completely get her. He couldn't help thinking there was something else going on there beneath her cool surface. But with her eyes so open and raw now looking up at him, he felt in his gut she was being sincere.

John slowly nodded his head in agreement, and she smiled, her sad face warming up like the sun.

It was a pact.

Veronica wiped a tear away before it had the chance to trickle down her cheek. "We're going to be late." She slid back into the passenger seat, and flipping down the small, light-up mirror, checked her face for damage.

"Okay." He got back into the car. He pushed the gear into drive but then turned to her again. "You sure you even want to go to this thing?"

She paused for a moment, and nodded. He hit the gas. The convertible pulled into the river of traffic making its way upstream along the twilight boulevard as the streetlamps came on and cast a gentle glow to light their way to the Diamond Ball.

Chapter Thirteen

As the convertible turned onto Constitution Avenue, it almost came to a complete halt. The security lines were three deep in black-suited men waving around clipboards and walkie-talkies. The paparazzi were also out in full force, their flashbulbs exploding like fireworks as the party guests in their limousines slowly rolled past the police barricades.

John had expected this mess, but what took him by surprise were the protesters. They stood yelling above the rush hour traffic's noise, waving their big signs, which read: *"SAVE OUR SCHOOLS, NOT THE WEALTHY'S TAX $!" "NO MORE WAR!"* And John's favorite: *"IMPEACH DICK SPENCER NOW!!!"*

The DC cops were already hassling them and trying to force the angry protesters down the block. The whole situation was a powder keg itching for a match.

The limos cruised by like big, black sharks, their tinted windows hiding well-heeled inhabitants from the angry mob. There were no cameras turned in the mob's direction. All lenses were focused on the money shot. Pictures of a bigwig's wife stepping out of the car in front of the entrance to the Smithsonian were what the tabloids paid the bucks for. Protesters in DC weren't worth the film it cost to shoot them.

John wondered if the same member of the paparazzi who had captured the infamous picture of Veronica lying on the steps of the Metropolitan Museum was here tonight. He wondered if Veronica wondered the same thing. It was hard to tell by looking at her. She had gone quiet, gazing straight ahead. She ignored the parasites who screamed her name trying to get her to look so they could snap a picture and take it all the way to the bank.

They had finally made it through the mess outside the museum and pulled into the main driveway. John handed over the car keys to a fresh-faced valet, probably a Georgetown student trying to work his way through a poli-sci major. He opened the door for Veronica who stepped out of the convertible as gracefully as a princess alighting from her pumpkin. She was cool and calm now, maybe because she was in her element as she entered the large, front hall of the Smithsonian on John's arm.

"We have to go over here," she said, pointing to an area behind the information booth. They passed more black suits who nodded their heads as she sailed past. Evidently, they were all up to speed on who got access to the back rooms of the museum. John and Veronica went through a door behind the information area and Georgette, Kay Hopkins' assistant, stood waiting with a clipboard gripped in her hands. She was wearing a pale fluttery chiffon dress and her hair looked stiff and over-coiffed. She plastered a stressed-out smile on her face as Veronica and John reached her. "Good evening."

"Good evening," replied Veronica. "I'm so sorry we're a bit late."

"No worries, no worries," said Georgette, sounding worried. "Let me take you back to the Adam's Parlor where the jewels are."

She took off at a fast clip down a maze of hallways lit with fluorescent lights and lined with glass-framed posters of all the museum's exhibitions. At last they arrived in a little salon beautifully decorated in matching green damask rococo furniture.

Mirrors in ornately carved, gold-leaf frames reflected back the warm candlelight of antique crystal chandeliers. Fresh peony tulips, apple blossoms, and jade perfumed the room with a pleasant scent. Over the settee, a lush bouquet of flowers bloomed in the Van Gogh that hung there. John felt his blood pressure drop the minute he set foot on the thick Persian carpet. The place was so gracious and comfortable it made you want to settle in for a nice game of cards or a long, intimate chat.

Georgette remained as wired as a wind-up toy. She pointed to Kay Hopkins, the museum's social director, who had overseen the rehearsal the previous day. Kay was dressed in a black evening gown with her white-streaked hair piled up on top of her head.

"Kay will get you all set up," chirped Georgette as she was already turning to trot off to some other business back at the ball.

"Thank you," said Veronica to the swirl of peach chiffon that was halfway out the door.

Kay Hopkins smiled brightly as Veronica stepped forward. The DC matron was standing over a table with burgundy velvet flung across it. Resting on the velvet was an eye-opening spread of some of the most fabulous jewels on the planet sparkling genteelly in the dim light.

John realized there were other people in the room besides Kay. The security team was doing a good job of blending into the wallpaper while First Lady Lillian Spencer and her daughter, Cynthia, sat on a loveseat in the corner. They both turned as John and Veronica entered the room.

Lillian rose and greeted Veronica warmly, kissing her cheek. "Veronica, you're going to be the star of our little ball tonight. Thank you so much for doing this. It's thanks to you that the children in Anacostia will have their library."

Veronica nodded her head and said rather coldly. "I hope they enjoy it."

Lillian's expression turned hard as she looked at her daughter, who still slouched on the couch in the corner. "Cynthia, don't you want to say hello to Veronica?"

Cynthia stood up like a trained lap dog and vaguely attempted a smile. "Hi, Veronica."

"Hello, Cynthia."

"And this handsome young man is?" asked the First Lady looking at John with a Stepford smile plastered across her face.

"This is John Monroe."

John stuck out his hand and smiled. "It's nice to meet you, Mrs. Spencer."

"Very nice to meet you," she responded while looking him up and down the way one might a dog you're not quite sure about. She turned to Veronica. "Your bodyguard?"

"My escort," said Veronica smoothly.

"Yes, of course." The First Lady smiled, taking this information in. She turned to Kay Hopkins. "Well, we better get going here. People are already arriving."

"I think that's a good idea," agreed Kay. "Cynthia, honey, shall we do you first?"

A reluctant Cynthia inched her way slowly toward the treasure table, as if she were afraid she would get nuked if she got too close to the high-voltage rocks. Kay picked up a massive diamond necklace that seemed to put a strain on her thin arms. As she raised it up to catch the light, rainbows of color flamed through the crystals. Everyone in the room, except for Kay who was used to the Smithsonian jewel collection, forgot their breeding and gaped.

"That's huge!" whined Cynthia, as Kay stepped behind her and fastened the clasp behind her neck.

The president's daughter stuck her chin down as far as it would go trying to see the rocks gleaming on her chubby chest.

"There are 275 carats of diamonds in that necklace. It was given by Napoleon to his empress to celebrate the birth of their son," said Kay beaming. "And this," she added, lifting a glittering crown of diamonds and emeralds from the red velvet, "this is one of the museum's most prized possessions, the crown Napoleon placed on Josephine's head at their coronation ceremony."

Kay turned and smiled at the First Lady before placing it over Cynthia's limp blond hair. "And now our own little princess will wear it tonight!" she piped.

"You might want to tell the good people of Boston about that," remarked John, "They threw a little tea party a while back..."

The icy smile and fiendishly arched brows of the First Lady and Kay Hopkins shut him down midsentence. He was relieved, however, to catch the corners of Veronica's mouth tighten as she suppressed her laughter.

"This thing is too fucking heavy," complained Cynthia as she adjusted the crown on her head. It was too big for her and it refused to sit straight.

"Cynthia, we need you to behave tonight," said Lillian sternly. "You've already caused enough trouble..." She sounded like she was going to say more, but she ended it there. "Go look at yourself in the mirror. You should be grateful. Do you know how many girls would give their eyeteeth for the opportunity to dress up in these lovely jewels to go attend a ball and have their picture taken?"

Cynthia just stood there sulking, but at least she didn't talk back. Evidently, the First Lady took that as a good sign.

"Oh, who's wearing that beautiful emerald

brooch?" exclaimed Veronica approaching the table, her eyes on a flash of green rock set in rows of sparkling diamonds.

"The Hooker Emerald?" asked Kay pleasantly. "Congressman Duly's wife, Gisela, will be wearing it. I wish she'd get here. I should have told the ladies to come earlier."

Cynthia snickered in the corner. With a frustrated sigh, the First Lady turned to her daughter. "What do you find so amusing, Cynthia?"

The president's daughter snorted. "It's perfect that Gisela Duly is wearing a brooch called the 'Hooker,' because she's slept with like...*everyone* in Washington!"

This time Veronica did not have as much luck suppressing an amused smile and John looked at his shoes trying to keep control. Ignoring the remark, Lillian and Kay turned back to Veronica as she reached out her hand to pick up the Hope Diamond. She held it there, fascinated, staring into the jewel's depths as the blue fire came alive against the palm of her hand.

Lillian and Kay came to her side and they, too, stood staring at the fabled gem. At last, Kay put a hand on Veronica's shoulder. "You're sure you don't mind wearing it? The curse doesn't bother you?"

Veronica shook her head. "I've already had my bad luck."

"Oh, yes," cooed Kay, "I heard about the theft. Have the police turned up any leads yet?"

"Not yet." Veronica still had not managed to drag her eyes from the magnificent gem that kindled before her.

"Well, let's put this on you, Veronica," said the First Lady, suddenly businesslike. "Since everyone is waiting, we need to get out there." She reached down and picked up the necklace, placing it around Veronica's neck.

The difference was amazing. Veronica was a beautiful woman at any time, but now with the blue diamond shimmering at her throat, matching the color of her eyes, she was extraordinary.

At that moment, Georgette trotted in with two more blue bloods. First was the aforementioned Gisela in a formfitting gown, which made good use of the push-up bra she had squeezed her ample breasts into. Following behind was none other than the dishy blonde Jessica in a sweeping Oscar De La Renta number. They gave Veronica a cool stare like a clique of the most popular boarding school brats might give a new girl on the first day of class. John knew they were sizing Veronica up, wondering if they could take her or not. Even with all of the expensive gowns and jewels, none of the women there could hold a candle to Veronica tonight.

Veronica didn't even notice they were in the room. She stood in front of a mirror and stared at the Hope Diamond resting against her flawless skin. She turned to John and said, "This is a night I will never forget."

"It's just a rock," he whispered, gently running his finger alongside the gem, grazing her warm skin.

She gazed at him with eyes sparkling as bright as the jewel around her neck, a smile of pure delight spread across her face. "That's what *you* say."

****

"For someone who hates publicity, you sure signed up for a lot of it," John observed as they entered the Beaux-Arts Rotunda.

Veronica showed off a bright smile for the cameras and waiting crowd. "It's for a good cause."

Overlooking the grand hall were three stories of balconies graced with several massive Doric columns. The effect was similar to walking into a splendid marble amphitheater. The room was decorated all in white with fragrant, ivory Boule de

Neige roses and the shimmer of tiny flames burning in crystal votives which made the hall sparkle and glow.

John's eyes immediately went to the security in their snappy tuxedos placed strategically around the room. In all his years at the FBI, he'd never seen so many men at one event. They sure weren't taking any chances.

"I hope *you* don't mind being caught on film," Veronica said, her eyes dancing.

He laughed. "My mother won't believe it's me. She'll accuse me of doctoring the photos and get angry when I insist they're real." His amusement faded as Nicholas Bezuhov glided up to them, as smooth as a ballerina, and, taking Veronica's hand in his, lightly kissed the tips of her fingers.

"What do you think, Nicholas?" she asked, gesturing toward the magnificent, blue diamond at her breast.

"I think you are very brave to face the curse," he observed in his thick Russian accent.

"Or maybe very stupid," she said.

"In any case very, very beautiful...as always," he replied.

The orchestra, which was tucked discreetly away in an alcove of the rotunda, kicked in with a swanky version of *Moonlight Becomes You.*

Nicholas bowed formally. "May I have the pleasure of a dance?"

Veronica glanced at John.

"With your permission, of course," said the Russian, just a hint of mockery in his voice.

"Veronica's a big girl and can make her own decisions. That's how we like to do things here in the good old U.S. of A.," John snapped.

"It'll be just one dance," assured Veronica, laying a placating hand on his forearm.

John nodded.

"We won't be long," said the White Russian, with the hint of a smirk. "Why don't you get yourself a drink? They have some good strong Russian vodka behind the bar, or maybe for you, a...how do you call it? A Shirley Temple." With that, he swept Veronica dramatically into his arms and waltzed her onto the floor.

John just stood there burning up as he watched the White Russian dancing with his girl. *His girl?* With a shake of his head, he opened his eyes to find her once again on the dance floor. They were obviously enjoying each other's company, talking and laughing. Veronica seemed at ease with Nicholas. She let her hair down and chattered, teasing him like a country cousin at a barbeque. John wondered how Jessica would feel about it if she walked in now and found her Nicholas with his arms around the most beautiful woman in the room.

John's attention was diverted when he caught sight of Quinn leaning up against the massive pedestal supporting the African elephant which was the centerpiece of the rotunda. Quinn was stuffed into an ill-fitting tuxedo and stood snapping orders into his headphone. He was trying to look subtle, but John could see him sweating clear across the room. He made his way through the black-tie crowd to his old partner's side.

"Tell them there is no fucking way," Quinn was saying in a low, strained voice into his mouthpiece. "I don't give a shit what the French ambassador's wife thinks about it."

Noticing John by his side, Quinn just rolled his eyes and shook his head to communicate his level of frustration with the person on the other end of the line. "Look, this is something we needed to be informed about at *least* a month ago!"

He paused as he listened and then shook his head. "I'll be right there," he barked. An irate Quinn turned to John. "Guess who Cartier has brought in at the last minute as their surprise entertainment?"

"Jerry Lewis."

Quinn didn't laugh. "No, just a little troupe called the Ballet de l'Aire."

John couldn't help himself as he burst out laughing. When he recovered, he said, "Do you want to take a guess who Veronica is dancing with right now? The same Veronica who is, in fact, wearing the Hope Diamond?"

Quinn snapped his head around and, scanning the floor, got an eyeful of the White Russian dipping Veronica as she smiled up at him. Quinn turned on John furiously. "Are you fucking crazy letting her dance with him?"

"Oh, I don't *let* Veronica do anything. She just does it."

"Look, I'd love to chat and all, but I've got to go *parlez* with the fucking French ambassador, his wife, and the President of freakin' Cartier," said Quinn. "*You* don't take your eyes off that damned diamond around her neck!" He pointed a stubby finger in Veronica's direction.

Before John could answer, Quinn was heading into the crowd, shaking his head and mumbling, "The Ballet de l'Aire my ass."

John watched the crowd on the dance floor. It was a regular who's who of the Washington political scene, but to his surprise, there were many foreigners present as well. Some of the men wore tuxedos and a few even wore turbans while their women were draped in piles of glittering bangles and necklaces encrusted with rare gemstones. All around him, he picked up conversions in Russian, Italian, and Urdu. All of the world's most famously wealthy and powerful families were present. Apparently it didn't matter what nationality you were, who you called God, or what side of the War on Terror you happened to be on. Everyone at this little library benefit spoke the international language—money.

With a musical flourish, the band finished their song. Veronica slipped out of the White Russian's arms and headed in John's direction. He liked watching her as she came toward him through the crowd, back straight, chin high, hips swaying confidently. With her pale glowing skin and graceful silk gown, she stood out next to the conservatively black clad matrons. Her youthful vitality was like a beacon in a dark ugly sea.

"Is it my turn now?" he asked, as she reached his side. She smiled and he was dazzled by the pure joy on her face.

"Let's just dance and dance all night!" she exclaimed.

"You're enjoying yourself then," he commented, as she wound her arm through his and dragged him onto the floor.

Unconsciously, she reached up and touched the diamond around her throat. "Yes."

He took her in his arms and the warmth of having her so close hit him like a wave. He pulled her more firmly against him and they swayed to the romantic music. "You see, if I have you close like this and I never let you go, no one can steal the diamond," he whispered into her dark hair.

She pulled back a bit with a wicked grin and replied, "But we want the Ghost to *try*."

"Veronica, as you know too well, when the Ghost tries, he usually succeeds."

"Not tonight," she said with a determined look in her eyes before snuggling into his shoulder again, her perfume encircling them like a magic spell blocking out the rest of the world. He closed his eyes and surrendered to the bewitchment.

They danced one song after another until an impeccably dressed, short, balding man took the mic and announced, "*Mesdames* and *messieurs*, as one of the sponsors of this evening's ball, we at Cartier would like to present for your entertainment, the pride of the Ballet de l'Aire, Marguerite Gateaux!"

The lights dimmed as a white beam shot up to the tightrope strung between the third floor balconies. The astonished applause of the audience below broke out as the flamboyant acrobat cartwheeled across the cable and posed theatrically like a vintage pinup shimmering in her red sequined leotard, a black eye mask standing out against her white skin and crimson lips.

Evidently Quinn had lost his argument with the French ambassador. John placed a protective hand around Veronica's neck, the clasp of the Hope Diamond secure beneath his palm.

Maggie proceeded to perform her intricately choreographed number, pirouetting and leaping across the slender cable as easily as a child scampering around a playground. As John watched the crowd, the delight of the spellbound audience was almost as entertaining as the act itself. She put on quite a show with her death-defying leaps and saucy wicked grin, her red hair streaming behind her like a comet's tail as she spun across the thin cable. It was easy to see why she'd never had a problem making her way over the most exclusive rooftops in Europe.

What is it about jewel thieves? John watched as she performed a final, impossible-looking spring in the air, flipped and hung by nothing more than the dainty curve of her ankle, smiling and waving down at the nail-biting audience. They were certainly a breed apart from all other criminals. Flamboyant and arrogant, there wasn't a one who didn't have a flair for the theatrical. John had to marvel as he thought about each of them individually—Maggie showing off at the Diamond Ball only one night after

173

robbing Senator Hayes' wife blind, the White Russian with his calling card and family crest, the Granny and her magician's slight of hand, and Zagen, far more dangerous than the rest. He knew each of them; only the Ghost was impossible to define. Maybe that was why the Ghost had never been caught.

John's eyes darted around the room as the audience broke into wild applause for Maggie. She stood above them, eighty feet in the air, no doubt already singling out her next victim. Her saucy grin froze on her face and for a moment, time seemed to stand still, as the wire snapped beneath her feet.

Chapter Fourteen

The audience watched in horror as the acrobat plummeted toward the marble floor. Veronica gripped John's arm as they watched a blur of red sequins and flaming hair tumbling through the air.

At the last moment, the wire tightened and caught on the sequins of her costume. With the lightning fast reflexes of the cat she was named for, Maggie stretched out her hands to grasp the broken cable just before hitting the ground where her weight would surely have torn the wire from her leotard. Catching the lifeline just in time, she swung across the room landing miraculously safe on one of the first tier balconies.

The sigh of relief was like a wave rising up from the audience, as ladies collapsed against their husbands and the men swore out loud, forgetting their surroundings.

"I don't think that was part of her act," said Veronica, her nails still digging into John's arm.

"It wasn't. Someone cut the wire." John scanned the third tier of the rotunda for signs of whoever might have tried to murder the famous acrobat.

Veronica relaxed her grip as she watched Maggie, ever the showgirl, jump onto the rail of the balcony to take her bow. "Why would someone do that?"

"That's Maggie the Cat up there," John informed her over the audience's wild applause. "She's one of the most prolific jewel thieves in operation. Maybe someone here tonight doesn't want to compete with her."

"You mean...another jewel thief?"

"That's exactly what I mean," said John. "Someone wants what's around your neck badly enough to kill for it, Veronica."

Veronica raised her hand protectively to the blue fire laying cool against her throat. "I'm not afraid."

He glared at her. "Well, maybe you should be."

"I'll be fine," she reassured him and turned her eyes back up to Marguerite Gateaux.

John followed her gaze. He had to hand it to Maggie, she was still pale as death, but the French cat burglar once again sported a broad smile as she blew a kiss to the audience and then disappeared behind the gauze drapes.

He shook his head. "Eight lives to go."

Veronica smiled, but John noticed she looked a bit pale herself.

When the crowd's applause finally died down, the lights came up on the red carpet, which ran through the center of the room. It was Lillian Spencer's turn to hit the mic. She stood in the spotlight smiling her best First Lady smile.

"Well, that was quite a performance, wasn't it?" she asked.

The audience laughed, letting out the tension.

"My goodness, I can see why the Ballet de l'Aire has such a magnificent reputation!"

More laughter. Lillian Spencer had covered up the catastrophe as easily as her husband covered up the corporate scandals and botched military operations his administration was involved in. Everyone knew what had really happened, but they'd play along anyway and pretend Maggie's fall had been part of the act, because that was the accepted protocol.

The First Lady smiled warmly. "I want to

welcome all of you and thank you for coming tonight. As you know, literacy is a cause near and dear to my heart. For all of us in this room it is the most basic of skills. We take for granted that we can pick up a book or newspaper and read the words printed there, but I'm afraid that for some children in the United States, those same words are as meaningless as a page full of hieroglyphics. I am committed to changing this!"

A ripple of polite applause went through the crowd. The First Lady paused, looking around the room as if judging the response. "Tonight we have pledged our support, and more importantly, our desperately needed dollars to build the new Donald Spencer Library in Anacostia. Because of your generosity, a child will be able to come after school and pick up one of so many reading choices. A new and magical world will open up to them." Lillian Spencer smiled beneficently at the crowd as once more they broke into applause.

"Meanwhile they're cutting hours and programs at all the other libraries around the country. Why doesn't anyone mention that?" whispered John to Veronica, but she just put her finger to her lips and turned her eyes back on Lillian Spencer.

"And now," said the First Lady, when the hoopla had died down, "I would like to introduce Kay Hopkins, one of the directors of the Smithsonian. Kay has graciously donated her time, this space, and some of the world's most breathtaking jewels to make this a night to remember!"

As Kay stepped forward, Veronica leaned in and whispered to John, "I have to get in place now."

He clutched her arm for a moment. "Be careful. I'm sure Maggie's still on the loose somewhere in this building along with God knows who else."

"Don't worry," she said with a smile. "What could happen to me while I'm on the runway with a wall of photographers snapping pictures?"

"Don't get cocky," he said, annoyed. "Remember what happened to Katherine Park."

"Don't worry, John, no one's going to get this diamond away from me."

John pointed to a place near the end of the red carpet. "I'm going to be standing right there if you need me."

"I'll be fine." She turned to walk away, but then she stepped back and lightly kissed his lips, sending a spark of electricity through every nerve in his body. "But thank you," she whispered and took off into the crowd.

The band swung into a jazzy version of *Diamonds Are A Girl's Best Friend* as the show began. Gisela, the smoldering beauty who had amused Cynthia Spencer so much by her allotment of jewels, was the first one down the runway. The massive Hooker Emerald was pinned squarely between her two jutting breasts, flashing green in the runway lights. The press went at it like a bunch of piranhas attacking a side of beef while Kay recited the history of the famous emerald that had once been the belt buckle of a Turkish sultan.

Jessica came next, dripping in her family pearls, which were rumored to have once belonged to the infamous Lucretia Borgia. She looked as stuck up and cold as ever, not even cracking a smile when the storm of flashbulbs went off as she stopped to pose at the end of the runway.

One dolled-up rich girl after another had her turn on the catwalk, each sporting bigger and better rocks than the celebutante before her. The crowd went wild for them. John couldn't tell if they were applauding for the individual young ladies or the extraordinary jewels they wore.

"Ladies and gentlemen," said Kay, as Lillian Spencer stepped onto the red carpet in a shimmering pair of massive baroque diamond earrings, "few objects in the Smithsonian collection conjure up more dramatic images than do these earrings. They were given to Marie Antoinette by Louis XVI and are said to have been torn from her ears as she tried to flee during the French Revolution."

The crowd really went crazy as Lillian Spencer, wearing her ill-starred gems, slowly made her way down the red carpet. She had her moment in front of the cameras, and as she turned to walk back down the runway, Kay introduced Cynthia and her imperial jewels.

John had seen a lot of ridiculous things in his life, like the thief in Palm Beach who left his cell phone at the scene of the crime, but the sight of Cynthia Spencer toddling down the runway looking like an overstuffed sausage encased in pink satin, shrinking under the glare of the public gaze with Josephine Bonaparte's crown slipping to one side of her head took the cake.

Miraculously, the crowd didn't seem to notice and gave her the same enthusiastic applause they gave her mother. John almost felt sorry for Cynthia as she tripped on the hem of her gown during her runway return.

"And now," gushed Kay, unable to keep the excitement from her voice, "for the first time in the museum's history, we have allowed our most prized possession to be worn at a public event. Our model is the lovely Miss Veronica Rossmore. I'm sure you've all guessed that the famous treasure I'm talking about is none other than the *Hope Diamond!*"

The crowd went silent in anticipation as they looked down the empty red carpet. Everyone held their breath, waiting to see the diamond that bore the most infamous curse of any jewel in history. John felt himself tense up as the seconds ticked by and Veronica did not appear. Almost starting to panic, he was about to push his way through the crowd and find her when Veronica stepped into the spotlight.

Cynthia Spencer may not have looked much like a princess while she walked the runway, but Veronica did. With the deep blue diamond shimmering and sparkling against her white skin, she cast a spell over the guests as surely as if she had waved a magic wand covered in pixie dust. As she made her way down the carpet, the audience rose to a standing ovation that sounded like an earthquake shaking the giant hall. Veronica, poised and calm, smiled at them; her face glowing and radiant, her eyes sparkling the same twilight blue as the Hope.

Someone who didn't know her might have thought Veronica was basking in the love of the crowd like an insecure starlet blossoming under the approval of the masses. John knew, however, that it was the diamond itself giving her this high. The feel of its cold weight against her breastbone, the subtle life of the gem radiating its energy to her, whispering all its dark secrets and infamous history. She communed with the gem the way some hippies hugged trees or a great jockey caught the rhythm of his horse.

She turned back down the runway and as she passed him she caught his eye and winked.

When the lights on the catwalk went down and the ball commenced, John had to fight his way through the crowd to reach Veronica. A throng of admirers, camera crews and, he feared, potential jewel thieves swarmed around her vying for her attention. As last she gave her final interview for the eleven o'clock news and came to his side. She grabbed his hand in hers and said, "Let's get a drink. I'm about to melt from standing under all those hot lights!"

"Over here," John pointed to a gap in the crowd at the end of the long bar. They moved quickly so any lingering press would get it that showtime was over.

Apparently, Cynthia Spencer had the same idea, and cutting them off, slipped ahead in the bar line. She leaned her elbows on the wood, her imperial diamond necklace scraping the bar, which was wet with splashes of liquor from the fast-paced pouring of the overworked bartenders. "Hey, let me have a rum and Coke," she called to the nearest man behind the bar.

He caught her eye and held up his hand to let her know he heard her and would be with her in a minute. She turned to Veronica. "Can you believe this? My sorority house has better bartenders than this! They needed to hire, like, *way* more people!"

John realized Cynthia had not tripped on the hem of her dress as she traversed the catwalk out of pure awkwardness. The president's daughter was completely hammered. Veronica ignored the girl, biting her lip as if holding something back.

Cynthia wavered on her feet a bit and turned back to the bar as the bartender handed her a drink. "Thanks," she said, her eyes fastened on the glass in her hand. Before stepping aside to let John and Veronica order, she took a deep drink. An infuriated expression squished up her piggy little face and she slammed the glass down on the bar. "Why is there no alcohol in this?"

"I'm sorry, Miss Spencer," said the bartender, looking uncomfortable. "Those were my orders."

"Whose fucking orders? I can't even have a drink at my own party?" she yelled. People nearby were turning to stare.

Veronica gripped the president's daughter by the shoulder and said softly, "Come with me, Cynthia. We're going to have a little talk..." Before

181

she could go any further, the lights went out, plunging the ballroom into darkness.

Like a blind man, John grasped for Veronica, his hands brushing up uselessly against the tightly packed bodies of panicked guests. He called her name, but in the chaos of voices, he was just one more babble of confused sound.

Then he heard her through the crashing chairs and women's screams. "Let go!"

John pushed his way toward her voice but he wasn't making it too far. Just as he was about to lose his temper, he heard a hum and saw the security lights snap on as bright as the afternoon sun.

The stunned guests instinctively stepped back to reveal Dornal Zagen dressed as a secret service agent. He and Veronica were in the midst of a violent tug of war for the Hope Diamond. The blue gem glittered on its icy chain between the white-knuckled fists of Veronica and the thief. The Austrian was gritting his teeth and John could see his temples pounding as Veronica held fast with every ounce of willpower she had. At their feet a wire clipper lay on the floor, evidently used to cut the necklace from Veronica's throat.

Like the flash of a camera, John took it all in. Then he sprang forward along with about fifteen secret service men.

Dornal froze. Something had gone wrong. The lights had come up much too early. Cursing, he wrenched the Hope out of Veronica's bleeding fingers.

John and the secret service men had almost reached him when the thief swung back his arm and threw the cursed diamond as far across the room as he could.

Stunned, the security men stopped in their tracks. The jewel caught the light and sparked like stardust over the outstretched fingers of the party guests until it landed on the down escalator that connected the rotunda with the lobby on the first floor.

A riot broke out as everyone from DC matrons to secret service men pounced, falling over themselves on the moving escalator like the Marx brothers in one of their classic movies.

In the chaos, no one noticed Zagen clamp his iron fist over Veronica's mouth as he dragged her toward the side exit. No one except John.

He could see the terror in Veronica's eyes.

"Put the knife down!" ordered Quinn, who, catching on, had crept up from another direction.

But Zagen ignored the FBI man and stared at John with hatred.

"Put the goddamn knife down!!" screamed Quinn.

"I'm going now," said Dornal, his voice frosty like Alpine air as he began to back away.

Not this time; John leveled his Glock at Zagen's face. He heard Quinn's panicked voice like a fly buzzing around him, telling him not to shoot. The chances of hitting Veronica were too great.

John met her eyes. She dropped her chin slightly. He got the signal.

Veronica smoothly lowered her hand and grabbed Zagen's balls, *hard,* digging in with her long nails. Taking advantage of the Austrian's momentary surprise, she ducked just as John squeezed the trigger.

The sound of the shot echoed off the marble floors and pillars. Everyone froze in shock as the room went silent.

He'd missed.

Just above Zagen's massive right shoulder, a bullet hole pocked the white marble column.

Cursing, the Austrian grabbed hold of Veronica even more fiercely than before and raised his knife to slice her throat open.

The women screamed and Veronica closed her eyes.

John felt the world slow down into a nauseating surreal moment. He had seen plenty of death in his career at the FBI, to the point where he'd become numb to it. But now, to watch Veronica's throat slit in front of him and be powerless to stop it was too much. In a moment of pure madness, he flung his gun aside and went for Dornal. There were no thoughts, no plans, just tunnel vision with the Austrian and Veronica at the end of it.

He realized later he must have yelled or made some sort of desperate sound, which startled even the cool Austrian enough to flick his eyes up for a moment and see John coming at him like a rabid animal. All it took was the flick of those eyes.

Before anyone understood what had happened, the convict's arms went limp, freeing a surprised Veronica. His pale face turned ashy blue and his gray shark eyes rolled back in their sockets before he collapsed into John's arms. Astonished, John looked down at the back of the Austrian's head. It took a moment for him to register what he was looking at. Someone had shoved a cake cutter deep into Dornal Zagen's brainstem.

Chapter Fifteen

John staggered under the weight of the Austrian's body, but even as he struggled to hold the convict, he caught a glimpse of an older woman with gray hair slipping down a dark corridor and out of sight.

As the security men recovered from their surprise, John found himself surrounded by helpful hands.

Quinn stepped forward, pointing down the hall where the old lady had just escaped. "Get down there!" he urged his men.

But John, dumping Zagen's body in the helpful hands, leapt forward. "No! I saw the killer. He was dressed as a security guard, too. He ran behind the crowd to that exit over there." John indicated a fire exit in the corner of the room.

Quinn turned a squinty-eyed look of distrust on John. "Are you sure?"

"Yes! You're losing valuable time!" insisted John.

Quinn shifted nervously on his feet and then made his decision. "All right, let's go!" His men took off toward the exit John had indicated.

All around them, a firestorm of flashbulbs went off and the cacophony of voices swirled. Through it all he saw Veronica crying quietly with her back against a pillar; one slender hand wrapped protectively around her naked throat.

John cut through the crowd, put his arm around

185

her waist, and began to lead her out of the ballroom. "Come on," he said, gently walking her past the gaping onlookers.

"As soon as the lights went out, I grabbed it," she said, looking pale and shaken. "I didn't even feel him cut it off my neck. Suddenly, it was just loose in my hands and he was pulling it away." Her usually soft white palms were cut and bleeding.

"I'm just glad you're all right. You saved your life by fighting back. Remind me to take you with me next time I'm in a jam," said John, smoothing back her hair.

She smiled, a bit of color coming back into her cheeks. "You're the one. I've never seen anyone look like such a complete maniac as you did when you came charging at him, but who do you think...," she paused and turned slightly pale again.

"Maybe if you're real nice, I'll tell you some day."

"You know who killed him?" she asked in a surprised whisper.

Before he could respond, Kay Hopkins appeared at their side, bug-eyed and sweating. "Dear God, Veronica, are you all right, honey?"

Veronica nodded.

"I can't believe you saved the diamond! You could have been killed!" she exclaimed.

"Where is the Hope?" asked Veronica.

Kay opened her hand to reveal the blue diamond winking up at them. "I have it right here. Secret service managed to grab the necklace before it was smashed to pieces at the bottom of the escalator."

"Oh, it wouldn't have broken," said Veronica, with a wan smile. "Diamonds are pretty tough."

Kay's brow puckered at the sight of the torn skin on Veronica's palms. "Look at your sweet little hands! Come along, honey. Let's get you and this diamond back to the salon." She put a motherly arm around Veronica's shoulders as she led her and

John, trailed by a small army of secret service men, back to the Adam's Parlor.

Veronica sat quietly on the green silk settee as Georgette scurried forward with a first aid kit.

"Allow me," said John, taking the kit from Kay's assistant. He pulled out a packet of gauze, a few cotton balls and a small bottle of antiseptic. "This is going to sting," he warned before gently applying the antiseptic to the cuts on Veronica's palms.

She grimaced a little but didn't pull away as he wrapped her hands in the gauze. "You look like the mummy's bride," he joked.

She smiled, but he could tell she was still shaken up from the drama in the ballroom.

The parlor was filling up with excited, chattering women coming to return their borrowed jewels, though the First Lady and her daughter had been whisked back to the White House by secret service at the first sign of trouble. Josephine's imperial crown and Marie Antoinette's earrings would have to wait until morning to be returned, but the Hope was now locked safely away in the Smithsonian's vault.

"Well, you look exhausted," said John to Veronica. "Let's get you back to the hotel."

"That would be heaven," she agreed, "but won't they need us here for questioning?"

"I'm sure as long as we promise not to skip town, Quinn won't object to us getting a little sleep. For tonight, let's just say you're under my custody."

She smiled. "I like that idea."

****

The wind was cool and refreshing as the platinum convertible sped down Constitution Avenue. The stars had come out and they twinkled sharply in the clear skies above. John and Veronica had snuck out the back entrance of the museum, avoiding the mess of TV cameras and news reporters who had arrived to cover the Ghost's grand finale.

Veronica rested her head against the seat with her eyes closed. "I'll be so glad when this night is over and I'm snuggled under the covers fast asleep."

John's cell phone started vibrating. He saw Quinn's number as the incoming caller and pushed the answer button. "How's it going down there?"

"Well, he's dead as a doornail!" announced Quinn.

"Did you find the killer?"

"Not yet, but we're dusting down the murder weapon right now looking for prints."

John knew they wouldn't find any.

"Guess what we did discover, though, in Zagen's pocket?" crowed the FBI man.

"What?"

"A friggin' journal and do you know what's inside?"

"Dornal's favorite Linzer Torte recipe?" joked John, blinking his eyes to stay alert.

"Every heist. The date, the time, even the rocks he stole. All our Ghost stories wrapped up in a nice, neat little bow. It's perfect."

John's eyes were open now. "You're kidding!"

"Nope. Can you imagine? Freakin' psycho, huh?"

John was incredulous. "He carried a notebook of evidence against himself?"

"Yup."

John digested this in silence as he turned onto Maryland Avenue. Who would do something like that? It was just plain stupid. Dornal Zagen may have been a lot of things, but stupid wasn't one of them. Of course the Austrian did have the kind of meticulous, methodical mind that would keep an accurate accounting of his life. Everything in its proper place. One more item checked off the list. Was it possible this journal was part of some sort of obsessive-compulsive ritual?

"Hey, you there?" asked Quinn.

"Yeah, yeah, I'm here. I'm just trying to get used to the idea."

"I know. A case like this...well, it goes on for so long and then when it's finished...you almost feel disappointed."

"It's crazy," agreed John.

"Well, I've got a few things to wrap up here, but then I'm going home for my first decent night's sleep in I don't know how goddamn long. I can deal with the rest of the details in the morning."

"You do that, buddy," said John.

"Sayonara."

They hung up. John slipped the phone into his pocket and glanced over at Veronica. Her head was still leaning back on the car seat and she was staring up at the stars flashing by.

"So, that man was the Ghost?" she asked.

John was still shaking his head in amazement. "Looks like it."

"Thank God that's over!" she said, before closing her eyes and drifting off.

When they reached the Monticello, it was well past midnight. John was tempted to swoop Veronica up from where she dozed, but she sleepily opened her eyes and stepped out on her own.

They didn't say much on the elevator ride up to the fourth floor, but when they arrived at her door, she turned to John and lightly kissed his lips. "Thank you for taking such good care of me tonight." She held up her bandaged palms.

"I'm just happy you're still in one piece." He slipped his hands around her hips and moved in closer, but she gently stepped away.

"We'll have plenty of time when we're back in New York..." She didn't finish the sentence but her eyes told him everything she didn't need to say.

He nodded. "Okay," and kissing her forehead, he

watched as she unlocked her door.

"You're sure you're all right?"

"Yes, I just need a good night's sleep," she said as she slipped into her room. "Good night, John," and she closed the door.

John stood there for a moment, scanning the hall for any nefarious activity, but there was none. The Ghost is caught, he reminded himself, still not quite able to grasp the concept as he slowly made his way down the hall to his own room.

He snapped on the lights as he walked in and tossed his jacket and pistol on the bed. He sat down to unlace his shoes when the *New York Post* article with the photograph of Veronica sprawled on the ground caught his eye.

He picked it up and looked at her lying on the floor where Derrick Chapin had thrown her in his jealous fit. How could he ever have believed this broken girl was the Ghost? Veronica wasn't a criminal, just a beautiful magnet for violent men. He cringed, thinking about the scene he'd thrown in the car on the way to the ball. He'd been wrong about her. Wrong about everything. *What else was new?* His fingers lingered for just a moment against Veronica's image before he put the picture away.

But then he frowned and picked it up again.

There was something about the photograph that bothered him.

He re-examined it. Nothing had changed, of course. Her legs still cranked to the same crazy angle, her dress was still up around her waist, her neck thrown back to expose the magnificent necklace...

Then it hit him.

He pulled the photograph directly under the bedside lamp to get a better look, but it was difficult to see. Still holding the Xerox photo, he picked up the phone and dialed the front desk.

"Good evening, Mr. Monroe," said a pleasant female voice.

"Hi there. This might seem like an unusual request, but would it be possible to have a magnifying glass sent up to my room right away?"

"I'll take care of it, sir," said the woman's smooth voice. "Is there anything else I can get you?"

How about a case of Maker's Mark and a carton of Marlboro Reds?

"No thanks," said John and they hung up.

A moment later there was a discreet knock at the door. He opened it up and traded a sleepy-looking bellboy a few bucks for a magnifying glass.

Closing the door, he went back to the light and laid the photograph down on the bedside table. He held the magnifying glass over the exotic necklace Veronica wore.

There it was.

The famous Winged Isis with its delicately engraved golden image of the Egyptian goddess and a pair of finely crafted lapis lazuli wings fanned out across Veronica's breastbone. The necklace was rumored to have been part of the magnificent Nefertiti treasures and was once worn by the fabled queen herself. It was the first article of jewelry the Ghost ever stole.

"No wonder you didn't want your picture taken, Veronica," he breathed.

Before he had time to think, John tossed the paper aside and headed for the door. But he stopped midway, and making a u-turn, walked to the sliding glass doors that led out onto the balcony. He slid the glass open and the hum of the traffic below and the cool air hit him as he stepped outside and scanned the rows of empty balconies lined up between his bedroom and hers. There were five of them, all about two feet from one another. It would be easy to make it across.

191

He pulled off his slippery black dress socks and climbed across the balconies as carefully and quietly as he could until he had reached hers. The curtains were half open. A big rectangle of light illuminated the balcony. He slipped into the shadows and held his breath as he watched her go to the closet and carefully hang up her fur wrap. Then she went to the minibar and, pulling out a bottle of white wine, poured herself a glass and sat down at the vanity table against the far wall of the room. She sat with her back to him, but he could see her beautiful face reflected perfectly in the vanity mirror.

There was nothing sleepy-looking about her expression now. She looked tense and glanced over her shoulder as if she wanted to make sure she was completely alone. Then she reached down into her cleavage. With her bandaged hand she fumbled at her breast for a moment and slowly drew the necklace out on its chain of glittering brilliants. Dangling it like a cat holding a mouse by the tail, she held it up so the cold blue fire of the stone blazed before her eyes. She stared as if hypnotized at the Hope Diamond, watching it sparkle and shine in red, purple, and green incandescence. John stood just outside the room watching her.

Veronica sensed something, shifted her gaze, and their eyes met in the mirror.

They were both caught.

Slowly, Veronica placed the jewel on the vanity table and turned as he slid open the glass door and stepped into her room.

"You're the Ghost."

For a long moment she did nothing. Just looked at him with her smooth, unreadable face. Then she nodded, defiant, and yet he sensed a flicker of fear in her eyes, the vulnerability behind the ice.

"You switched the diamonds. When? During the blackout?"

She nodded again and then dropped her dark blue eyes to the floor.

His head spun. Anger, betrayal, and an annoying desire to protect her all whirled through him. "Why?" he demanded, coming to stand above her chair.

She looked up at him but said nothing.

"You certainly don't need the money!" he fumed as he paced the room trying to clear his mind. "You know how I knew it was you?"

She wasn't looking at him now and she didn't answer.

"I saw the picture of you in the *Post* with the goddamned Winged Isis around your neck! What in the hell is that about Veronica? Did you just prance around Manhattan in all the loot you've picked up over the years?"

"Maybe I did!" she said, her eyes blazing. "Who are you to judge me anyway? Have you never done anything wrong in your life? Anything you regret?"

"Sure I have, but the difference is, I don't do the things I'm not proud of anymore."

She shook her head. "You don't understand."

"I understand one thing," he said. "We're returning that diamond tonight. We'll figure out a story." He ran his hands through his hair, massaging his scalp trying to think up a plan. "We'll say you were protecting it from Dornal Zagen, or..."

"I can't do that," she said, her voice cool and even.

"I'm not going to give you the choice," he responded, and before she could stop him, he snatched up the diamond and held it in his fist. Her eyes flickered over him, sizing him up.

"Don't bother," he told her. "You don't stand a chance."

"But I do," said an all too familiar voice from the entrance hall.

193

John snapped his head around to see Quinn closing the door quietly behind him, a Smith and Wesson 640 revolver clutched in his right hand pointed straight at John's heart.

Chapter Sixteen

"Give her back the diamond," commanded the FBI man.

John slowly opened his hand and Veronica stepped forward and took back the Hope.

When he'd recovered his breath, John asked, "What the hell are you doing, Quinn?"

"I'm just following orders," said his ex-partner still leveling the gun at him.

"You want to put the piece down and explain all this to me?" asked John.

"When Miss Rossmore's safely on her way, I'll fill you in," promised Quinn.

John turned around to see Veronica wrapping the diamond in a silk scarf and placing it in her bag.

"Where are you going, Veronica?"

She stopped and looked at John, her eyes pleading with him not to ask.

"Where are you going with that diamond?" he repeated. "Even you wouldn't be crazy enough to wear that to your little Park Avenue parties. So what are you going to do with it? Are you going to lock it up somewhere for your own private enjoyment? Never mind that it's a national treasure and belongs in a museum..."

"Do you think I'm that selfish?" Veronica couldn't take any more; her veneer cracked and the words rushed out in a torrent of emotion. "Yes, I suppose you must, but I'll tell you what I'm doing with it. I'm taking it to Amsterdam where I'm going to have it cut and sell it to the highest bidder! You want to know why? It's because…"

Quinn stepped forward and grabbed her arm. "That's enough, Miss Rossmore. The less he knows about it, the better for him."

Furiously, she stared at Quinn's hand on her arm, slowly raising her eyes up to his red, sweating face. He unclenched his fist and stepped back a pace.

"What have they got back there at the Smithsonian?" asked John, nailing her with his eyes. "Some fancy fake Nicholas Bezuhov knocked off for you?"

She didn't answer.

"Shut up, John," barked Quinn.

"What about your jewelry?" John refused to back off. "What happened to that?"

"It was never stolen. I had it all along," she said, unwilling to look at him.

John could tell she was lying. "Then show it to me, Veronica."

"That's enough!" said Quinn, once again aiming the revolver at John. "No more questions."

John didn't like it, but he wasn't going to argue with a man holding a gun. Even if that man was supposed to be his friend.

Back to business now, Veronica snapped her purse shut and walked to the closet where she pulled out a small suitcase and a camel-colored wrap-coat, which she put on over the elegant evening gown she still wore. She slung her purse over her shoulder and, picking up her suitcase, headed for the door.

"Everything should be all set." Quinn took a step toward her while still keeping a watchful eye on John. "The car's waiting downstairs and I got word right before I came that the plane is ready, too."

She nodded and then turned to look at John. He could tell she didn't want to look at him but couldn't help herself. She bit her lower lip and he felt as if she were bursting to tell him something. "Goodbye,

John." She turned to leave the room.

Her hand was on the doorknob when he said bitterly, "I thought we were going to trust each other, Veronica."

Her face was as cold and hard as any diamond in the world. "Yes, I thought we were."

And then she was gone.

John turned angrily on his ex-partner. "You want to tell me what this is all about?"

Quinn wiped his shining forehead with the back of his shirtsleeve and motioned with the gun for John to sit down. "Let's watch a little TV," suggested Quinn.

"You watch some fucking TV," growled John, stepping toward Quinn, but his old friend raised his gun and aimed it once more at John's heart.

"The last thing in the world I want to do is hurt you, but you need to chill out for few minutes." Quinn's voice sounded desperate and shaky, not a sound John had ever heard before.

John stopped where he was and examined his ex-partner. He looked like hell. His mousy hair was plastered to his skull, his flabby jowls hung down, the lines in his face were etched so much deeper than they had been only a year ago. John could probably get the gun from him, but that was probably, and he had learned a long time ago that the margin for error when it came to handling loaded firearms had better be zero. He threw up his hands in defeat and sat down on the edge of the bed.

Some of the tension in Quinn's face melted away and he slipped his gun back in the holster. "I'm thirsty as hell. You want something to drink?" he asked as he walked over to the minibar and took out a can of beer.

John shook his head.

Quinn pulled up a chair opposite him and opening his beer took a long, deep drink. Then he sighed, took another pull and put the can down on the end table next to him. He laced his hands together and leaned in toward John.

"Look, I know this all seems fucked up. It *is* fucked up. I mean...it's fucked up, but not the way you think, Johnnie."

John just stared him down.

"I just don't want you to think this is me." Quinn was obviously feeling the heat of John's glare. "I mean, we worked together for a long time and we're friends and..." He grimaced and, grabbing the can of beer, took another long drink and sat nervously fiddling with the aluminum tab.

John still said nothing.

"Okay, you want to know?" asked Quinn finally. "I'll tell you, if you want to fucking know. I'll tell you, but I mean, this cannot leave this room. The fact you're even *in* this room is already a problem, a very big problem, which..." He shook his head.

"Why don't you just tell me what's going on?"

Quinn looked up and then back down at the floor. "Okay, here's the story. You know that this ball tonight was a benefit for the Library Fund?"

John nodded.

"Well, the organization heading up the whole thing is a charity group called The Donald Spencer Children's Library Fund. The chairwoman for the group is Lillian Spencer. She runs a lot of these things, as the president's wife, which you can imagine. But here's where we get to the problem. The *treasurer,* if you can believe it, is Cynthia Spencer. Apparently, the First Lady thought it would teach her kid responsibility." Quinn laughed at the absurdity of the idea. "But that's not how it all played out. See Cynthia, as treasurer, had access to all the donations, which have come pouring in over the last six months. This event was a twenty-five-grand-a-ticket affair, and with over 350 takers, we're talking about close to ten million dollars here."

Quinn paused to take another drink and shook his head in disgust. "So anyway, spring break rolls around, and Cynthia and her little coke-addicted, Yalie boyfriend head south to a little island called Nevis. Well, I don't know if you've ever been to Nevis, but apparently they have quite a casino there, and in the casino, they have a special private VIP room where it's a million dollars just to walk in the fucking door. Well, I guess Cynthia and her boyfriend cranked up a few too many lines and she decided she was a big shot. So she goes back to her little hut on the beach, or wherever the fuck she was staying, and pulls out the checkbook she just happened to bring along with her for the Library Fund. She goes back to the casino and writes them out a big one million dollar check. Within minutes the casino, which is run by a bunch of crooks, verified the account and the cash, and our little princess is off and running. Well, by the end of the night, Cynthia and her boyfriend have ripped through over six million dollars and the kid's library charity is shit out of luck."

Quinn shook his head in disgust and then, fumbling in his pocket, pulled out a pack of cigarettes, lit one up, leaned back in the chair, and took another swig of beer. John could tell he was starting to enjoy himself now. Quinn always loved to tell stories and this one was a doozy.

"So," he continued, "when Lillian Spencer finds out about this, she loses her mind, right? Because what Cynthia's done is illegal, immoral, and it's going to start a scandal that could rock her husband right out of the White House once the press gets their hands on it. So she wracks her brains about what to do."

"Why didn't she just replace the money herself? God knows the Spencers certainly have enough."

"Well, that's what I thought," said Quinn nodding his head in agreement, "but apparently there's rich and then there's *rich*. The Spencers are rich but they're not super rich to the point where coming up with six million dollars wouldn't seriously set them back." He shrugged. "So anyway, the First Lady's trying to come up with a plan, when suddenly she remembers something. She remembers that her dear old family friend Veronica Rossmore is the most accomplished jewel thief in the world." Quinn leaned forward, excitement glowing in his eyes. "You see, they caught her, John. It was three years ago, right before we snagged Zagen..."

"Before I snagged Zagen," John corrected him.

"Whatever," Quinn waved his cigarette in annoyance. "The point is, Veronica Rossmore goes to Spain and she's partying in some nightclub in Madrid. She makes a few friends, Carmen and Lorenzo Mandosa. She goes home with them for a little after-hours entertainment. So they're all back partying at her new pal's apartment and she says she's got to go use the powder room. Lorenzo points her in the right direction. She heads down the hallway but she can't stop herself from slipping into the master bedroom and rifling through Carmen's jewelry box. She hits the jackpot and finds a Cartier dragon necklace, but before she knows it, they catch her in the act and call the Madrid police. Well, Veronica Rossmore sure didn't want to spend the next twenty years rotting in a Spanish prison. So she called her mother's old school chum, Lillian Spencer, to see if she could pull a few strings and get her out of the jam. It wasn't easy, but the First Lady pulled it off. The thing is, now, Veronica owed her big time."

John shook his head in disbelief. "If Veronica was the Ghost and the Spanish police captured her, how could we not have known about it?"

Quinn rolled his eyes. "Johnnie, we don't know a lot of what goes on. We know what people like Lillian Spencer want us to know and that's it!"

Quinn looked angry for a moment, but after a drag of his cigarette and another gulp of beer, he calmed down and resumed the story. "So, on top of all this, the First Lady is incredibly superstitious, to the point she had the friggin' White House feng shuied."

John nodded his head, remembering the story being featured in the papers. But something was bothering him. "There's one thing I don't get. The Ghost was the best of the best. If Veronica really was the Ghost, how could she get caught in such an amateurish heist?"

"Well," Quinn explained, "the thing about your little friend is, she's got a bit of a psychological problem. I don't think that young lady was ever stealing for profit." Quinn laughed derisively. "I mean, the girl is loaded. She's got more of what you might call a compulsion."

"You mean she's a kleptomaniac."

"Bingo. It seems like toward the end she just started getting sloppy and was caught in the grip of her illness or something." Quinn shrugged. "I don't pretend to understand crap like that."

John understood it, but he wasn't about to share with Quinn how it felt to be so totally out of control you couldn't stop yourself from rushing down the road to self-destruction.

"Anyway," Quinn continued his story, "they've got this infamously cursed diamond right here in the nation's capital spreading its bad juju all over the place. It's been bugging Lillian Spencer the entire time her husband's been in office. So she thinks to herself, maybe she can kill two birds with one stone—no pun intended." Quinn snickered at his own bad joke.

John wasn't laughing.

Quinn sighed and shook his head. "Okay, so Mrs. Spencer thinks she can get the Hope out of the country and sell it to our enemies. The Library Fund gets its money back, the bad guys get the bad luck, and Veronica Rossmore has to help her do it!" finished Quinn triumphantly, spreading his chubby hands wide in the air like a barker at a circus.

John narrowed his eyes. "What about Bezuhov? How's he mixed up in all this?"

"He's not," said Quinn.

John took it all in for a moment. Then he asked, "Who's she selling it to and when?"

"That I don't know," said Quinn. "And neither, I think, does anyone other than Veronica Rossmore. The First Lady felt the less she knew about the whole thing the better. So as long as the money shows up in the Children's Fund bank account within the next few days, I don't think there will be any questions asked."

"Lillian Spencer sure puts a lot of trust in Veronica," John observed dryly.

"Not really," Quinn snorted. "If that money doesn't show up in the account on schedule, it won't be too hard to track down Miss Rossmore and put her behind bars for life."

"And what if Veronica told the truth and put the First Lady and Cynthia Spencer behind bars instead?" asked John angrily.

Quinn looked at John with pity. "Don't be an asshole, Johnnie. You know how rich people are. They all stick together and cover each other's asses. It's how they're able to get away with so much shit that you and I would fry for."

John knew it was true. No matter how much Veronica probably resented being forced to ply her trade for the benefit of Cynthia's Spencer's coked-out gambling spree, he didn't see her stepping forward to make a federal case out of it either.

"Well, now you know," said Quinn, taking a deep drag of his cigarette and exhaling. "So I'm going to have to kill you."

John looked up sharply at his ex-partner's threat, but Quinn just sat there grinning.

"Under the circumstances, I don't think that's very funny," growled John.

Quinn's grin broadened, but then he said seriously, "You know, Johnnie, this can't go anywhere."

John nodded his head. He was as bad as all the rich people Quinn had been talking about. He'd keep his mouth shut and let it go on, just like Veronica. He wondered if he'd even tell Simon.

You're only as sick as your secrets, he could hear the old AA fart cautioning him. John felt about as cheap and crappy about himself as he had in a long time.

Quinn looked at his watch. "Well, I guess I can let you outa here now. Miss Rossmore should be safely on a private jet to Amsterdam, and you and I can go home and get some sleep for once."

John said nothing.

"Hang on, I'm just gonna take a leak," said Quinn heading for the bathroom. "Then we'll both leave here together. I'll walk you to your room and make sure you're tucked in nice and cozy with a glass of warm milk and a good book."

"You're the man with the gun."

"Don't you forget it."

John frowned. "There's still something I don't understand. Why hire me if you didn't want me to know what you were up to?"

Quinn shook his fat face, his jowls waggling back and forth. "That was the old man's idea. Of course, Mr. Rossmore knows nothing about Veronica stealing the Hope and he legitimately wanted to make sure she was protected. When I found out he was planning to hire a bodyguard, I knew that was trouble. The last thing we needed was someone snooping around, but then...," the FBI man hesitated and shifted his eyes.

"Then what?" John knew he wasn't going to like the answer.

"Well, I thought of you. I knew I could keep tabs on you, and if you started to find anything out I'd know about it. Let's face it, Johnnie, you're not the guy you used to be...I mean, after your crack-up. I know you don't drink anymore or anything, but I figured your brain's so scrambled, I wouldn't have to worry about you putting two and two together." Quinn shrugged his pudgy shoulders.

So that's what everyone thought. John had figured as much, but it was still hard to hear.

"How much is Lillian Spencer paying you?" John shot back.

Quinn smiled, but his eyes froze up. "Hey, it's not like that, Johnnie. This is a matter of protecting the president's family. There's so much crazy shit going on in the world right now, the last thing we need is a big scandal to stall out the administration and keep the President from just doing his job. It's for the good of the country."

John shook his head. "The good of the country, huh?"

"Listen, partner, don't make me nervous about you," said Quinn glancing down at the revolver still griped in his hand.

"I'm the last thing that should be making you nervous."

Quinn exhaled and wiped his short, shiny forehead. "All right, I can't wait for this freakin' night to just be over."

Quinn stepped into the bathroom and John looked around the suite. Something shiny sitting on the corner of the vanity table caught his eye. He walked over and saw it was Veronica's car keys on a silver chain. Acting on instinct, he picked them up and slipped them in his pocket just before Quinn emerged from the bathroom.

"Come on," said his ex-partner, "let's get the hell outta here."

Quinn marched John down to his room, and just as he'd promised, he stood there chain-smoking and waited for John to brush his teeth and strip down to his boxers before climbing into bed.

"Well, I'd love to read you a fairytale, but I gotta get back to my own room and get some friggin' sleep," said Quinn approaching the bed.

"How 'bout you just tell me real quick about how Zagen was involved in this whole thing," said John.

Quinn raised his brows and swallowed hard. "Listen, I had no idea he'd behave like such a freakin' psycho. For all he knew, he was scoring a get-out-of-jail-free card and all he had to do for it was steal the Hope Diamond. At least that's what he thought. Of course, it was a setup to catch him in the act and end this damned Ghost story once and for all. We could pin all the robberies on him and allow Veronica to get out of town with the real diamond."

"Veronica think that one up?" asked John bitterly.

Quinn shrugged and looked away. "No, buddy, I did. But you know, obviously I had no freakin' idea Zagen was going to go crazy and try to kill her."

John just glared at his ex-partner, but before he knew it, Quinn had slipped a pair of handcuffs out and was fastening John's wrist to the decorative wrought iron bedpost. "Sorry, pal," he said with a smirk. "But I can't have you doing anything stupid tonight. I'll be by tomorrow…"

But that was as far as he got before John clocked him in the chin with his free hand. Quinn's head jerked back and he fell into the end table.

"That's for almost getting Veronica killed!" shouted John as he got out of bed, no easy task with one hand cuffed. He slugged the FBI man one more time, knocking him unconscious. "And that's for almost getting *me* killed too!"

John breathed hard as rage flooded him. He could murder Quinn with his bare hands.

He flexed his knuckle and shook out his wrist, inhaling deeply. Closing his eyes, he repeated the serenity prayer over and over in his head as he sank back onto the bed.

God grant me the serenity to accept the things I cannot change, the courage to change the things I can, and the wisdom to know the difference. God grant me the serenity to accept the things I cannot change, the courage to change the things I can, and the wisdom to know the difference.

He said it until it became a mantra. Then he just sat there for a moment with his eyes closed and willed himself to calm down. His anger subsided as his blood pressure slowly returned to normal.

He leaned down toward Quinn and frisked the unconscious FBI man until he found the key to the handcuffs. After setting himself free, John awkwardly lifted his ex-partner's chubby frame onto the bed, cuffing him to the headboard and leaving the key just out of reach on the side table. He pulled a blanket up to Quinn's chin and tucked him in for the night. He'd have a nice black eye and a sore chin when he woke up tomorrow. John shrugged. His ex-partner had been complaining about needing a good night's sleep for the past forty-eight hours—now he'd get it.

John dressed quickly and switched out the light as he left the room making sure to post the "DO NOT DISTURB" sign on the door.

He made his way down the back stairs to room

211. He listened at the door, but no sound came from the White Russian's suite. John glanced around quickly and jimmied the lock.

The door clicked opened. He slipped into the pitch dark room as quietly as possible. He stood in the entrance hall listening for a moment, but the place seemed dead to him. Carefully he took a few steps farther in and snapped on the lights.

The suite was empty.

John searched the closets and drawers, but came up with nothing.

He left the suite and headed down to the front desk. A thin, unfriendly-looking woman stood behind the polished wood staring at him as he came toward her. Self-consciously, John ran his fingers through his hair. Did it show on his face that he was involved in some mysterious doings? He quickly flashed the concierge one of his bright, disarming smiles. "Hello there, how are you?"

"Very well, sir."

"Um, I was wondering, is Nicholas Bezuhov still in residence here?"

"The prince?" she asked, coming a bit more to life.

John bit his tongue. "Yes, that's him."

She shook her head. "No, I'm sorry, sir. He checked out around six o'clock this evening."

"Right before he left for the ball...," muttered John to himself. Then remembering the concierge, he smiled again and handed her a few bills. "Thanks."

****

The platinum convertible flew down the highway as fast as John could push her. At well past two a.m., the road was almost empty. The air was sharp and cold; the wind smacked his face as he pushed a hundred miles per hour, but he didn't feel it. Pennsylvania was a blur in the dark whipping by him, but he didn't see it. There was only one thought on his mind—getting the Hope back from Veronica. There was only one person who could help him do that. Old Buzzy Rossmore.

The idea had come to John as Quinn was walking him to his hotel room. He had realized, as he watched his sallow, potbellied ex-partner, that he hated what Quinn had become—just a scared little man doing what he was told with no more moral fiber than a rodent.

Maybe John had once been like that, too. Maybe that was part of the reason he drank. His mind flashed back to where he had been this time last March. He had woken up and gone into the office as usual. He'd brought his coffee thermos filled with cheap vodka—just for maintenance. He would drink steadily all morning, sneaking shots in his cubicle until he found himself in a stall of the men's room with his thermos in hand just sitting there drinking.

Then something had happened. Even though he'd already put away almost the entire contents of his thermos, he hadn't gotten drunk. The alcohol wasn't working.

A wave of panic had hit him hard and he'd looked around the industrial bathroom for something to help. Of course there was nothing. He'd stood there disoriented with his heart pumping and his adrenaline flowing. He'd felt his chest tightening up and he couldn't breathe. He had rushed to the sink, and turning on the faucet, caught up handfuls of clean, cold water and doused his face in the icy blast. He hadn't stopped until his cheeks were numb and the fear was a little more under control. Then he had raised his head and stood there with the water dripping off his nose.

One question had stood out in his mind. *What now?*

With shaking hands, John had picked up his

thermos again and sucked down the last remaining drops of lukewarm vodka. Then the strangest feeling had washed over him. He had felt as if he stood outside himself and saw clearly for the first time the desperate, angry man standing there trying to chase the demons away, trying just to get through another Tuesday afternoon.

He had examined his face in the mirror, as if looking at a stranger. It struck him then that he was an alcoholic just like his dad. His expression was the same as his father's had been, the trapped secretive look in his eyes. There was no denying it. John had wondered in that moment how he'd managed to justify what he'd been doing for so long.

He hadn't known then that he would have to leave the FBI, or that he would have to go sit in musty church basements and listen to a bunch of people whine about their lives, or that he'd have to make coffee for those same whiners, or take orders from a crotchety old bastard like Simon. He hadn't known anything except if he didn't stop then, that day, that hour, he never would.

Since that time a year ago, if he'd learned one thing it was that he could never hide from the truth again and he had to do the right thing.

He still didn't know if there was a God or not, but he knew the devil intimately and he knew when he stood at the crossroads, too. If he wanted to find a God to watch over him and guide him, he couldn't just close his eyes and pretend. He couldn't just say Cynthia Spencer and the Children's Library Fund weren't his problem. Or that it didn't matter if a hunk of sparkling blue rock, the color of Veronica Rossmore's eyes, sat in a museum for the people to see or not. Maybe other people could do it and live with themselves, but for him, it would only be a matter of time before it ate away at his soul and he reached for that first drink. Maybe it would take awhile. Maybe even years, but it would mark the turn down the wrong path at the crossroads.

He reached in his pocket and fingered the beat-up black box that housed the photograph of his father and his WWII medal. He thought about the hero his father had once been and then about the wax-faced man with the poisonous liver lying dead on the kitchen floor. That was where a wrong turn at the crossroads could lead you.

At a quarter to four, John pulled up in front of the red brick town house on Ninety-First Street. All the homes on the block were dark and quiet. Maybe the city didn't sleep, but this particular section of the Upper East Side sure did. John parked the car, and fighting an attack of nerves, walked up to the front door and rang the bell.

Chapter Seventeen

The musical chimes echoed through the silent house. John tapped his foot nervously on the doorstep. He wasn't exactly sure what he was going to say, or even why he thought Buzzy could help him. After all, the old man seemed to have about as much control over his strong-willed daughter as he had himself.

He heard the sound of slippered feet shuffling down the stairs. John swallowed and stood a little straighter as the door opened. There was Buzzy Rossmore in his Japanese *yukata*, his gray hair rumpled, a curious look on his face.

John noticed for the first time that the archeologist had the same eyes as his daughter, only hers were cold and hard on the surface with yearning haunted depths beneath, if you could get that far. Buzzy's crackled with good-natured intelligence and had almost an innocent quality, like a baby's eyes.

"What has she done now?" asked the old man.

"She's stolen the Hope Diamond."

Buzzy raised his bushy, white brows and just stood there for a moment. Then cocking his head toward the stairs said, "Then you'd better come in."

The old man led the way up to the same parlor where John had first encountered Veronica. The room looked peaceful and quiet, lit by the lamplight spilling in from the street outside. John thought once again how much it looked like an old-fashioned room out of another century.

Buzzy turned on a few table lamps and motioned for John to sit down. "Can I get you anything to drink, Mr. Monroe?"

"Oh, no thank you," said John, feeling awkward now for having woken up the old man in the middle of the night. "I'm sorry to have disturbed you. I probably should have waited 'til morning."

"Nonsense," said Buzzy firmly. "It's not as if I were asleep. It seems the longer I live, the less sleep I need."

John didn't know what to say, so he just nodded.

"Anyway," said Buzzy sitting down in the ancient leather chair by the fireplace, "maybe you should tell me about Veronica and the Hope."

John explained the situation as well as he could, making a great effort to emphasize that it had not been Veronica's choice to steal the famous jewel. When he finished, Buzzy sat quietly, his old face sagging like a hound dog's.

"I'm sorry about all this," said John, not really knowing what to say but wanting to break the silence and somehow comfort the old man.

Buzzy Rossmore looked up. "Why should you be sorry? I'm grateful to you for telling me." He sighed and rubbed his heavily lined forehead. "Lord knows Veronica certainly wouldn't be volunteering the information. If anyone is to blame, it's me."

"Listen, Mr. Rossmore, maybe I'm speaking out of turn, but it seems to me Veronica's a big girl, and no matter how much I like her personally, she's the one who decided to become a thief."

"You're not a parent," observed the old man with a sad smile, "or you would never say that. You're also wrong about your premise. Veronica may be a big girl now, but she wasn't always. You see, all this began when she was still a child, after her mother died. I didn't know at first. We were in Luxor and I was working on a dig in the Valley of the Kings.

That's how I dealt with Marie's death. I went back to work and put everything I had into it. I didn't want to think about my wife's suffering and what I had lost. No amount of mourning could bring her back, but when I was doing the work I loved, at least I felt like I was building a future for myself and Veronica. Only, I'm afraid, maybe what was best for me wasn't necessarily best for her. It seems glaringly obvious to me now. She was left alone too often in a foreign country with very few friends her own age. She put on a brave front and never let me see her cry; I just assumed she was all right.

"On Veronica's first birthday after her mother died, I wanted to do something special for her. So I brought her to Alexandria. The minister of culture was throwing a New Year's Eve party aboard his yacht and I thought Veronica would enjoy getting out on the water and watching the fireworks display over the harbor. Everyone seemed to be having a good time, including Veronica. I suppose the champagne flowed rather freely and some of the guests got a bit feisty. There was one woman in particular, Rachida, the beautiful wife of a Moroccan pasha who was famed for her exotic looks and such. Perhaps we spent a little too long engaged in conversation. At any rate, I don't think Veronica liked the woman. I imagine she was still missing her mother. I suppose we both were missing Marie." A wistful expression crossed Buzzy's careworn face.

"It's difficult to lose someone you love," said John sympathetically.

"Yes, yes it is," replied the old man, his face still folded into a frown. "At any rate, the long and short of it is, Rachida wandered up on deck to watch the stars over the Mediterranean. Having had a few too many cocktails, she nodded off in a deck chair. The rest of us were below in the ship's grand salon playing charades, of all things. I never noticed

Veronica slip away. Later that night when the pasha went on deck to look for his wife, she was still resting in the deck chair, passed out from the alcohol. Her necklace, the priceless Winged Isis, had vanished." The old man shook his head still not quite able to believe it.

"I never dreamed Veronica could have taken it," continued Buzzy. "The necklace was one of the great treasures of antiquity. It was a protection amulet, very sacred. The ancient Egyptians recognized no difference between the ornamental, magical, and even medical. Veronica, of course, knew this. In retrospect, I think it was the talisman she wanted more than some decorative piece of jewelry." Buzzy shrugged his shoulders. "But as I said, I had no idea she was the one who had stolen the thing. She was only twelve-years-old and a very well-behaved girl, too. Rachida had a reputation for being wild and careless. I simply thought she was responsible somehow for losing the necklace herself."

Buzzy grew silent for a moment as his mind seemed to drift back. John shifted in his chair and Buzzy refocused and continued the story. "The following year, when we returned to New York, we were exhausted from traveling, so we spent a very quiet New Year's Eve. I took Veronica to the Russian Tea Room for a birthday dinner with her grandmother and then we stopped off at Serendipity for ice cream sundaes before returning to our suite at the Pierre to watch the ball drop on television. The Pierre does such a good job of keeping their guest's business private, I never even realized that damned diamond bracelet had been stolen from the South American widow down the hall. I didn't hear about it until the following year when the press starting talking about the Ghost and mentioned that a bracelet had been stolen from the hotel while we were guests there."

"That's when I first learned about the Ghost—about Veronica." John shook his head still trying to get his mind around it.

Buzzy smiled sadly. "It was on her fourteenth birthday that I discovered what my daughter had been doing. We visited the Baroness Hull in Vienna. She was sponsoring my next expedition in Turkey. It was New Year's Eve, and she had a fantastic holiday party after the Kaiser Ball. Everyone in Vienna was there, and of course, since it was a formal party, they all wore their best jewels. Like Veronica and myself, many of the guests were staying with the baroness. That night a diamond tiara, which was once owned by Queen Victoria, disappeared from one of the lady's rooms."

The old man shook his head and looked heartbroken, "and I knew Veronica had taken it. I think it was her way of feeling important, like she mattered, at least in the beginning before it turned into a compulsion. Or perhaps it was a way to compensate for losing her mother. I didn't have the heart to confront her about it. I knew that was wrong, but I thought it must be a phase. At any rate, I decided what she needed was companionship, so I sent her to boarding school in Switzerland where she could be with other girls her own age. I think that only made things worse. I'm afraid what she really needed was me. If only I'd spoken to her then about the thefts, perhaps I could have stopped her kleptomania before it got out of control. I should have been there for her." Buzzy wrung his old hands together and his kind face was riddled with guilt.

"But you seem to be close now," said John.

"Oh, don't misunderstand me. My daughter and I are good friends, and she has been invaluable to me in my work over the past few years, helping me catalogue all my discoveries and organizing the mess I scribble into legible books." Buzzy's face brightened a bit and some of the good humor returned to his eyes. "As far as I know, she stopped stealing after she divorced Derrick. I think when that marriage fell apart Veronica made a decision to change a lot of things in her life. She began seeing a therapist and stopped spending time with some of her friends, whom I had never felt were very good for her in the first place. At any rate, she's seemed happier and more at peace. Since then no reports of the Ghost have turned up. Until now, of course." He looked worried again. "I cannot believe Lillian would use Veronica like this!"

"Believe it," said John.

The old man just shook his head.

"There are still some things I don't understand," said John. "Like who sent her the note you received warning her to stay away from the Diamond Ball?"

"That's right." The old man looked perplexed. "I still have it." He rose, went to the mantle, and opened a little ebony box. "Here it is." He handed the note to John.

John unfolded the paper and read it aloud.

"Stay away from the Diamond Ball, Miss Rossmore, or you could find yourself an unwilling character in the latest Ghost story and the ending won't be a happy one for you."

The old man frowned. "I never could understand why someone would send this to Veronica and pretend to be the Ghost."

"But that's just the thing," said John, the truth dawning on him. "No one was pretending to be the Ghost. This is a note to the Ghost not from the Ghost, probably from someone who didn't want the competition."

"You mean some other jewel thief?" asked Buzzy astonished.

"That's my guess."

"Well!"

"Okay, that explains the note," said John, still not satisfied, "but what happened to her jewels? She tried to say tonight that they weren't stolen, but I could tell she was lying. Why would she do that?"

"I don't know," said the old man, looking mystified. "Maybe she was telling you the truth."

"She sure put on a show when she first came to tell me they were gone, crying and sniffling like her childhood dog had just been flattened under a Mack truck," said John confused.

"It's not like her to lie and pretend," said Buzzy. "I know that's hard to understand considering all the thefts she's committed, but really, I've never known her to lie outright or to fake tears."

"Well, she did seem genuinely heartbroken," admitted John. "I can't say I understand getting that upset about a bunch of rocks. You have insurance, don't you?"

"For all the jewelry she legitimately owns, yes," replied Buzzy. "But I hope you won't think she's too materialistic," said the old man, appealing to John. "It's not greed. It's just...well, haven't you ever owned anything that you really cared about? A family heirloom maybe or something from your childhood? I believe somehow her compulsion to hold onto these jewels was tangled up with her feelings about her mother's loss, about being vulnerable and alone in the world. After all, diamonds are one of the few indestructible, seemingly eternal things in our ephemeral world where people can die or desert you. A world where all too often disaster seems to be just around the corner."

The WWII medal with the wrinkled black-and-white photograph of his father immediately sprang to John's mind. He felt a slight, painful tightening around his heart when he thought of losing it. "Yes, I guess maybe I do understand, but that still doesn't explain what happened to her jewelry."

Buzzy frowned. "No, it doesn't."

They both sat in silence for a moment pondering the situation. Then the archeologist thumped the arm of his chair. "Well, it seems we have no choice but to go straight to the source!"

"That's what I thought when I drove down here tonight."

"All right, then." Buzzy stood and walked across the room to a pile of neatly stacked files. He lifted them up and handed the pile to John. "My eyesight is not what it used to be. Too much hanging around dimly lit tombs," he laughed. "Tell me if you see a file marked *Amritsar*."

Confused, John took the stack of files and looked through them until he came to one marked by that name. "Here it is." He handed the file to the old archeologist.

Buzzy beamed as he flipped open the folder and pulled out a yellowing, tissue-thin map. "All right then!" he said, excitement lighting up his face, making him look about ten years old.

"Mr. Rossmore, are you okay?" asked John, suddenly afraid the old man had gone senile or cracked under the stress of his daughter's escapades.

"Never better," crowed the old man and he leaned down to John, a twinkle gleaming in his eyes and asked, "Do you know how I got my nickname?"

"No, sir."

"Well, come dawn, you'll find out! Just give me a moment to get some decent clothes on and we'll be off." The old man dashed out of the room leaving a confused John still sitting on the parlor sofa.

****

John did indeed get to find out how Buzzy Rossmore got his nickname as the platinum convertible pulled into the Westchester County Airport. The archeologist led him through the washed-out grayness of dawn to a small plane. With

218

the brightly lit eyes of a maniac, he told John to climb aboard.

An engineer was carefully examining the engine with a flashlight, doing his preflight check. John couldn't help feeling some concern and evidently the look on his face must have reflected his thoughts. The reliable looking young man nodded his head in an encouraging way, so John took Buzzy's advice and climbed the steeply pitched steps into the cockpit.

Buzzy exchanged a few polite pleasantries with the young engineer outside and then came aboard himself, wincing as his arthritis kicked in. He sat rubbing his knee after parking himself in the pilot's seat of the flimsy-looking plane.

"Well, what do you think?" asked the old millionaire beaming. He reminded John of Veronica when she was excited about a particularly bright, shiny diamond.

"I saw an old movie once with Cary Grant where he played a pilot. In the movie, they had to kick one of the pilots off their squad because his eyesight was shot," said John nervously.

Buzzy laughed, "Oh, that was in the old days before we had high tech gadgets like this." He tapped the elaborate dashboard of bells and whistles in front of him. "You better fasten your seatbelt, though."

John fastened the buckle around his waist and white-knuckled it as Buzzy eased out on the throttle and the plane shot forward down a runway which looked much too short.

"You want to tell me where we're going?" asked John over the roar of the engine.

Buzzy's eyes twinkled. "You'll see." He turned his attention back to the runway, but then said as an afterthought, "I hope you've had all your shots."

The plane lurched and rose sharply into the air.

John swallowed hard and tried to breathe long and deep like his friend Bethany had shown him. After the initial terror had subsided and his adrenaline level had returned to normal, the lack of sleep hit John like a ton of bricks and the drone of the plane soon sent him into a coma-like sleep.

****

He didn't wake up again until the ear-popping descent of the plane brought him back to consciousness. They landed in a private air field outside Lisbon, refueled, and stopped in for some lunch at a little fado café where they ate a Portuguese version of seafood piala and thick cut, greasy French fries before returning to the jet and resuming their flight.

The archeologist still wouldn't tell John where they were going and seemed to take a gleeful pleasure in the prospect of surprising him. The old man reminded John more and more of Veronica with every passing hour. Buzzy amused them both by telling John stories about his days as an archeologist in Egypt, Mexico, and the Island of Crete. It turned out Buzzy Rossmore had been a regular Indiana Jones in his time. At least that was how he told it and John didn't doubt the older man one bit.

Finally, they landed again just outside Bangkok, in an airport that was really no more than a glorified field with a rusty control tower, a snack shack, and a gaggle of very territorial chickens. After all of their hours of flight, John insisted they find a hotel and Buzzy get some sleep. The old man put up a fight, but finally agreed, and they bunked down at the house of the friendly man who served as engineer, air traffic controller, and baggage claim boy at the "airport."

They ate a good noodle stew with some ingredients John didn't recognize and knew better than to ask about. After the meal, they slept on the brightly colored wool blankets in their host's living room for about four and a half hours before Buzzy, all bright-eyed and bushy-tailed, thanked their host in his native tongue, handed him a generous wad of American money, and they were off again.

"You never really know a man until you've shared a pig intestine or logged fifteen hours of flight time together in a two-man plane," said the archeologist once they hit their flying altitude.

"Pig intestine, huh?" said John, trying not to get too queasy.

"Oh well." Buzzy smiled and his soft wrinkly face became a happy mandala of lines and light. "You're in love with Veronica, aren't you?"

John didn't know what to say, so he simply answered, "How did you know?"

"You never would have come this far," said Buzzy, smiling warmly at John.

"Has this whole trip been some kind of test?" asked John suspiciously.

Buzzy's smile grew even broader. "I like you, John."

John shook his head and looked out at the miles and miles of pale blue sky and fluffy white clouds.

"Have you ever heard of the Hindu goddess, Sita?"

John frowned. He had heard of her, but he couldn't remember exactly where. "I think so."

"Mother Sita is one of the great goddesses of the Hindu religion. She rules over purity, grace, perfect beauty, the harvest, and constant prayer," the old man informed him. "Though she was a goddess, she once incarnated into the form of a mortal woman and that woman was a queen. Well, one time Sita found herself in a situation where her purity and goodness were in question. So she gathered all the court together and she said this," Buzzy's voice took on the cadence of one reciting something from

221

memory, "'I am as pure as fire. Hence, I will prove the purity of my character by passing through the raging fire of flames.'"

"And do you know what she did?" asked the old man.

"She walked through a fire?"

"She walked into a raging fire and stood there until the flames burned down into ashes. Not one bit of her was burned because in her soul she was pure," the old man told him gravely.

"I think I finally know where we're going."

"Where you're going," corrected Buzzy.

John raised his eyebrows and looked at the crazy, old man. "Excuse me?"

"I have a friend in Delhi I'm going to drop in on. I haven't seen him in at least twenty-five years."

"Aha."

"You, of course, will be going on by train to Amritsar," the old man informed him.

"To the temple of Sita."

Buzzy beamed. "That's my boy!" He squeezed John's arm warmly.

Chapter Eighteen

India was beyond anything John had ever imagined. The smell of burning trash and pollution was so strong he had to cover his nose with his sleeve just to breathe. Delhi was like Manhattan times a billion, with cramped avenues jammed with cars, brightly painted trucks, and big-horned cows, all clogging up the road. Everyone stared at him and not all the looks were friendly. Hordes of children hung on him begging for money in their fast-talking little voices. It was hotter than hell. There were no traffic lights in the entire city. He had to make a dash for it through the chaos of honking cars and hope that he'd make it to the curb on the other side safely.

Aboard the old-fashioned train that chugged slowly northward toward the little town of Amritsar, there was no air conditioning and no toilet. Just a hole in the floor to squat over and no toilet paper in sight. At least the throbbing, sweaty mobs of desperate humanity were left behind in Delhi and John was alone in his train compartment.

Deep green fields, bright jungle flowers, and ancient twisted-up trees flashed by outside his window like nature on some kind of psychedelic fertilizer. By the time the train pulled into Amritsar, John had counted sixteen skinny, bronze-skinned men he'd seen pooping in the fields. He made a mental note to himself to stay away from the produce on this trip.

Outside the train station, he hired a bicycle

rickshaw. The ride was about as hair-raising an experience as he'd ever had as the flimsy vehicle skidded across broken streets and weaved through crowded, medieval-looking alleys, so narrow John had to pull his elbows close to his body to avoid banging them on the faded stone buildings. They sped past men in turbans stirring large vats of milk over open fires and barefoot women in brightly-colored silk saris with mud clinging to the hems of their skirts. Horns blared, other rickshaws whizzed by. John clung bug-eyed to his seat hoping the wizen-faced driver had understood the place he'd shown him on Buzzy's old map.

At last, they broke away from the wild little town and jolted down a long dirt road bordered by more of that incredible lush forestland on either side. After they'd gone for a while, the driver hit the brakes and they skidded to a stop.

John didn't see any temples around. Just road and forest.

The driver smiled a toothless smile and waved his hand indicating for John to follow him. "Ji, come this way, Ji," he said and bowed his head slightly.

The ageless Indian man started barefoot straight into the woods. As John followed, he saw that there was a small trail, and wiping the sweat and dust off his face, he followed his driver down the path until they came to a little clearing.

A one-room, whitewashed house stood there with its doors thrown open. A string of orange and yellow marigolds were draped around the entrance, but aside from that, the place looked humble.

The driver turned to John, smiled his big gummy smile again, and nodded in the direction of the little building. "I will wait for you."

"It could be a while," said John doubtfully.

"It's okay." The man sat down on a fallen tree at the edge of the clearing, obviously making himself comfortable.

John shrugged his shoulders and tentatively walked toward the doorway and peered in. He started to enter when the driver called out in an agitated voice, "Ji! Ji!" and motioned frantically at his shoes. "You must take them off!"

Feeling awkward, John kicked off his shoes. The driver smiled and nodded his head encouragingly. "Okay."

John entered the little building and found himself in the first really clean place he'd seen since landing in India. In fact, it wasn't just clean; it was immaculate. The inside of the shrine was whitewashed just like the outside. Even the floor was white. A circular fountain stood in the middle of the tiny room with water bubbling up from its center. The temple smelled like honey, roses, and tropical jasmine mixed with some kind of incense, which burned in the corner on a brazier. Clearly someone was taking excellent care of this place, but at least for the moment, John was the only one there.

In the back of the temple, a solid gold statue of the goddess Sita sat cross-legged and serene, a blissful smile on her lips, her eyes half closed in ecstasy. She was draped in scarlet silk; her wrists, ankles, fingers, and toes where encrusted with richly-colored gems. A garland of yellow daisies hung around her neck, but at the center of her forehead an empty crater gaped.

On the altar at Sita's feet, more incense burned and more flowers were heaped; rose petals were scattered across everything. A golden tray with little cups of what looked like tea fought for space with a golden bell, and there were two large candlesticks, which lit the goddess softly, making her skin glow.

It was cool in here and John gratefully splashed some of the water from the fountain over his face and rinsed his hands. Then he stood there not quite sure what to do. The place had such a stillness about it. He realized he hadn't done his morning prayers or any meditation in too many days. He walked to the altar and sat down on the floor in front of the goddess.

For a long time, he just sat there and stared at her. Something about her half-closed eyes made him feel safe. This was a little corner of the world that operated on a different psychic playing field, a place where time stopped, or maybe had never begun in the first place. A time of eternity.

He didn't say any of his usual prayers or do any kind of formal meditation. He just sat and felt the shadows of the sun setting outside the temple, listened to the soothing ripple of the fountain, and soaked up the emanations of the golden goddess on the altar.

Dusk was just starting to settle when she came. He didn't have to look behind him to know Veronica stood in the doorway.

If she was surprised to see him, she didn't let on. She moved to his side, by the altar, and kneeled down next to him. She was wearing an amber-colored sari with birds and flowers embroidered along the hem and a silk scarf covering her dark hair. She looked as natural in it as if she had been sporting Indian garb all her life, but of course, for much of her childhood she probably had found it necessary to dress in the exotic clothing of the many countries her father had dragged her through.

"How long have you been here?" she asked softly.

"Since early this afternoon."

"I'm glad you came." Her smile was so warm he could almost feel it against his skin.

"So am I," he breathed as he really took her in. He felt as if he were looking into a part of her very few people had ever seen. With newly enlightened eyes, he witnessed the graceful humility at her core, which had been hidden beneath that ever-changing protective exterior. Her inner beauty shone like an interior lamp illuminating her dark blue eyes and he felt a quiet intimacy between them so much deeper even than the passion they had shared or the flashes of painful hidden scars revealed.

"Do you know about Sita?" she asked.

"Your father filled me in."

She smiled. "Poor Daddy."

"You've given him a tough time over the years. The man is wracked with guilt," said John seriously.

She met his gaze unflinchingly. "Do you know why Sita and her husband, Rama, incarnated into human flesh?"

"No."

She turned to the golden goddess and said, "They incarnated to end the evil and wickedness in the world and to re-establish the rule of the righteous."

Before he could comment on that, she reached into the folds of her sari, part of which she had tied up like a hobo's knapsack. The Hope Diamond and the white brilliants fell into the palm of her hand. She laid the smaller stones that had made up the chain on a little golden plate that matched the bell and tea set on the altar. Then she rose, and leaning into the shrine, firmly pressed the fabled blue diamond into Sita's third eye where the gaping hole had existed for the past three hundred years.

The goddess looked complete as the stone exploded with blue fire. For a long moment, they both sat and watched the diamond shine. For the first time, John understood what Veronica meant about gems possessing a magical life of their own. He could feel that magic now in the tiny, whitewashed temple. It didn't bother him anymore that a fake was on display in the Smithsonian Museum. Sitting here, he understood the diamond had never really belonged outside of this temple in the first place.

"What are you going to tell Lillian Spencer?" Even at a whisper, his voice sounded loud in the stillness.

"I'm not going to tell her anything," she said evenly. "Her money will be waiting for her in the specified bank account just as planned."

"How's Nicholas Bezuhov mixed up in all this?"

She tore her eyes away from Sita and smiled at him. "Nicky has all the jewelry I've pinched over the years. He's cutting it down and selling it for me. That Children's Library Fund is going to be getting their money back plus a sizeable donation I think will knock their socks off!"

"You're selling everything?" he asked, stunned at the thought of the incredible collection she had amassed over the past fifteen years.

"Everything that didn't originally belong to me."

John whistled. "No wonder you were crying so hard that night."

"It seems silly now, doesn't it?" Her face looked so peaceful and serene, she almost reminded him of the golden statue above them.

"That's quite a risk Bezuhov took for you."

"Yes, it is," agreed Veronica. "I told you he was a good friend. You must understand, over the years Nicholas was the only person in the whole world I could confide in. He kept my secrets and I kept his."

John thought about what she said and it made sense. Maybe Bezuhov wasn't his favorite person in the world, but for Veronica's sake, perhaps he could keep more of an open mind about him in the future.

"So does this mean you're retiring for good?" John asked, even though he already knew the answer.

Her eyes sparkled mischievously and licking her lips with the tip of her tongue she almost purred, "I've decided to move on to bigger game." And she looked at him in a way that sent a shiver up his spine.

Suddenly the heat was so palpable between them, he move to pull her into his arms and settle things for good. She gently put out a hand to block him and said, "Close your eyes. You may never be in a place this sacred again. Soak it up so you can carry a little bit of it with you wherever you go."

Obeying, he closed his eyes and said a silent thankful prayer to this goddess who, until recently, he had never even known existed. He felt his heart open and faith, pure and joyful as a bubbling spring of clear water, flooded him for a moment bringing a smile to his face and tears to his closed eyes. He had walked a long, strange road trying to grasp that intangible, fleeting thing called faith. Tomorrow morning, when he woke up, it would probably be gone. Or maybe, as Veronica said, maybe a little bit of it would seep into his heart permanently; a building block upon which to grow.

He opened his eyes and turned to tell her, but she was gone—the Ghost in action.

He knew she couldn't have traveled far and jumping to his feet he ran outside. Night had fallen and he could just barely make out the black outline of ancient trees against the dark background of the sky.

"It is good, Ji?" came a voice from the darkness.

"Are you still here?" asked John surprised, trying to see where his driver was.

The man silently stepped forward into the light that spilled from the temple. "Yes, I am still here. I told you I would wait," he answered good-naturedly, as a skinny, walnut-colored hand opened in front of him. A man's ruby ring winked up at him. Even in the dim light John could tell it was a perfect blood red and weighed at least ten carats. It looked somehow familiar.

Then he remembered. The last time he had seen this jewel it had been kindling hot against Veronica's breasts. Now that the gem had been restored into its original setting, he recognized it for what it was—The Fire of the Maharaja.

"The lady says to give this to you. She says the man who owns this before, he is no longer alive."

John just stood there staring.

"Take it. It is for you, Ji," urged the man with his toothless smile as he pressed the ruby into John's hand.

It was true. The Italian businessman Veronica had stolen the ring from so many years ago had since crashed his sports car on the Ponte Milvio in Rome, leaving no heirs behind. The ring felt heavy and finely crafted in his palm. Slowly, he slipped it onto his finger.

"She says to give you this, too." The driver handed him a note.

John took the paper and turned toward the light to read it. It was written on elegant stationery with the crest of the Royal Alpine Hotel in Lech at the top. The address and phone number were printed on the bottom in dark blue ink.

According to the ancient lore of India, in order to bring good luck, a gemstone must be given freely, never coveted, and never taken by fraud or force.

By the way, do you like to ski?

- V

He didn't like to ski, but that was okay. Somehow John had a feeling they'd be spending most of their time curled up by the fire telling Ghost stories as the snow floated down outside the window of Veronica's cozy chalet—that is, when they weren't otherwise occupied.

Epilogue

Nicholas Bezuhov poured a glass of champagne for Jessica as she settled next to him on the fresh green grass along the Thames. It was a fine day for the Henley Regatta. They sipped champagne and watched the handsome young Oxford and Cambridge crew teams straining in the sunlight as they rowed toward the finish line. British aristocrats milled around the gaily striped pavilions that had been erected in the Royal Enclosure, the ladies showing off their pretty hats and the gentlemen in classic bow ties and straw boaters. Nicholas was also properly attired, although the diamond pin stuck in his lapel was perhaps a bit more flashy than those of his British counterparts. Jessica, however, fit right in. She wore a wide-brimmed hat adorned with a becoming pale blue bow.

With lazy elegance he pulled a little box from his breast pocket and presented it to the American debutant. "For you, *slatkaya*."

Her face flushed with pleasure. "Oh, Nicholas, how exciting!"

She carefully opened the black velvet box and her eyes nearly popped out of their sockets as she took in a beautifully designed bracelet of pink and yellow diamonds crafted into exquisite little daisies on platinum stems.

"Nicky!"

"You like?" he asked, pretending he didn't know she was about to explode in a shuddering orgasm in the middle of the genteel affair.

"Oh, Nicky!" she gasped again.

Nicholas smiled. He had sold the majority of Veronica's hot collection and deposited the cash in the bank, just as he'd promised he would. But a few small gems, here and there, he had kept for himself. The bracelet now shimmering in the sunlight on the debutante's slender wrist had been made from some of those jewels. Whether she was aware of it or not, Jessica had run part of the risk when the stones were hidden in her car. It seemed only good sportsmanship to see to it that she reaped at least a small reward.

"Oh, I just can't wait to show Mummy!" breathed the debutante.

"Please, *slatkaya*," said Nicholas smiling indulgently. "You are going to make a scene."

"Oh," Jessica flushed slightly, and lowering her hand to her lap brought her voice down to a more demure tone. "Of course. Forgive me, Nicholas."

****

Delores Pigeon poured out nice, piping hot cups of cocoa, sprinkling them with nutmeg before Antoine thoughtfully carried the tray with its old-fashioned Wedgwood china and home-baked cookies into the rose garden. The Welsh mists were burning off as the sun peeked out and smiled over the charming little cottage garden that overlooked the sea.

"You have settled in a lovely place," said Antoine as he pulled out a chair for her.

"Oh, I'm so pleased you like it!" exclaimed Delores beaming. "And I'm so happy you brought your nice friend Gaston," she turned her smile on the good-looking young man dressed in pinstripe pants and a tight white T-shirt stretched across his well-muscled chest.

"Well, we had to go to London anyway for the nineteenth-century Swedish antiques auction at

Christie's, so I thought it would be best to bring the rest of your money to you in person," replied Antoine.

"Always so thoughtful," said Delores, pinching his cheek. "So how did I do?"

"We did better than expected on the Puck. It turned out one of the Saudi princesses has this wild thing for Katie Park, and when she found out she might be able to get her hands on the Puck Diamond...well, let's just say Daddy went all out to make his princess happy."

"Every girl deserves such a good father," glowed Delores.

Antoine leaned over, placed a friendly hand on hers and put on a sympathetic face. "I know you really were wanting to get the Hope, but I have to tell you, I think it would have been a nightmare to sell.

"But, you know," Antoine changed to a more upbeat tone, "with all the other nice jewels you were able to grab, I think we did even better than you would have with the Hope."

Delores nodded understandingly. Things certainly had not gone according to plan the night of the Diamond Ball, but she hadn't made it as far as she had in the jewel thief racket without being able to think on her feet. So when the lights had gone out and everyone was in a panic, what better time to grab as many handfuls of jewelry as she could?

"And I'll tell you this, Granny," said Antoine, lowering his voice and giving the rose bushes a paranoid sweep with his eyes, "A lot of people think you're a big heroine for what you did."

"Oh," she blushed and shook her hand at the boys, embarrassed at the compliment.

"No, no!" insisted Antoine. "You are a heroine, really you are!"

Gaston nodded his head in agreement.

"It was pure luck. I just happened to be escaping out into the hallway right behind that nasty Dornal Zagen, and I still had the cake cutter in my hand from serving up my famous double chocolate sin cake..."

"Ah! I love that cake!" gushed Antoine. Then realizing his rudeness, "I'm sorry to interrupt. I just...I can't even hear you talk about that cake. It's so magnificent."

"Anyway," said Delores with a sigh, "that Austrian has been causing trouble for everyone for so long. It was such a relief when they locked him up, but then he breaks out of prison!"

"I know," Antoine agreed, "good riddance to bad garbage."

"That Veronica Rossmore is such a pretty girl. I just thought what a shame it would be to see that lovely milky-white throat cut."

"Yes," Antoine nodded his head in a show of support.

Delores' eyes lit up. "Oh, I almost forgot! I have something for you. Now you just sit there and let me get it."

Delores scuttled inside the cottage, returning a moment later with a pale blue afghan tied up in a big white silk ribbon. "I crocheted this for you, for being so helpful and nice."

Granny placed the afghan in his lap.

"You know this is my absolute favorite shade of robin's-egg blue," he turned to his partner, "isn't it, Gaston? Don't I always point out how much I like this shade of blue?"

"You do!" agreed Gaston.

Antoine turned and looked Delores straight in the eyes. "I absolutely, positively, L-O-V-E, love it!"

Granny's heart glowed with happiness. Everything had come out just right in the end.

****

Even the usually unflappable Parisians couldn't help turning their heads as Marguerite Gateaux made her way into Au Chien Qui Fume, the fashionable Les Halles bistro. She sauntered in on the arm of Placido Del Toro, the handsome young Spanish bullfighter who had set the continent abuzz with his daring antics in the ring, and lately with his sizzling hot romance with France's favorite criminal, Maggie La Chatte.

The flaming-haired star smiled as she slipped into a choice, burgundy leather banquette. Settling in, she allowed Voltaire out of his Hermès carrying bag. The King Charles spaniel was in good company. Lining the bistro walls were paintings of various canine breeds smoking pipes or cigarettes in long, elegant holders. Behind Marguerite, a boxer terrier dressed in a suit and cravat held a fat cigar between his teeth, his bug eyes staring relentlessly at Placido. Fortunately, the handsome bullfighter saw only her.

"Tonight, you will let me take you back to Barcelona," he said in a divinely low, masculine voice.

"Placido, you know my new show opens at the Paris Opera tomorrow," replied Marguerite as the waiter poured her a glass of her favorite bordeaux.

"Give it up!" cried the Spaniard dramatically. "Come home with me and become my wife!"

Maggie only laughed and then playfully slipped off her red satin shoe and rubbed the tip of her toe against his crotch. "Cher, you know I don't want to get married."

"You will kill yourself," complained the bullfighter, his brow darkening. "You cannot expect to escape with your life after every fall like the one you took at the White House."

"It was the Smithsonian, chere, and let me tell you—that was no accident." Her green eyes glittered with feline intensity. "Someone didn't want to compete with me."

"That whole business you certainly must stop," he complained. "It's crazy. You are crazy."

"Certainly it's no more dangerous than chasing an angry bull around a ring?" she observed with an arch of her brow.

"It is different," fumed her lover. "I am a man."

Maggie only laughed again and pushed her foot more deliberately against him, feeling his arousal. She leaned across the table and whispered, "I can tell."

Grabbing her foot firmly in his strong hands, he placed it back on the floor. "I'm serious. How can you have children if you are running around rooftops or falling off high-wires?" he demanded.

"Don't you worry about me, mon petit chou," she said leaning in to touch the tip of his nose with her finger. "I have a little magical protection." She raised her hand to her stomach and gently rubbed the stone that nestled comfortably against her navel fastened to the thin gold chain that encircled her waist.

When Marguerite had snatched the Mogul Emerald from Senator Hayes' DC townhouse, she had known it was inscribed with powerful Islamic prayers. However, it was only after the near fatal fall at the Diamond Ball that she realized just how powerful that magic was. She had worn the gem that night carefully concealed beneath her costume, hoping its fabled good luck would enable her to make off with the Hope. Instead of assisting her theft, she now credited the emerald with saving her life. As skillful as she was, she knew it was not her acrobatic genius that had kept her from smashing her bones apart on the marble Smithsonian floor. It had been some kind of supernatural intervention.

It wasn't too hard to understand why Zagen had

tried to kill her that night. She couldn't blame him for wanting to get rid of the competition. After all, wasn't she guilty of the same thing? Of course, she hadn't resorted to attempted murder, but she had seen to it that a few notes were slipped under Veronica Rossmore's door to frighten the spirits away. It wasn't that she disliked Veronica. Quite the contrary. She had admired her ever since she spotted the fifteen-year-old schoolgirl sporting the very hot Fire of the Maharaja along with tons of costume jewelry and a trendy, punked-out mini dress at the Hippodrome, a fashionable London nightclub, ten years earlier. No one else had guessed the massive ruby was real, but Maggie's trained eye had picked it up in an instant. That was a girl after her own heart, Maggie had thought at the time. Being territorial by nature, as her cat name implied, Marguerite had decided to stake out her claim this time around in the hope Veronica would stay away.

As it turned out, Maggie and her notes were nothing for Veronica to be afraid of compared to Dornal Zagen. Fortunately for everyone, the Austrian would never be a problem again.

"What are you thinking about now?" asked Placido peevishly, his darkly handsome face looking like a cranky schoolboy's.

Maggie smiled. "I'm thinking that when I get you back to my apartment...," she leaned over to whisper in his ear.

The petulant expression changed to an excited grin. Maggie thought her feisty bullfighter might be ready to charge before she even got him in a taxi. That was just fine. The dark alleys of Les Halles had witnessed the more sordid, urgent side of romance for several centuries. When it came to l'amour, nothing fazed the French.

****

Veronica, clad in a pair of worn Levis and a

vintage, white lace top, trotted in with a bottle of fresh milk and warm scones that she'd picked up at the little bakery in the medieval town half a mile down the mountain. The summer breeze carried the smell of wild flowers through the open door and John turned to give her a kiss as he finished brewing coffee in the little chalet's kitchen.

"I spoke to your father this morning," he told her, lingering over her ripe lips.

Veronica snuggled into his arms so that the cold milk bottle pressed against his back. "Really, what did he have to say?"

"He said it looks like Dick Spencer is going to lose the election in November. He's way down in the polls."

"Karma," quipped Veronica, pressing her nose against John's neck and breathing in the fresh smell of soap. "What else did he say? Does he want me to call him back?"

John did not reply. Instead, he unwound her arms and led her out to the front steps where the clear blue sky rose up from mountains still capped with snow. Lower down, the hillsides were covered in a riot of white Edelweiss, purple Gentians, and maroon Lady's Slippers with bees buzzing good-naturedly around and clean fresh streams gushing icy water along their slopes. It was the most magnificent view he had ever seen, but it couldn't quite compare to the beauty of Veronica's face smiling up at him with open, trusting eyes. It had taken a while for John to win that trust. Slowly, he had seen the change come over her during the months they had ensconced themselves in their alpine Shangri-La.

Every evening they lit a fire and, one by one, revealed their secrets, their stories and deepest scars. Finally, one night, there was nothing left but the love that had grown up between them and he knew it was time. With no more secrets to keep, maybe love could finally work.

John inhaled a deep breath of fresh mountain air and took the plunge. "I've had an interesting day today."

Veronica nestled in closer, "Really?"

"I called Simon and had a little chat with him. Then, after that, I called my mom and had a little chat with her, and then I called your father because, I had to ask him...," and John, still gripping her hand in his, sank down onto one knee, "I wanted to ask him for permission to ask you to marry me."

Veronica, the ice princess, gasped, covered her face with one trembling hand and started sobbing.

"Oh wait, wait before you answer," he slipped his hand in his pocket and pulled out a very small diamond ring. It was less than a carat, but it had a pretty antique setting. "This, I can promise you, is not hot. It belonged to my grandmother. I had to explain to my poor mother how to FedEx it to me last week. It's not the Hope..."

Before he could finish, she had taken the ring and slipped it on her finger. Though her cheeks glistened with tears, he had never seen her smile so bright.

"Johnnie, this is one diamond I'm never going to let slip through my fingers!" and she collapsed into his arms, sending them both rolling across the dew-covered grass in a kiss that felt like it might just last forever.

A word about the author...

Lydia Storm was raised in Manhattan's Greenwich Village and went on to receive her Bachelor of Arts from Vassar College in Dramatic Writing.

Currently, she resides in Saratoga Springs, NY, and is the author of two produced screenplays: "Desperate But Not Serious" and "Embrace of the Vampire." "Moonlight on Diamonds," which finaled in The Heart of the West Writer's Contest, is her first novel.

Lydia would love to hear from her readers at lydiastorm@gmail.com.

Breinigsville, PA USA
01 September 2009
223398BV00004B/5/P